OTHER

OTHER

THE 2024 SPECULATIVE FICTION ANTHOLOGY

Cover art by Ilan O'Driscoll.

.

The story "The Shape of an Eye" by Halli Reid first appeared as "Joint-Eaters" by Halli Lilburn in *Alchemy and Artifacts* by Edge Publishing in 2019.

.

The Spanish-language version of "Word Thief" by Silvina Palmiero first appeared in the Uruguayan magazine, *Revista Mordedor,* in 2021.

.

The story, "Maybe She's Made with It" by M.H. Bavlsik uses brand names and trademarked goods in a fictional story to express critical commentary on society. Any brand or product mentioned could be exchanged for any other brand or product, and in no way is the story meant as an attack or defamation against any brand or trademark. The full list of trademarks can be found at the end of this book.

.

About the Artist:

Ilan O'Driscoll is both a visual artist and a professional actress, and has won awards for her work at fine arts festivals, as well as for her performances on stage. Most recently she starred in the psychological horror feature *Believer,* and will next be seen in *Fear Street: Prom Queen* for Netflix. Instagram: @lilwheemo

A note about language:

Throughout this book, you will find artistic licence has been used with the English language. You will find made-up words, portmanteaus, and other liberties taken. We encourage creativity with the written word. Also, our contributors are from all over the world, so within each story you will find spelling and language used in the native form of each writer.

CONTENTS

FOREWORD

This feeling of *other;* that we are on the outside looking in, wanting desperately to be *over there* while tethered to the *here;* this is more than seeing the grass as greener on the other side. It's a deep-rooted sense of not belonging where we are, uncomfortable in our own skin, and of hoping that we might ultimately thrive somewhere else.

The stories in this anthology show us versions of ourselves shaped by the events of our lives, and not always by our own choices. The mother relationship, for instance, is the one that gives us a foundation in our identities, letting us fall and get up on our own while never abandoning us. Many of the ideas in this anthology reveal broken relationships with mothers– and isn't it interesting that *other* is broken from *mother*.

Some of the stories reveal our developed masks or shells; how we struggle with thinking we're not whole until we *define* our otherness, only to discover the thing we need most of all is our own true selves, long since lost and adrift in our past.

Other: the 2024 speculative fiction anthology celebrates what makes us unique, for the human experience *is* individuality even amidst community, and maybe that means our differences don't divide us after all. Maybe our outlier qualities mean we are exactly where we belong.

Sara Walker-Howe
Bannister Press
December 2024

PART ONE

THE CALL

Your shift is almost over, but the line at your register is longer than ever. You drop the items from the conveyor belt — a pomegranate, apples, porridge, nutmeg— into a canvas bag for the young woman in front of you.

"16.50," you tell her.

She puts her card in the machine and smiles, her winged eyeliner disappearing in the creases at the corner of her eyes. It's clear she's said something, but pretty much everything's a loud thrum in your ears right now.

"Pardon?"

"I *said,* I heard it's going to be a bloodbath this weekend. Are you going? Everybody's going."

Everybody's going.

You stand there, lost for a second. "Busy." You smile back and hand her the bag.

"I don't think I love you," he'd said.

"Pardon?"

You hadn't expected it, because you'd been making plans to go to the Mountain. With him. You'd booked a room at the inn, and reserved a small table at the *Gather*. Anyone who was anyone ate at the *Gather*, and you wanted this weekend to be special. The cost of the tickets for the event had set you back weeks.

"...Why?" you'd asked, your voice barely a whisper. You shouldn't have, though. It wouldn't have mattered.

It's not you. We just don't fit.

It wasn't till later, when you were walking to work that you remembered an off-hand remark of his about the low status of your job. Or the way he'd often mention *her,* and his weird smile when he'd say her name.

Seeing things in hindsight is a bitch of a thing.

You run to the back alley behind the grocery and throw up. When you return, wiping the vomit on the back of your sleeve, you pass the bulletin board and see it. And it hits your chest like a hammer all over again.

GLASS MOUNTAIN
Wanna go? Don't have a car? We have space!
20 zlot per person.

You could still go, something inside your mind tells you, till you harshly dismiss it. But it won't stop. *Go. Go to the Mountain. Everybody's going.*

You clock out, but as you switch out your apron for your jacket, another thought hits you out of the blue: your grandmother's old trunk up in the attic. It's where she'd kept her armour, wrapped in worn, moth-eaten silk. The pauldrons, the greaves, the bracers, they'd need polishing, sure, and the gorget was rusted last time you looked, but nothing a good oiling couldn't sort out. Your Vans will have to do, however, till you can afford new shit kickers. Paying full rent by yourself yesterday cleaned you out.

As for a sword...

Fuck it

You go grab the ad off the bulletin board and reach in your pocket for your phone...

THE SHAPE OF AN EYE

HALLI REID

Fairies do not like potatoes. 'Tis cos of the eyes. If the eyes of a potato can see them, they run a' hide. A fairy won't chucker any shenanigans if the eyes are watching them.

When the blight came from America in '45 all the lumpers got the dry rot and every small plot o' land that grew spud crops were lost. True, we were starving but 'twas the fairies that turned all of Ireland to hell.

Father returned from a bout o' work in England where they fed him real meat all winter. I thought he'd be healthy looking at least, but he was weak, and his flesh hung off his bones like a naked, baby bird. His eyelashes were falling out and his teeth were loose in his mouth. He said 'twas from the water; that fairies went in his mouth when he drank and ate half the food down in his stomach. He called them joint-eaters. I suppose they were starving too with nothing to eat and without the eyes, nothing was putting fear in them. They could take whatever they wanted.

"There's no cure for joint-eaters just as much as there's no cure for the blight," he says to me.

"That is false, Da. We need eyes," I say.

He picks up a lumper lying dead on the ground and crushes it in his hand. "And where will ye find some?" He drops the remains and they float down like dust.

I stomp on the dirty rubbish left of our garden. "We'll make some, won't we."

"I'll try anything," he says.

Paint is easy to make if ye don't mind stirring bird droppings and alkali and whatnot. That's for white colors. Black is easy too. Ye just burn some wood and scoop up the remains. Our cottage is made of rocks. That's where I paint the eyes and some on the walls and on the path, all the way to the road. All Ireland's made of rocks, so I find the closest looking to potatoes and build nice-sized piles round the door. I get a wee bit creative and put some character in them. I make them angry and penetrating, stacked up four or five pair at a time.

"No fairies will be cursing us now," I say.

"Siobhan Slack, what have ye done?" Father grabs his beard. "I cannot work nor sleep with all these eyes on me. Even on me cup and me plate? I cannot ate on this. 'Tis bird shite."

"Don't fret Da, there be nothing to ate besides," I say.

The yard is quiet. No bird songs, not even any wind. I lay awake waiting for me Father to go snoring but he don't start. He's awake too, listening to the nothing outside. We stay still in our beds half the night looking into the dark and waiting.

In the morning I pluck a dandy lion root and make some tea. Father stays groaning in his scratcher.

"I'm so thirsty," he whines, so I give him the tea.

"More, lassie," he begs, so I give him mine as well.

I realize that even if no more joint-eaters invade our gaff, there is still one down in his belly that must come out.

"Come on Da, git up. We got work to chucker," I say.

"No Siobhan, the life has left me. You must go on without me."

I've seen people starving. A load of people. They fall asleep and don't wake up. Father should not have reminded me.

"Why do men do so much whining?" I say. "You know, Mother never let out a peep when her time came."

"Oh Siobhan, I'm so sorry. Bless your mother, her memory gives me strength to hold on." He wrestles with himself to sit up and swing his legs over. "I'm so thirsty."

"Let's go down to the stream and fetch water for tea." I carry the bucket cos Father is too weak.

On the way I think of how to pull the blight outta his belly but I can't scheme up anything. Why would the bugger want to leave? He's got a warm, cozy place that's safe and feeds himself.

"He's got to want to leave cos his living space is undesirable," I say to meself.

"I need a drink fiercely," Father sighs. He sees the creek and hobbles faster.

"No Da." I catch him round the collar. "Ye cannot drink. Keep your wee belly dried up." I pull him back to the house.

"I'm dying of thirst." He gets desperate and strong.

"That's it." I find a rope to bind him to the post.

"Ye'll not restrain me," Father shouts and puts up his forks like an American boxer. His mustache quivers.

It might have terrified me when I was young, when his shirt fit properly, and he had muscles to go with those arms, but now his hollow cheeks and knackered eyes gobsmack me. I notice how skeletal he's gotten; thin as a willow and ready to snap. Still, his eyes are lit with a strange fire. His need for a drink is driving him mad.

"Yer missing a full shilling. Don't fight me Da." I hold the rope up ready to toss it round his middle.

He swings out and grabs it, but I tear it out of his poor hands, throwing him forward onto his hunkers. I wrap the rope round him and drag him to the post.

"Demon wane!" He screeches and kicks the back of me hunkers.

I fall into the post but keep my grip on the rope. I land hard on me shoulder and roll away as his foot comes looking for me noggin.

It slams into the dirt beside me head, like he was an elephant crushing a peanut.

I imagine what my brain would look like smooshed into the dirt and I scream, "That's it!" and yank that rope so hard he knocks his noggin against the post and passes out.

I lash the rope round him as many times as it'll go. Me shoulder isn't working so I wrap it up in a sling. Eejit. Fool. I am trying to help, and his crazies will kill me. While the ol' lad sleeps, I go and get meself a water bucket. Me cup is painted with eyes. As I'm drinking I gawk into the liquid. Would Father's belly get dried up enough to expel the joint-eater or would it kill him first? What if he's tied up for days? There must be a way to make it happen faster.

I look round the room trying to fen something to help. Me eyes land on a wee box of salt. I haul the box to Da who's leaning on the post with his gob wide open. I spoon it down until his throat is clogged and he starts choking. It wakes him up and he coughs up salt for donkey's years.

When he can talk he yells, "What the bleeding hell have ye done?" He struggles under the rope but gets nowhere.

"Tis for yer own good." Once his gob is empty I give him another dose of salt.

He spits most of it out. "I need a drink right nigh!" He howls.

"No, ya don't." I stomp me foot. "Ye can't give it what it wants. Ye need to starve it out."

"I'm gonna die," he cries.

"Think before you speak, Da."

He huffs and grumbles to himself for a donkey's years. Tears fall down his bake. "'Tis everything happening 'round us. 'Tis more than I can handle. We gotta go."

"Go where?" I ask.

"To America. Before we land in our graves like yer ma." He looks out the window towards her plot under the garden.

"We are not taking that fairy with us to America. He is staying right here. So, open yer gob and ate this." I shove the box in his bake.

"'Tis bleeding dear." He pouts for a moment, shuddering, then spoon after spoon he forces it down.

I set the water bucket in front of himself.

"Ye torture me." He can't reach the bucket but the fresh peggy dell floats under his nose.

"Not ye. The fairy." I make a soothing mud on the floor and smear it on his cheeks, trying to make the outside of him more happy than the inside.

Night falls. I light a fire to ward off the chill outside. The day has drained me soul, and misery weighs on us both. I try laying down for a rest but the ol' man is sweating and gagging. His throat starts wobbling like the buggers are trying to crawl out. His whole body is heaving like he might explode, and it scares me.

"Da, what do I do?"

He can't answer me. His eyes roll back into his noggin. A blackness fills his gob and he coughs up a dark liquid. In his heaving, out squirms a salamander, quite unnatural in shape and size, its features slightly human looking and down-right evil. The creature pulls its squishy body out from inside me father, leaving a trail of black slime running down his chin, mixing with the mud. I hold me hands over me gob to stop meself screaming. Then another wicked slug crawls out with a sloppy sound. Then another. Father pukes it out with a gush of slime. How he could survive, starving from the famine and having three joint-eaters, I'll never know. Bless me poor ol' man.

The black creatures slither over to the bucket in a hurry but that drink they were so desperate for didn't come. A black and white eye painted on the bucket stops them short. The magic in the sigil starts working. The iris of the eye that I painted there looks straight ahead, but suddenly it turns to focus down on the monsters. Anywhere they go the eye has them in its sight. They stumble over each other trying to back away from the staring eye, but, as they turn round, there's another eye glaring from the wall, and another on the peg of the table. Each one has come alive to move and fen the salamanders wherever they run.

Writhing in agony, they squeak and scream, leaving trails of black goo as they scatter. I throw me cup at them. It bounces over and hits one, stamping a bird shite eye into its black skin, searing the mark into its flesh. They escape out the west door, but their panic rises even outside cos of the cairns and the wall and the path. All the rocks I painted were moving and tipping, chasing those blasted things away. Eyes stacked up upon eyes following them into the darkness of night.

When the eyes can no longer fen them wicked slugs, the magic fades and their pupils hold still. The wind picks up, the crickets chirp and the land returns to normal.

Father slumps over and I pick his head up to rouse him. "Wake up, Da," I say.

He comes 'round, and he groans. "Water."

I untie his arms and give him the bucket. He plops his whole bake right in and drinks himself for donkey's years.

Epilogue:

There is a half-acre site in Manhattan named the Irish Hunger Memorial to remember the one million Irish people who died during the Great Famine. One million more immigrated to America during the years 1845 to 1849. On this site grows grasses and vegetation native to Ireland. Rocks were brought over from every county with their names carved into each stone. A cottage was also transported from Carradoogan in County Mayo, donated by the Slack family. The roof is gone but the stone walls remain. On the door on the west facing wall, under the lintel, is painted the smudge of a symbol. The marking is made of charcoal and bird feces. It is in the shape of an eye.

Halli Reid has short stories and poetry published in *We Shall be Monsters* with Renaissance Press, *Tesseracts* with Edge Science Fiction and Fantasy, *New Spaces* with Lintusen Press and many others. Her genres range from horror and science fiction to fantasy and poetry. She is a creative writing instructor and a structural editor with essentialedits.ca.

WHEN WE HAD WINGS AND SMOOTH SKIN

MICHELLE KOUBEK

I began my search over a year ago, two months after the first Runic Blossom wilted in one of the Mathematician's gardens. It stood out in the blue brush like a wart on the cheek of a fairy and elicited a similar response: eradicate it before it tarnishes the beauty. The town's top Seedsman was immediately summoned to the unsightly flower that he very unsystematically plucked and claimed the rest of the plant had been healed. We collected some soil samples and logged the occurrence as closed, but by the next morning, the entire plant had shriveled up. Our top Seedsman had no clue what he was doing. Some whispered that he had killed the plant.

This is when I became involved via a team of Reviewers, so named because we were trained to ask the tough questions and understand the mysteries of the world. We began by extracting samples from the crinkled leaves of the dead plant and comparing them to leaf samples of healthy Runic Blossoms. Every chemical analysis offered the same results. After several weeks, we were forced to draw the conclusion that the withered Runic Blossoms were not dead at all; they had simply become ugly.

For the week that followed, the Crease, named for the prominent wrinkles that inevitably formed across every afflicted plant's stem, advanced into more sentient plants like the Gilded Flower Bells. These plants were more evolved than the Runic Blossoms and chimed whenever visitors approached one's home. The Crease also afflicted the Stone Spiral Tulips that spat pebbles at guests who had overstayed their welcome. Interestingly, in addition to their wilted forms, the behaviors of these flowers also changed as if they were falling asleep. By the end of the week, every flower in town was as inactive as a rotten tree stump. We became accustomed to silence as we entered our homes as the Gilded Flower Bells ceased their songs.

We continued searching for a cure with no luck, and as our discouragement grew the affliction began to show in the fauna of the town as well. Just like the plants, their behavior changed dramatically. Hares that typically leapt in and out of our homes as they pleased resorted to lingering near and around the burrows where they slept, snuggled closely as if they found us fearful. In addition, the perches we kept in our bedrooms for the great horned owls that served as natural alarms suddenly became unoccupied each night.

In desperation, we managed to trap a few hares and examine them. When we did, we found the same striations on the pads of their feet that were on the stems of the plants. We never found the owls, but I predict some part of their body would have reflected a similar state, because I knew what it was. It was the Crease. It was infecting everything.

That is why two months after the affliction was discovered, I gathered a sack of unperishable food, a map I had inherited from my great-grandfather, and a blanket to sleep on, and I ventured towards Juniper's Peak. This is a legendary mountain that is said to be where all living beings came from, as well as where the Creator lived. The map was hand-drawn with archaic messages instead of clear directions, and the only reason I brought it was because my great-grandfather had insisted it was the only way to reach Juniper's Peak. He was quite odd, especially before his death, so I was not sure what to expect from the first instruction on the page.

Close your eyes and make a wish on the first star you see in the sky, I read.

I considered turning back around at this point. How was I supposed to travel anywhere with my eyes clenched shut? I would be more likely to find myself in a ditch than to walk in the right direction. Not to mention the nonsense about wishing on a star. Everyone knows that wishes were never granted that way. It's a story that mothers tell their children, nothing more. My great-grandfather must have meant something more literal.

So, I resorted to assessing the trees and rock formations nearby that might resemble a star, hoping this was somewhat in line with what my great-grandfather wanted. After an hour of evaluation, I settled on an unusual coil of bark on the trunk of a willow tree and marched in the direction the topmost of the star points indicated. I walked into early afternoon, keeping the second instruction in mind:

When the road ends, use your wings.

The first part of this was straightforward, so I had no trouble walking forward until the road stopped. When it did, the dense woods broke and a cliffside emerged before me. The latter piece of the instruction was less obvious. Wings! As if human beings were light enough to become airborne like pixies. Yes, we have wings, but they are stubby and could hardly be considered suitable for fanning someone suffering from heat exhaustion, let alone flying.

Clearly, 'wings' was code for something that would transport me across like a hidden bridge or perhaps, if it was more figurative, a synonym for human ingenuity. Yet there was no bridge. So, I leaned on human ingenuity by finding a decent-sized dandelion (it stretched from my feet to my chest) and plucking it to use as a kite to carry me to the other side of the cliff.

Once I alit on the ground, I paused briefly to snack on the grapes I brought, enchanted by the town's Spellworker to multiply on command, before reading the next instruction:

Be the magician. The magic will show you the passageway.

I had no idea what a magician was. I was aware from my studies that there was a mysterious and unexplainable energy called magic that lived in the flowers, animals and even humans like me, but a magician? What would a magician do? The closest profession would be the Spellworker. Our town Spellworker could apply magic that existed to other objects via enchantments and see what happened. Their work was based on trial and error. Always they were experimenting and making predictions, but magic was not something we understood.

This map was useless.

Without any other choice and knowing I should be close to Juniper's Peak, I wandered the area aimlessly, hoping that I might get lucky and end up in the right place. I scoured the thick brush and scaled the tallest elms; I lifted strange boulders and tried to ask the nearby squirrels for help, but they merely told me I was insane. I stood on the rocky overlooks and gazed down at everything beneath me to see if there was a shimmer that snagged my sight. I searched for the entire first day, then into the next and so on, until the days became weeks and then months. To this very day, one year from when the Runic Blossoms wilted in town, I have not found Juniper's Peak. I can see it, looming in the distance as it always has, but it remains out of reach.

I have not found the Creator who may be able to save us.

Today, I am ending my pursuit. I am less than a mile from town, back in the part of the forest I know well. I put my return off for as long as I could, not desiring to reunite with my fellow Reviewers without explanation for the affliction. But enough is enough. I must return. And as I approach, I hear joyful music, so I sprint through the trees to see what could be worthy of such a celebration.

The humans of town are frolicking in joy like eager fawns. I approach the nearest townsman, a middle-aged fellow whose singing is known to be healing for both the mind and body. I examine his face. He scowls with wobbly mouth at me, because I have disrupted his dancing. I note nothing of interest on his features that might indicate disease.

He spins in his revelry!

Then, I see that his back is flat as a meadow. This man has lost his wings!

I frantically assess the others and find that the same horrible disfigurement has occurred to each of them. What foul beast must have invaded town while I was away and torn their wings from their shoulder blades? Or is this again the Crease?

"Come dance with us!" the man beside me pleads. I am about to ask him where his wings have gone when I am struck by his smile. There are thin creases around his cheeks.

The Crease is etched into his face.

"You are afflicted!" I scream. "You have the Crease!"

I stumble backwards, crashing into a townsperson behind me. To my horror, I see another grin on their ecstatic face surrounded by crinkles. It's like the lines might cut the woman's skin if they run any deeper. I've never seen anything more unsettling. It is a nightmare.

Swiftly, I scan the expressions of the humans about me, hoping I've somehow gone mad in my wanderings. Yet every deceitful grin is swaddled by the same, familiar indents I know as the Crease. It's like the town folk are wilting as the Runic Blossoms did. They are wrinkly as if they are dead.

Why do none of them seem to care about what they've lost? Why are they so happy with these lines sabotaging their skin?

Uncertain of what else to do, I flee back into the shelter of the woods, the darkness creeping around me as the torchlight of the town becomes distant. In those shadows, I sob. It is not loud enough to drown out the celebration of the townspeople behind me, but it brings me some catharsis. Someone has to weep for them. They are too lost to grieve for each other.

"They are called smile lines," a gentle voice says to me.

I flinch like I've been struck by a rock.

"Who's there?" I plead to the evening.

"I am the Creator," the darkness replies. I look about and see no one. I know then that I am truly out of mind.

"You are not mad," the voice says. "You just cannot see me. If it makes you feel better, imagine I am a fox sitting on a stump. That is a form I often take."

"The Creator?" I repeat. "Impossible. I never made it to Juniper's Peak. What would you be doing here?"

"What you see is an illusion of a mountain that used to be. Juniper's Peak is no more," the voice sighs. "In truth, I've been with you for some time without you noticing. It's taking all of my powers to speak to you."

The dark woods groan like there is something massive swinging from the trees. I still cannot see anyone in the blackened forest, so I accept that there might be some truth to the voice's words. It does not make me feel better though. If this is our Creator, why does he not help the townspeople a few yards nearby? Does the Creator not care?

"What are smile lines?" I whisper.

"Side effects of what you know as the Crease."

"But the Crease destroyed the flowers," I say. "Is everyone here going to be okay?"

"They will wither as the plants have, but they will survive," the voice hums. "After all, it is the magic that keeps them beautiful and with the Crease that magic will be gone."

"I don't understand," I whisper.

"The smile lines are scars," the voice explains. "It is where the magic leaves. The magic of your kind is fading."

"No," I close my eyes. "How could I not have realized the magic was fading?"

"Because your magic is nearly gone," the voice hisses. "It's been gradually happening throughout the generations. Why do you think it was so difficult for me to appear to you?"

"But we have just begun to study the magic," I argue. "You can't take magic from us now!"

"I am not taking anything," the voice grunts. "You are giving the magic away. It's been a long time since your kind have been able to accept the unexplainable."

I cover my face. The voice continues.

"You only began studying magic because you have forgotten what you already knew. You're trying to recover what you've been losing over centuries. You are an outsider to magic now."

"I don't believe you!" I tremble.

"Look in this puddle and see," the disembodied voice soothes.

A blue glow rises from the forest floor like sanctuary in the shadows. It comes from a body of rainwater leftover from the shower the night before. I approach cautiously, unsure if I want to look upon it, but my curiosity spurs me onward. I must know what mysteries are being kept from me. I must understand everything. After all, I am a Reviewer and answering questions is my job.

I must see.

So, I lean over the shimmering pool.

At first, the reflection shows me as I have always been, which makes me consider that my mind has played a cruel trick with the voice and the preceding conversation. Then, the edges of my lips flinch like feathers dance on them. I do not feel joy, but I must grin. The smile is being yanked out of me. And even though I no longer believe in magic, it feels like the closest thing to magic I've ever experienced.

I grin as the skin around my mouth wrinkles like a prune. I feel the dents of what I know must be the Crease, the smile lines, dig crevices in my smooth skin. I can't recall why the Crease was bad though. They're just lines around my mouth. Why would that bother anyone?

I feel the new indents in my skin carefully as the blue light of the water dies. I have forgotten what I am doing in the forest. It's the middle of the night. I should not be out here alone.

I hear carefree songs somewhere in the distance that I predict might be my townsmen, so I head in their direction. I am lost and hoping for respite, which I sense can only be found in the celebration. As I walk, an owl hoots somewhere above from its home where it has always lived, safe in the treetops. For a mystifying reason, the sound saddens me, so I frown. I cannot say why hearing an owl in a tree would make me sad. It's just a bird; it's not important.

A gust of wind blows past my face and for a moment, I think I hear whispers in the breeze like soft rustles. I feel my cheeks, touching the lines around my mouth. They remind me of the smile that has escaped me. And in that forest, with merriment a few yards away, I wonder if that is all I have lost.

I sense that there used to be more to my existence.

I don't know. I have forgotten.

Michelle Koubek is an autistic writer with other recent work of hers either published or forthcoming in *Strange Horizons, Star*Line,* and *Factor Four Magazine*. Her website can be found at www.michellekoubek.com. She dreams of owning a castle one day.

DIVERGENT PATHS THROUGH THE UNKIND WOOD

D. M. BEUCLER

You have to get through the woods. Your sister is sick and you have to get through the woods. It's a common plague, the kind that peels the flesh away in long red black strips and sets a cough, but there is a cure.

You make the journey with your sister, eking out precious bits of energy to get her to a bed in the healers' tent at the start of your pilgrimage. You aren't alone. Everyone with a sick child, or sibling or love has considered making the journey and many of them do. You've prepared for the journey, carrying a bag with day-old pease porridge slices, a bottle made of red fired clay, and a knife from the kitchen. You wear your warmest woolen hood, a wool cloak over your dress, and your sister's shoes that have the most wear left in the leather.

At the start of the path is an old man who gifts you a badge of pewter to pin to your breast so that anyone you meet knows that you are on pilgrimage seeking the cure and can ask you for a boon.

There is another man starting on the path with you. A lordling of some sort. He is finely dressed in wools that have been beaten until you can no longer see the warp and weft. There's a sword at his side, trimmed in something that might be gold, or maybe brass. His badge is pinned to his hat.

"Shall we go together," he asks and you agree. It's always best to share the journey.

You walk together. You walk until the blisters on your feet scab over and blister again. The wood is large. It will take days, maybe weeks to cross. You don't know if your sister has that time.

Of course, the path is hard. You knew it would be. Footfall after footfall through brush that clings and roots that bind. And when you hear the cry for help you don't hesitate. He follows you willingly enough, and if there is recrimination in the set of his shoulders you ignore it.

It's a child lost in the wood. You know the tales. You have to help others along your path. And you do. You share your food, your warmth, and when the boy is brought safe home, in a roundhouse that seems more tree than house, you smile and set your way to find the path again.

Your companion is amiable enough. He takes his turns leading the path, pushing a way through the bramble briers and tanglevines. It's hard, and takes all your concentration to get by, or almost all. You are the one who spots the doe caught in the snare. The cord is around her throat and one leg is caught up in it and she stands so still, her nose near the tangle of her forelegs.

Your blade is not the sharpest but the lordling lends his sword and the leg is still sound. The doe bounds away, in the way of her kind, fleeing everything. And you struggle back to the path.

The next obstacle is a river. It's wide and fast flowing and you have never swum before. The lordling has. He helps when the water is too much and pulls you to the other side. Perhaps you were simply one of his trials, for when you wake by the fire the next morning, he's gone.

But there must be an end to the forest. You go on. Your sister is waiting. It's harder now. The calls for help come thick and fast. A mouse with an injured paw, an old woman gathering wood, a child in a tree, the progress forward is measured in steps not strides. Impatience cries at your back and you want to say no. You think of your sister, but they are someone's sister too and this wood is not kind to those who limit their empathy. You help, burning hours of daylight, walking until the woods are dark and you can hear things moving around you.

The soles of your shoes are worn thin. You can feel the brambles pushing against the wool of your stockings. Maybe you have always been here. Maybe it is your sister who is the dream and there exists nothing more but the push forward, carrying this man's bundle a little while, sharing what you have foraged along the path, your provisions have long since spent. Your cloak is gone, a woman with a baby dressed in only a tattered shift needed it more. The hood went to another child crying with the cold. Your underdress now reaches your knees, so much of it has been torn away for bandages. You've emptied yourself into this forest. It isn't enough.

When you reach the end you don't believe it. The forest never ends. Your feet are bare now, the only things you have are the badge and the battered dress you wear, seams frayed, rents unmended.

There is the cure. A root. You've tripped over so many other roots, but this one is deathly pale in the dark earth. It feels like ice under your fingers when you dig it up. You can't cut it; you have no knife. Your knife went to a peddler in exchange for a chicken to feed a family of eight on the eleventh day of this journey. Or was it the twelfth. The days have merged together into a mire of walking, walking, helping, walking. But this is the end. It has to be.

You break off a hunk of root the width of your hand. It's cold and oozes white under your fingers. You cling to it. You have what you need, surely that means you will get what you want. You start back to the path.

It's clearer now, easier to find your way out than in. But the calls for help keep coming. You've given everything away but the root. Still you empty yourself more. You give your time, time to gather wood, scour the wool, tend the fire. It's the only way through the forest.

And when your bleeding feet find the edge of the wood you stumble out into twilight. Has it been enough?

The lordlings' horses are still there, saddled and waiting to carry him and whoever he was curing home. You stumble into the healers' tent. The beds are filled with groaning bodies. But now of course you can afford to only look for her. Your sister's is the last bed on the left. You find one of the healers standing nearby. You point to the bed where your sister is lying, still so still.

"I'm sorry," the healer says. "You didn't make it fast enough."

The lordling's loved one is near the center of the tent. They are sitting up, laughing. You watch as they stand and walk away.

"I helped all I could," you whisper. "Why was my journey so much longer?"

"They asked you because they knew you'd answer," the healer said.

D. M. Beucler is a fiber artist, writer and professional chaos manager from Ohio. She has 2 kids, 3 cats, and enough crafting supplies to outfit a small army. Her debut novel *Memory and Magic* releases in the fall of 2025 from Luna Press.

STRANDLINE

EMILY MACKAY

There's no myth that hasn't a little truth to it. Sometimes it's a deep truth of the dark eras, a long-obscured ghost of flood or fire. Sometimes it's a symbol-truth, a reflection of how we know the world to really be, underneath. Sometimes, very rarely, there's a literal truth, a real and present truth, the grit at the heart of the pearl.

So often we've damped the pages with blooming yellow water-stains and curled the corners of your history books. Not just in the obvious ways: Atlantis, the mermaids, all your hippy-dippy water ladies. We lurk in the tales of mysterious drownings, the liquid, lyrical poetry, the pseudoscientific backwaters that insist on humanity's essentially aquatic nature. Yes, there's an orphaned hunger in your briny blood that pulls people like you and your friends down here to mope on the wet shingle under the dark of the pier.

You can get back to the party in a minute, don't worry. If you lean in close here, you can smell it. Don't be afraid, I'm not going to kiss you, you idiot. But there's a dampness, feel it? Like the back of a wardrobe in a cold room, like a window in winter, like a hole in the riverbank: dank. That sharp smell. Weed and water, sand and salt. Wild.

Well, you might wrinkle your nose, but oh, your lot covet our free fluidity; just so, we envy your solidness, the confidence of two feet on firm ground. Over the years, we've let go to envious lust here and there – a soggy mess it's made, too. Yet still we can't seem to keep away from the land.

Of course, you must know all those men in the folk tales didn't find us singing on the shore by accident. We watched them from the water for days; heads peeking up like slick rocks, black eyes following as they moved about the strand. We all want what we can't be, don't we? Like you, we rail and punch against the hard limits of our bodies, hating our pale wetness, our smooth, rippling lumpishness; we long for dry, soft-haired long limbs and hair that jumps up to meet the wind.

But for those who did let themselves be found – just singing to themselves, as you do, combing their hair among the pools, as you do – happiness was short, the ending inevitable. In the wind-nipped north of Scotland, they tell of the Grin Iron Wife, who stalks beyond the shallows in the shoals and reefs, watching and waiting to pull unwary children into the depths. She had infants of her own once, was beaten alongside them by a drunken fisherman whose face set hard and stupid and sunburnt against her as soon as their first baby started to squall. It's not just any child the Grin Iron Wife seeks, but those half-human children she knew would not make it back home.

Things have changed since then, and then again they haven't. Your world, like ours, has grown more complicated, smarter and stupider, and still we can't resist it. It's easier for us to hide, now, when we come among you, easier for us to stay. And like all immigrants, we work hard to survive.

In any picturesque seaside town, you'll find a colony of older women sitting quietly in shops stacked with seascapes, driftwood forms, picture frames and mirrors ringed with pebbles and shells and sea glass. (And in the back, the weirder stuff.) Some of us can't bear to go far from the borderline, one toe always in the rock pool.

Me, I wanted to go as far inland as I could. I had no patience for painting, or writing, or beachcombing. I had no human skills at all, I realised, as I panted on the rocks that poked sharp into my soft belly. Damp and salty, in a decades-old dress taken home by my aunt, I sat at a bus stop and waited for a driver to take pity on me. Then I headed to the city.

It took years to scrape up from nothing, with no history, no identifying numbers, no money. I stole, and I sold all that I had, and I begged for food and bed and work. And after half a lifetime – our lives, closer to animal, are shorter than yours, and we must seize our moments harder – I set myself up on my own in a boutique on the mildewy edge of the garment district.

Though small, my shop was a cave of treasures, and my dresses slipped on with something of the shapeshifting magic of my other skin. The fabric transformed, braced and bolstered and boosted in a way that elasticated underwear could only dream of. Those of our kin found me fast; the signature in my sinuous lines sang a secret song to them through the window panes, and they fell into the gleaming folds like a homecoming. As word spread among the students and the artists, the strongest reactions, strangely, often came from your kind, their hands hovering softly over the gleaming weave; unsure if it was for them, if it was OK to touch it.

We are not the same. Yet over the years I have learned that you know as well as us what it is to feel dislocated, exhausted, utterly empty. To fear that you made, long ago, a rash choice whose consequences have spiralled and set around you, your course now fixed until the end. You know loneliness. A beautiful coat can't make that better. A gown can't fix it.

Except that, just for a second, it can. When you see the workings of a mind that echoes your own in the shifting colours of a piece of carefully chosen shantung, in bold and exquisite detailing, in structure that is now ruthlessly rock-hard, now flowing easy as rainfall, just for a moment you feel that you, in this, could be better. You could be more really yourself.

I can remember the looks of shock, of joy, of growing desire, as women and men held in gentle fingers the corner of a garment, pulling it out to reveal its truths and glory. And I remember their money, and how it felt to belong in your world, unassailably now, because I could give your people, over and over again, these versions of my own skin.

I hoped they felt free to be who they wanted, for a while. It was when I felt closest to you – at that distance. I rarely admitted it to myself, but a lot of the time I found the squawking and smell and clamour unbearable. I tried your men once or twice, but they were so earthbound: heavy, loud, like livestock. It's a hard thing, to have longed for something so, and then to slowly feel that longing curdle into disgust. The problem is with me, not you. I know that. It's sad, all the same.

Only one of you ever recognised me. A young woman and her small daughter came into the boutique. I'm not being cruel when I say she obviously couldn't afford my prices; hour after hour sitting in a small shop, you come to know on sight who will splash and who will scuttle out as soon as they've read a tag. I never made them feel unwelcome; I'd been a browser for so long myself.

This woman, with fine, dirty-blonde hair, hung like a coatrack with heavy bags, kept one hand lightly but firmly on the crown of her child's head as she grazed her fingertips over dappled grey velvet. "Ah," she sighed with sore regret. "It's like a selkie dress, Della."

The small girl, without looking up from her screen, pointed her chunky little paw right at me. "That's because she is a selkie lady, mama."

The mother ruffled the child firmly into silence, pantomimed credence. "Of course, Della, silly me." She rolled her eyes at me. "Sorry."

"No need," I said, smiling at the girl with my teeth. "She's quite right."

They moved on to admire a display of hats. I slipped over to where they stood, and, under the pretence of adjusting the flowers by the dressing room, I slid the grey dress off its hanger and in among their groceries.

Years later, I saw the girl again. By then, she was a young woman; I recognised the dress first, its silvery, sliding shimmer catching the eye, just as I had made it to. She was on the opposite side of a local train, confiding and laughing with a friend. But she had a separateness about her beyond that conferred by the dress; she was a little back, a little aside, a little waiting. I caught her eye, smiled; I didn't need anything more from her, or she from me. They got off at the next stop, and I listened as their voices faded beneath the clattering of the carriages as the train sped onward.

Children always seem to know when there's something fishy about a person. There was one earlier, at the station, heading back with her family from a day at the beach, dragging her bucket and spade behind her. She clocked me straight away and was dragged away gawping by her bemused father. I mean, the fact I'm wearing my very best hat on top of the most operatic gown I ever made was probably part of it – you have to go out with a bang, don't you – but this is Brighton after all, and fancy frocks are hardly out of place. It was sweet. Mostly I can't stand children these days; I find myself less and less able to stand any of you.

You're only young, pretty much a child yourself, behind all that glitter. I expect you could feel something off about me, too. Maybe next time you'll recognise it. Go on, leave me now, go back to your friends. And don't chase too hard after the sparkle. It doesn't last.

Emily Mackay is a Scottish writer and editor based in Hertfordshire, England. She has written about music for the *Guardian, Uncut, NME* and more, and is a news copy editor for the *Guardian*. In 2017, she wrote *Björk's Homogenic*, a volume in Bloomsbury's 33 ⅓ series on classic albums. She has since edited several books in the series, as well as in the Manchester University Press series British Pop Archive, and contributed the chapter, "Kenickie's At the Club," to *33 ⅓: The B-Sides*. Her first published story, "Tin Can Alley," appeared in the journal *Riffs* in 2021.

PART TWO

ALLIES

You arrive just as the sun breaks against the horizon, and though you think you're prepared, the otherworldly grandeur still manages to take your breath away. It's everything they said it was: a true mountain made of glass. The sun's rays hit its peak, bending back the light, evaporating the rolling mist that blankets the valley.

"Oh. My. God," you whisper.

Your traveling companions emerge from the rusted car, leaving their doors ajar too.

"Jesus. How are we gonna...?" Piotr lets out a low whistle as he stares up and up. His girlfriend, Daria, appears way more amused.

"We're gonna die!" She giggles, still high from whatever the pungent shit is she's been smoking in the car. To be honest, it's given you a headache.

You'd called the number posted on the store's bulletin board, almost hoping no one would answer. *Sure, no problemo. There's loads of room in our car,* Piotr assured you. It wasn't till they'd shown up in the tiniest Fiat known to man that you reminded yourself you get what you pay for. 20 *zlot* indeed. *Idiot,* you'd told yourself.

Three and a half hours of Piotr waxing garrulous on how the *Golden Liberty* are absolute bastards, and two pee breaks later, and *voila:* you're here. Not alone, but not with *him*. You let the sting sit in your chest for all of ten seconds, and then you mentally slap yourself. *Stop it.*

The *szlachta* had formed the Golden Liberty, cutting the king's power off at the knees, and in retaliation the King and his *Volkhv* created the mountain of glass. He then put his daughter at the top of the mountain, and proclaimed that whoever could reach her would win immeasurable wealth and his kingdom when he died. Give the people what they want, you guess. Bastard dad move, though. And so there is the *Climb*.

No one's made the Climb.

The odds aren't great; they're zero, but it doesn't stop people from chasing this dream. Every month people come from further and far to attempt it. Priests hold token ceremonies, blessing the climbers, the blessings useless. So smaller, more plentiful skirmishes, with smaller rewards are offered too. You have no illusions about the climb. You're not doing it; you're here for the mêlées.

An industry's sprung up near the mountain; a service village with inns, smithies, apothecaries, brewers, carters, knock off t-shirt sellers, it's a damn festival, with a large market square decorated for the festivities. Adjacent to the market square are the tourney fields, quiet at the moment with only a few scattered crows pecking at the detritus, but soon enough they'll be popping.

"Should we sign up for the fights, or find lodging first?" Daria scans the buildings. "I'm kinda tired."

"Let's get some coffee. Then the lists. Mmm. *Chrust!*" The smell of fresh dough sprinkled with sugar beckons, and Piotr heads off towards the food stalls.

You'd rather feel anything than this goddamn rejection bullshit. Before you'd left, you couldn't believe your luck when you found an old style sabre tucked away behind the men's winter coats at the local Thrift, the grip missing some of its leather but the blade well balanced. *Please don't let me down too*, you tell it as you follow Piotr into the crowds.

BECOMING A HOME

CAMDEN ROSE

I pull at the window glass Shedding from underneath my fingernails and knock on Mom's door.

Aunt Rosa answers, her body as young as the day I left. Her black hair drifts over her shoulder and down her waist like a waterfall. I tug at my frizzy curls without thinking.

"Alex?" she says with a slight tilt of her head. Her hair cascades down her shoulder and hits the door frame. Light from the kitchen streams in between her strands, making her glow like a goddess.

Everyone always used to whisper about her, saying she was wasting her beauty by not Becoming a home for someone. Even after Dad passed, the neighbors belittled her for taking his place instead of finding a man to raise me. And when I was the age where my Shedding every month filled me with roof shingles instead of beautiful windows, I believed them.

"I, uh..." I want to explain everything, but instead, I just stand there wide mouthed as Rosa tilts her head, perplexed.

"Well, come inside. I'll start some tea." She backs away from the door and shuffles toward the kitchen, barely picking up her feet as though to stay connected to her sister.

I take a deep breath of the cool air outside then step into my mother.

The floorboard creaks under my weight like a comforting hug. I slip off my shoes and let my feet relax into the warm hardwood. I've forgotten what it was like to live in a home, not just a house.

Rosa reaches for the kettle and fills it with water from the sink. "So," she starts. "Why are you back?"

"I—" I sigh and lean against the counter. "I lost my job."

Rosa arches an eyebrow at me, then closes the lid of the kettle and puts it on the stove.

"I just need a place to stay for a while. That's all." I don't mention that my boyfriend Paul offered me his house until I Became. That instead of breaking up with him, I told him I'd think about it.

Maybe it's a sign, he said when I told him about getting fired from my receptionist job at the dentist— budget cuts is what they claimed. *Maybe now we can... build a home together.*

After that conversation, I've had nothing but nightmares. Visions of fully Becoming, of pushing a kid out of my walls, but no one can hear my screams because I'm a home and I've surrendered my voice. In my nightmares, Paul pulls my child from my drenched plaster before I'm ready and raises them as he wants: full of ambition, pride, and an understanding of how the world works for men and women.

The next morning, I go to the store so that we can be stocked for two people instead of one. I don't mention that I just need a moment of fresh air, a second to stop thinking of my mom and Rosa every time I see a new roof shingle pushing its way through my skin.

I go to a local grocery store, one somewhere between a mom-and-pop and a chain store. As I'm debating my cheese selection, I hear a slight gasp behind me.

"O.M.G., Alex?" says Daisy, while putting her hands to her face as though she's genuinely shocked.

I give her a brief smile and act like I'm in a rush, but Daisy doesn't seem to buy it. She stands next to my cart and puts her hands on my shoulders as though we were best friends in school. Her nails are perfectly manicured—a French tip with a small daisy on the thumb.

"Hi, Daisy." For a moment, I wonder if there are other alumni still in town.

"How've you been? How's the job? I heard you moved out of this godforsaken town. Good for you. You look great. Are you working out? You know I've been trying this new thing called yochi and it's done wonders for my body. My skin, too. I could get you a referral, if you'd like, and you'd get a discount on your first session." She pauses to take a breath, then slows down. "Sorry, I'm a little starved for company. Everyone around here seems to be Becoming and it gets quite lonely when you're one of the last ones left. Rowan and I keep trying but—" She shrugs. "—nothing's stuck yet." She looks down briefly in shame, but when she looks back up at me, her eyes shine. "Enough about me, how are you?"

"Good." I grab the cheese closest to me. I hope she'll take the hint and move on, but if anything, she only gets more determined. She taps on the cheddar cheese wrapping with her fingernail.

"I heard that cheddar cheese is good when you're Becoming. Helps encourage the homeliness, you know?"

I hold the cheese in my hand, caught in a permanent limbo between what she says and what she implies.

Daisy grips her cart handle, holding it so tight that I'm surprised her nails don't loop back around and stab her in the palms.

"Well, either way, if you ever wanna grab coffee or something, let me know. You never know how much time we have left at this age," she says with a wary smile and continues down the aisle.

I wait until she's turned the corner to put the cheddar cheese back and grab some Swiss instead.

On the way home, I see what Daisy mentioned. Half the homes are new, though it takes a few glances to notice. The daughters who used to live in their moms have Become mothers themselves. Different iterations of the same thing.

I drive through the neighborhoods, trying to map which homes are who, which daughters became mothers, and which mothers pulled up their foundations so their daughters could put down their floors.

My neighbors to the left, the Gustons, no longer have light blue shutters on a white A-frame house. Now the home is more curved, somewhere between an A-frame and a dome, and the shutters are a light green instead. Mary Guston always loved green. Her parents, living in their own lifeless home, must be so proud of her. Her mom must enjoy being herself again.

I look back into our driveway. Somehow, I'm tearing up, even though I know conceptually that once Mary is done Becoming, she'll turn back into herself and live out her days as a person, happy she contributed children and a loving home to society.

That's what she said she wanted to do after all.

As I get out of the car, I glance across the street at the Jenkin's home. It's the only one that looks the same after all these years, though vines grow up the bricks, tracing the mortar like a dance. No car sits in the driveway and all the lights are off.

Even from across the street, the home seems to sink into itself.

"Need any help?" Rosa asks, popping her head out of the door.

"Yeah." I open the trunk, but I keep glancing at the Jenkin's home. It looks the same as it did when I left six years ago.

Rosa catches me staring but says nothing. I follow her inside, grocery bags looped around each arm. I sweat plaster dust.

That night, Daisy messages me on social media.

Hey, free tomorrow?

I wait for her to send a follow-up message, but nothing comes. Eventually, I shut my phone off and go downstairs.

Rosa sits on the couch, eyes glued to the TV like always. I join her silently.

We watch the characters run around and gasp dramatically at the hardening wood on a woman's arm. Then, Rosa turns the volume down, so much so that we hear the hum of the heater over the screen chatter.

"So, how long do you think you're going to stay?" she asks.

I shrug. "I don't know. Just until I get back on my feet I guess."

Rosa nods. We sit there for a moment, avoiding eye contact.

"Have you always known?" I ask, pulling at the loose thread on my jeans. They smell like basement must, so I don't wash them until I'm done Shedding each month.

"Hmm?"

"That you don't want to Become. Have you always known that you don't want to raise a family?"

Rosa's lips disappear in her mouth. "Did something happen with you and Paul?" she eventually says.

"What?" I shake my head. "No, I just, no. Just curious."

She puts her hands in her lap. "Yes, I think in some way, I've always known."

I nod, but before I can respond, Rosa turns the volume up again and we go back to watching TV.

The next morning, I wake up with shingles in my hair, scraping my face. While icing the burns, I message Paul a good morning message that he responds to with an equally cutesy good morning. Then, I message Daisy that I'd love to do something.

She agrees to meet me at a coffee shop down the street. I decide to walk there, just to feel the ground under my feet for a bit.

I'm glad when Daisy doesn't mention the shingle scars. She waves me over. A blue coffee mug in a saucer sits on the wooden table. The latte in it is already half-drunk. The white half-faded milk leaf globs together.

"Hey!" she says, then wraps me in a hug. I'm surprised how long she holds onto me, as though she's afraid I'll disappear.

"Hi." I break away and put my hands in my pockets.

"Do you want to order something? On me." She smiles and I feel even worse.

I want to ask her if she's hanging out with me because I'm the only person her age left, but I crave company as much as her, so I say nothing.

"Sure," I mumble and order a coffee at the front. While I'm waiting for the drink at the front counter, she looks over at me and grins. I scratch my hair, feeling the shingles underneath pushing their way through.

Other customers glance my way and I hold my stomach. I'm supposed to not want people to see this side of me unless it's pretty; I'm supposed to not want people to see anything ugly until I've Become.

I grab my coffee and sit down, across from Daisy. She takes another sip of her drink. Her hands shake a little bit, but I don't comment on it.

"So, how are you? Really?" she asks.

"Good. Just visiting my aunt."

She nods. "Dating anyone? I know when you left, you were dating that... what was his name?"

"Darren. We broke up." He had wanted kids and I couldn't give him a definitive answer about what I wanted. Eventually, he got tired of waiting. "I'm dating someone named Paul now. We met in college."

When I met Paul, I told him that I wanted kids, that I wanted to Become. It was easier than explaining the complicated space of my mind. I figured that either we'd break up and it wouldn't matter, or by the time we'd been dating long enough to have children, I would have decided.

"Oooooh," she coos. "What's he like?"

"Uh, he's... nice. Charming. Sweet." I try to come up with other descriptors that seem less generic, but my mind draws a blank.

"He sounds wonderful." Daisy looks off into the distance. "It's so nice, being able to find someone who makes you feel loved."

"Yeah," I agree, but when I try to picture Paul fitting that description I come up short. It's not that he isn't loving. He's wonderful, an ideal boyfriend according to everyone. But, even though I know he's trying his best, he doesn't make *me* feel loved.

He'd be a great husband though. A great father. He'd fit the part perfectly.

"You know, I got accepted into State a few years ago," Daisy says. She traces the rim of the mug with her nails.

"Oh?"

"Yeah. But then I met Rowan and..."

I'm not sure if I should say *sorry* or *do you need help,* so I keep my mouth shut. After a moment of staring at her drink, Daisy laughs and looks back up at me.

"I'm happy though. You know, with him. Rowan's great. And who needs a degree when I'll Become a home anyways?" She chuckles and picks up the coffee with both hands, cupping it like it's a baby bird. Her hands tremble and a few drops spill over the top and down her perfectly manicured nails— this time sky blue with a different colored flower on each finger. After a moment, she puts her drink down on the table— so hard I'm surprised the cup doesn't break. She smiles wider than I expect her to. "I'm so glad I found him."

Daisy picks the drink up again, holding it so tight her hands go white and I see small scars on the edge of her palms from her most recent Shedding. She takes a sip and I follow because I don't know what else to do. The coffee is dark and hot on my tongue.

"So, are you and Paul thinking about, you know?"

I know what she's asking, but I don't want to discuss it, so I tilt my head instead, hoping she'll move on.

"You know..." She leans in and whispers as though it's a secret. "Becoming."

At the mention of the word, I feel the shingles pushing their way through my hair, the nails budding out of the skin on my legs like ingrown hairs. "I don't know... I uh..." I look at my drink.

She frowns and grabs my forearm. "Oh, I'm so sorry. I didn't know that you couldn't. I just thought that—"

"I can."

Daisy pauses, then laughs and relaxes into her chair. "Oh, I'm glad."

I nod, unsure how to explain that I'd rather not have the choice than have the false sense of one.

"I think about that sometimes. You know, if I couldn't. It would be so hard, seeing everyone, knowing I couldn't join." She sighs, then gives a small smile. "At least I wouldn't be alone though."

"Hmm?"

"Well, you know, because your aunt can't—"

"She can. If she'd wanted to, she could." I ball my fists up under the table to stop myself from standing up and leaving. The window shards under my nails threaten to dig into my palms. I hate that people think Rosa can't Become, instead of thinking that maybe it was a choice she made.

"Oh!" Daisy laughs at herself. "Rowan always jokes that I just *love* making assumptions. I guess he isn't wrong."

After coffee with Daisy, I get in the car and pull up Paul's contact information. I should call him and be honest about my intentions, about the fact that I can't decide even though everything around me demands I follow my path. I'm supposed to want to have kids, want to Become, want to give away 18 or more years of my life to being nothing but a home for someone else.

But then I get a text from Daisy apologizing for taking over the conversation and assuming Rosa wasn't able to Become. She asks if she can make it up to me.

I tell Daisy I'm free tomorrow and put my phone away.

The days go by slowly and I find myself stuck in the limbo that comes with being twenty-something with no kids. No one wants to hire me in case I Become. My social media is covered with pictures of friends Becoming—posted by their spouses, of course. I can't go to the store without some older cashier making some silly comment about how I'd be such a pretty home. Even my ads are cluttered with different furniture that could fill my home: elegant chaises with roll arms, tall wooden cabinets, sheer linen drapes.

"It's so sad about Patrice Jenkins," Daisy says on our fifteenth coffee date.

"What about her?" I ask. At this point, I've learned to ask questions and let Daisy carry the conversation.

We've been seeing each other more and more over the last month and a half, though I think it's because all her friends have Become. For me, I just need a break in routine, something to get me out of my home. Something to make me leave my mom's embrace and Rosa's stares.

"Her husband and kids left, but she never Unbecame. Guess she thought they'd return or something." She sips her coffee with gloved hands. Maybe she got a manicure she didn't like. Maybe she thought her Shedding was ugly.

Mom also could have returned to herself after I left, but she didn't. Sometimes I wonder if it's because she thought she needed to take care of her sister or she feared what she'd return to. Maybe she knew I wouldn't take her place.

"Which brings me to some news." Daisy smiles.

I tilt my eyebrows up as she pulls off her gloves. Her fingers have turned to wood underneath, though she can still move them back and forth. Her nails are no longer beautifully decorated—just dark and splitting. She grins wide.

"Wow, you're..." I start.

She squeals, "I'm Becoming!" She grabs my hands, softwood against my palms. "I'm so happy. I hope it's a boy," she says through tears and at some point I start crying too.

On the way home, I drive past Patrice Jenkins and Mary Guston and the blank lots waiting for Becomers— one of which will be prepared for Daisy. Then, when I get home, I call Paul. He picks up on the third ring, after I've already started pacing the bedroom, trying to make the space feel bigger than it is. I glance around at the posters peeling off the walls and swallow.

The homeliness feels constricting sometimes, like a hug that's gone on a bit too long.

"Alex?" Paul answers, his voice calm though I know he's been worried. I keep refusing to meet up or call.

"Hi." I lay down on the bed like I'm a teenager in some movie. That lasts about three seconds before I sit up again, my arm itching with the pain that comes right before I Shed each month, before the window panes and bricks and nails force their way through my skin.

"Hi. You want to talk?"

"Yeah, I... Let's build a family."

"Are you sure?" he asks. I think part of him knows.

"Yeah. Are you free tonight?" I say.

"Sure, yeah. Yeah, I am." He chuckles. "Where do you want to meet?"

"Does my mom's work? I'll send you the address."

He agrees and we hang up, neither of us really wanting to chat.

I lay down on the bed, the countless pillows altering my normal posture in uncomfortable ways. Downstairs, Rosa watches her drama. Same thing she does every night.

She'll always be there.

Sometimes I feel bad for her. Sometimes I wish I were her. But then I think about how everyone whispers about her choices. They say that no one would ever choose to not Become, so she must be infertile.

If I follow her path, they'll whisper about me, too.

Paul texts me when he arrives, so I run downstairs and open the door. He stands there, flowers in hand and a sheepish smile on his face as though he's in high school about to go to prom.

I pull him inside and upstairs before Rosa can say anything. We make love to the sound of her TV.

When it's over, my arms no longer itch and I wonder if it's a sign, if moments after, I can Become just like that.

Paul wants to hold me close, so I let him. When he falls asleep, I sneak out from under his arms and downstairs. The second to last step creaks and I pause. Rosa turns off the TV.

"Is this what you want?" she says to the screen.

I finish walking down the stairs and sit next to her. She doesn't look at me, nor I at her.

"Yeah." I sit up straighter. "It's what I want."

Rosa nods. With a deep exhale she gets up and heads to the kitchen. I follow her when I hear the kettle on.

After a moment, she hands me a green mug filled to the top with yellow-colored tea. It smells like grass and outdoors.

"It'll help you. Ease the sickness, the building pains."

I nod and take a sip. Tea slips down my throat like a massage.

Rosa sips her own drink. "You know, it was never easy for me," she says, "but I'm happy. I never saw myself growing into a home, Becoming a mother like that."

I don't mention that she's Become in her own way, choosing to raise me after Dad passed, choosing to stay after I left. Instead, I cup the mug between my hands and stare at the steam as it drifts into the air.

"I wanted you to feel more than just the warmth of a home growing up."

"I know." I hold the mug tighter, as tears drip into the tea. Rosa puts her own mug down and holds me. We cry together. When my bones shift to studs and my skin to walls, I know that I'll still have her.

I sit for a long time in front of Daisy's house debating backing out and never talking to her again. Eventually, I rack up the courage to ring her doorbell. I hear it echo throughout the house before she answers.

"Alex!" she practically squeals and grabs me in a hug. She's gotten bigger since the last time I saw her, but I guess so have I.

"Hi, Daisy," I say, hugging her.

When we break apart, she steps back and gives me a once over. Her eyes stop on my fingernails, which have fully transformed into small clear glass windows. "Are you...?"

I nod. She squeals even louder and wraps me in another hug.

"Now we can Become together! Oh, it'll be so much fun! I've already been thinking about what color I'll paint my walls, how many windows I'll have." She laughs. "As though I haven't been planning this since childhood." She waves me in and walks to the living room where she sits down on the couch.

I follow behind her, a step at a time. The house feels cold and lacks the warmth of a mother.

Daisy pats the spot next to her and I remember how exhausted I am. I sit down next to her, my body sinking into the couch.

"Oh, I'm so excited. I thought I would be alone in this, but I won't. And then, in 18 glorious years, we can all laugh about it while we drink mimosas and wave our children off." She sighs to herself, then turns toward me. "Do you think you'll miss it?"

"Hmm?"

She looks at her hands—the wood has traveled up her arms almost to her shoulder. "Do you think you'll miss this? You know, being able to sleep and work out and eat food and have a social life?"

Of course I'll miss it. But if I want my mom to return to her body, Paul to stop pressuring with his kindhearted messages, Rosa to stop staring at me with those knowing eyes, I have to Become what they want.

A nice, quiet, beautiful home.

But I can't say all that. I've surrendered my voice.

Camden Rose is a queer author who loves seeking out magic beneath the everyday world. She can often be found at the ocean's edge taking notes on the local mermaid population. She lives in the Pacific Northwest with her spouse, black cat, and collection of books and board games. You can find her online at www.camdenscorner.com.

A UNIVERSE CUPPED IN THE PALM OF HER HAND

J. L. GEORGE

It was a Tuesday afternoon when Annie found the universe at the bottom of a teacup.

She remembered the goddess who'd left it because they were such a rare sight around here. Deities on walkabout tended to frequent more upper-crust establishments, and if they went in for baked goods, it was French pâtisserie rather than Suzanne's banana loaf.

This one had asked for a pot of Earl Grey and a toasted teacake. She'd glanced around at the other customers, and in a blink, her flowing robes had been replaced by a pink puffball skirt and a t-shirt bearing the name of a local record shop. She could almost have been any other artsy young person dropping in for an afternoon caffeine fix. It was like she didn't *want* to be noticed, or worshipped.

Annie had never met a god like that before. Most of them, when they deigned to visit this universe at all, strode around with their feet barely touching the ground, accepting the awe of passers-by as nothing more than their due. The teacake goddess– as Annie had privately called her– avoided the stares of the other customers and, once Annie had taken her order, blotted out their excitable whispers with oversized headphones conjured from a pocket somewhere within the folds of her skirt.

As Suzanne emerged from the kitchen, Annie jerked her head in the newcomer's direction. Suzanne looked nonplussed, and she mouthed, *Goddess!*

Suzanne just about managed to contain her curious stare. She huddled close to Annie behind the counter, and whispered, "Are you sure?"

Annie nodded. "I saw her change clothes, like that!" A snap of her fingers.

Still sceptical, Suzanne raised an eyebrow. "In a place like this? Come off it, Annie— we live in the real world, not a bloody soap opera."

A small flurry of customers flooded the shop, and by the time the whirlwind had passed, the goddess had finished her teacake and left. Annie felt oddly deflated, and started to wonder if maybe her eyes had been playing tricks on her after all and the goddess had only been a student or one of the local museum staff popping in on her break. After all, Suzanne had been telling the truth: nothing ever happened to people like them.

Then she'd noticed the left-behind teacup, and the strange glow inside it. When she lifted the cup and saucer closer to her face, she found herself mesmerised by bright whorls of galaxies against misty blackness, myriad glittering points of light. A whole universe, cupped in the palm of her hand. If she gazed at it too long, she started to feel dizzy.

Neither she nor Suzanne had a clue what to do about it. They could hardly leave it in the lost property box with the forgotten umbrellas. In the end, Annie carried it carefully over to the shelf behind the counter and set it down next to her cacti. It felt ridiculous to leave it there, shining in a corner of her humdrum little world and waiting for its creator to come back, but she rather liked the faint glow it cast on the walls, the way it made the coffee shop look like a stranger, brighter version of itself.

They were almost ready to close up, and Annie was wiping down tables and wondering what, exactly, a universe would *do* if you left it alone overnight, when the goddess burst in.

Now that Annie looked at her— really looked at her— there was no mistaking her for an ordinary person. Her hair was a black cloud pricked with stars, her skin a deep brown that seemed to glow from within. If she were human, Annie would have said the concerned furrow between her brows was adorable.

"I think I left something here," she said, a hint of breathlessness in her voice. "I only just made it. If I don't get it back..."

When Annie lifted the cup down from the shelf, cradling it gently as a baby bird in both hands, relief broke like a sunrise across her face.

"I wanted to do something. To say thank you."

Annie hadn't expected to see the teacake goddess again. It had been a long shift, the morning rush bleeding into the lunch rush without a minute's breather, and she was painfully conscious of her red, sweaty cheeks and the fact she'd got steamed milk down the front of her apron an hour ago and hadn't had time to change it. Plus, Suzanne was yelling for her to see to the old gentleman on Table Three, who was complaining that his cappuccino kept staring at him.

She blinked a few times, not sure she'd heard the goddess right. "Sorry, what?"

There was that little frown again. "Is this... not how you do things here? Only, you kept my universe safe for me." A tiny, tentative smile, one that echoed something inside of Annie. "I thought maybe you'd like to see it." Annie's stomach flipped. She'd heard stories about those who, chosen by the gods, walked between universes– about the danger and the wonder, and how special one had to be to do it. She'd never been quite sure she believed them. And now here was a goddess, holding out the possibility like she was offering to take Annie out for lunch.

Except that the way she spoke made it sound more like a shared secret than a simple invitation. Like a flirtation.

Annie swallowed, noticed that the goddess's smile had begun to falter, and nodded vigorously. "I finish at half four," she said. "Cuppa while you wait?"

The goddess's face lit up. Gazing into it felt like looking at the sun reflected on an ocean. "And a toasted teacake?" she said, hopefully.

Annie tore her eyes away and grinned. "You're on."

She picked up the new cappuccino, dropped it off at Table Three, and collected the old cup, noting that whatever was wrong with the coffee hadn't stopped the old guy from drinking two-thirds of it.

It was the same cup she'd found the universe in – blue ceramic, with a rough surface that was satisfying to touch. Annie peered into the leftovers, but there was nothing there except milk foam. The guy was probably just a bit dotty.

The sun had begun to sink by the time she locked up, painting the clouds coral-pink and fiery orange. The goddess leaned against the front wall, hands tucked into the pockets of her fluffy hoodie, staring up at the blooming colours with her lips parted in silent wonder. The sight took Annie by surprise; she'd never imagined a goddess being fascinated by something so everyday.

Then again, this wasn't her universe. Annie wondered what sunsets looked like there, and if it even had suns at all, and shivered with anticipation.

The goddess lowered her eyes to meet Annie's. "Shall we?"

Annie took the hand she proffered. She'd thought there might be an electric charge to a goddess's touch, but the skin was warm and soft as any human's. "I don't know your name," she realised, aloud. "I probably should, if we're going..." *On a date.* She didn't know if that was right, and wasn't sure she'd have dared say it anyway.

"Oh! Of course." And the goddess said something that started out like a word shaped by human lips, but was somehow also the shushing of waves, and the rustle of an autumn breeze in a hedgerow, and a pure note struck from a crystal in a cavern deep beneath the earth.

The sound brought tears to Annie's eyes. She blinked them away. "I'm... not sure I have the equipment to say that," she admitted.

"I listened to you and your friend," the goddess said. "You call the people in the coffee shop by their orders."

That was true of the regulars. There was Oat Chai, who came in every Sunday afternoon to stare gormlessly at their laptop screen, and Weak-Tea-One-Sugar, who started her mornings with them every weekday before shuffling to the Co-Op for her shopping, and Flapjack, who'd talk the ear off anyone unfortunate to get caught in his blast radius.

"But that makes it sound like you're just a customer," Annie said, and cut herself off, wondering if she'd been too familiar.

The goddess cast her a shy, sideways look. "I would like to be more than that."

"Then how about..." What had the first couple of syllables of that name sounded like? "Sara." It wasn't exact, but it was close.

"Sara," the goddess repeated, and again, as if tasting an unfamiliar dessert: "Sara. Yes. I like it."

Annie squeezed her hand. "Okay then."

She'd never been to another universe before. She didn't know anyone who had. She sort of expected it to be like a teleporter on a TV show – that she'd disintegrate in this world and reassemble, only slightly discombobulated, somewhere else.

It was not like that. Sara reached into the pocket of her hoodie and pulled something out, a million tiny points of light glittering in her palm. She let her universe slip gently from her hand.

Annie's stomach lurched. But instead of plopping to the floor like a melted ice-cream, the universe expanded, grew to something the height of a doorway and the colour of a night sky. Sara tugged her hand, and they stepped somehow both sideways out of this universe and into Sara's.

Annie got a brief impression of tall buildings made from weathered, golden stone. Of a sky that glowed violet and teal, and bold brushstroke clouds; of air that sparkled inside her when she breathed it. For the space of a heartbeat, it was beautiful.

A wave of nausea and pain slashed through her head, so intense she felt herself begin to deliquesce around it like butter cut with a hot knife.

She couldn't breathe. She doubled over, retching and trying to curl in on herself at the same time, as though the pain were something outside of her, something she could be protected from, and not burning inside her skull. Somewhere above her, Sara was saying her name, asking, "What's wrong?" But she sounded terribly far away.

There was a hand on her shoulder. Even the slight, warm weight of it was too much, and she tried to shrug it off, but it held her in a gently inexorable grip.

"Come on," Sara urged, and guided her to her feet. Dizzily, Annie moved with her. They were side-stepping again, out of the world, a tapestry of the heavens folding around them.

And then they were back beside the coffee shop, and Annie was vomiting her lunch onto the solid, familiar pavement.

Suzanne had been locking up, but stopped, startled, at their reappearance. Annie let herself be led back into the coffee shop and slumped into a chair. A steaming mug of ginger tea appeared before her, and she closed her eyes and sipped gratefully. It was somehow sharp and bland at the same time; perfect for settling stomachs and clearing heads.

At last, she felt herself enough to open her eyes. Suzanne sat opposite her, prodding at her phone. When she noticed Annie looking, she set it down, with a smile that was mostly sympathetic – though Annie knew from experience she got antsy if she wasn't home in time for *Pointless*. "Feeling any better?"

"Yeah." Annie squished the teabag in the bottom of her mug with the spoon. "Where's Sara?"

"Sara?"

"The goddess. We went– we were supposed to go to her universe, but– "

Suzanne patted her hand. "She said she had to go."

"Oh."

Annie deflated. But of course Sara was gone. She'd been stupid to get carried away, to think she was one of those people you heard of in rumour and myth, special enough to go universe-hopping with the gods. Well, it was very clear now that wasn't true.

She swallowed the last dregs of her ginger tea, over-strong and so bitter the tart smell went right up her nose and made her sneeze. With her eyes squinched half-shut, she caught a glimpse of something in the bottom of her mug.

An eye. Watching her.

She blinked; it was gone in a swirl of stardust. Perhaps she'd imagined it.

"Do you remember what mug it was?"

Suzanne glanced up from the crossword she'd spread out on the coffee shop counter (Sunday afternoons were always dead) and pushed a curl of greying hair out of her face with her pen. "Hm?"

"After I had that... episode, and you made me ginger tea."

"The throwing-up-outside-my-cafe episode?"

Annie winced. "Yeah, that. Do you remember what mug you used? Was it this one?" She lifted the blue ceramic mug, the one in which she'd found Sara's universe. "I was too out of it to notice."

Suzanne shrugged. "Might've been."

"Right. Helpful."

It had been a week with no sign of Sara. The wound was still raw, and most of Annie wanted to slam the lid shut on the whole thing and tell herself it had been a stupid daydream.

Only she kept thinking about that half-second glimpse of someone watching her in the bottom of the mug. Kept wanting to pick the scab.

"Keep it, if you want," said Suzanne. "I think it's gone funny in the dishwasher."

On her break, scarfing down a cheese and ham toastie with one hand, Annie turned the cup one way and the other. There *was* something odd about it. Something about the way it caught the light that made it look as though galaxies shimmered in the blue glaze, swirled in the bottom of the mug. Whenever Annie looked closer, though, the illusion dissipated.

She took it home, as Suzanne had suggested. Leaving it in her kitchen seemed risky– her flatmates had no respect for mug etiquette– so she put it on the nightstand in her room and managed, mostly, to forget about it.

Late that night, as she sat up in bed watching one last episode of *Bake Off* on her laptop, something shimmered in the corner of her field of vision. Annie rubbed her sore eyes and resolved, as she so often did, to cut down her screen time, but it was still there.

She took a deep breath, closed her laptop, and reached for the blue cup. The shimmer, as she'd half-expected, came from inside, shifting from the ghostly blue of bioluminescent plankton to the purple of a ripe plum. This time, when Annie took it in both hands and looked closer, the light didn't fade. The afterimage of a universe lingered in the bottom of the mug, moving and changing from moment to moment as though it lived.

A sigh escaped her. This was where she could have been, if only she were stronger, adventuring through the stars with a goddess. She slumped back against her pillows, the mug falling into her lap.

"Annie?"

At first, she couldn't tell where the voice had come from, and she peered around the room in confusion. The glow from the mug caught the edges of the furniture, the fur of her old soft toys, the mound of clothes on the floor that had been there all week and that she couldn't muster the energy to wash, but that was all. There was nobody here.

The voice, though– that, she knew.

She looked into the mug. "Sara?"

The goddess gazed back at her, the light of a galaxy glancing violet and blue off her cheekbones, reflecting in her eyes so Annie couldn't read their expression. "Yes," she said. "I – "

"You didn't even say goodbye," Annie blurted out. Her voice sounded high and childlike, pathetic.

But Sara only looked bewildered. "I didn't think you'd want to see me again. My universe *hurt* you."

And Annie's indignation dissolved like sugar in water. "It didn't mean to," she said. "At least, I don't think it did?"

Sara shook her head. "Of course not."

"I'm just not built for it, I don't think. For leaving this universe. I'm so sorry."

"Sorry?" Sara echoed. "For what?" She paused. "Wait a moment."

"Don't go!" Annie called, but her image shivered and vanished. Annie stared into the cup, bereft.

And something opened up in the dim light of her room. A door that shimmered like a night sky.

Annie should have been embarrassed. She was in her pyjamas, hair sticking up every which way, still awake at– she glanced at the clock– two AM and probably not smelling too fresh. Sara, though, smiled at her like she was a prom date in a fairytale dress.

"Can I sit?" she asked, and Annie nodded dumbly. Sara perched on the mattress beside her, the warm brush of her thigh through the bedclothes a sudden, startling revelation. "I could show you, if you still want to see."

"Yeah," Annie whispered, "I want to."

Sara's gentle fingers threaded through her own around the mug. Inside it, Annie saw the colours of an alien sky, teal and glowing violet. She tensed, waiting for the sickness to hit her, but it didn't come. There was only the quiet of the night, and the warm touch of her goddess's hand, and the universe they both held.

JL George (she/they) was born in Cardiff and raised in Torfaen. Her fiction has won a New Welsh Writing Award, the International Rubery Book Award, and been shortlisted for the Rhys Davies Short Story Award. In previous lives, she wrote a PhD on the classic weird tale and played in a glam rock band. She lives in Cardiff with her partner and a collection of long-suffering houseplants, and enjoys baking, live music, and the company of cats.

THE SILVER COURTESAN

ANJUM NOOR CHOUDHURY

Her sarcophagus is on display in Gallery 3, between a life-sized display of Galle's prehistoric fishing community and an eight-foot-tall effigy of Lord Buddha. Only two other sarcophagi have ever been discovered in the Indian subcontinent and they both pre-date the Common Era. Hers is newer. It was excavated from a shipwreck carrying silver coins emblazoned with the seal of Mughal Emperor, Aurangzeb.

Legend, according to the audio-visual presentation at the exhibition's entrance, has it that a wealthy merchant trapped the empire's finest courtesan in the stone case so he could ship her to the Caliph and thus prove he'd renounced all carnal indulgences.

Your stomach coils and clinches with wet, squelching pain. It's not the misogynistic horrors some dead guy from the seventeenth century inflicted that distresses you. Well, no more so than such stories usually do. Besides, there were no signs of a body inside, so even if there was a courtesan trapped inside the sarcophagus, she must've managed to get out. No, this is your uterus, its awful timing, and its old friend, menstrual diarrhea, here to make your day trip to the southern coast of Sri Lanka hell.

The gelatinous wetness spits out in violent bursts and pools between your legs. You worry the pad you've got on is already drenched to capacity from the bus ride over. Following the signs down the antique wooden staircase to Gallery 4, you hurry past an empty administrative office bathed in harsh fluorescent light and furnished with mismatched filing cabinets. Your toes begin to claw into your sandals as you weave through displays of colonial bullets and torpedo-shaped soda bottles recovered from the depths of the Laccadive Sea.

"Something in particular you're looking for?"

A thick clot explodes in your pants as you bite back a yelp and turn to face the voice. Taking her in, for a second, you're sure your bladder might add to the mess as well.

She's wearing a curator's lab coat over a magenta saree, the full, flared sleeves of her blouse peeking out from underneath those of her coat. Lush raven hair cascades down to her chest in sleek waves. Her round face, full lips, and thick, perfectly arched eyebrows are held together by skin that appears untouched by the country's harsh, salt-infused sun, and glows not so much with youth, but with impeccable genes.

You're tongue-tied as you notice her looking you over, and gulp as she inches closer.

"Bathroom, actually," you manage. "Could you tell me where it is?"

The curator inhales deeply, as though contemplating the balance between life and death. You notice her shoulders droop the tiniest bit as she nudges her chin towards the back exit. "Through there."

You take your time getting your stomach settled in the outhouse (not bathroom), change, and pack your fresh pad with two-plied toilet paper you've hoarded from the hotel bathroom. You're able to roam the rest of the museum in peace after that. You even loiter by the administrative office for a while, hoping to run into the curator again.

The steaming ocean air slaps you in greeting when you step out of the Marine Archaeology Museum. The sky over the white walls and red-tiled roofs of Galle Fort is overcast. The gloom seems to have chased everyone off the cobblestoned streets. You feel their eyes on you though, through souvenir shop windows, café balconies, and tuk tuk doors. They call to you as you pass, mostly to buy their wares and enlist their services. Some try to guess where you're from. Some ask if you're on the market for a boyfriend, and you pick up your pace.

That they all seem firmly planted indoors, a safe distance away from you, is the only reason you don't break into a run.

Otherwise, you hate it— traveling. You hate that you can't tell if your pad's leaking or your thighs are just sweating. You hate that you've got to watch how much water you drink for fear of having to use another outhouse, or worse. You hate that you're constantly afraid, even though most of the locals have been gracious and helpful so far. You hate that, time and time again, in a world that's hardwired to match everyone into pairs, you're the only one doing this alone.

But passing up the opportunity to travel feels like you'll get your strong-, independent-, feminist-woman card revoked, so you suck it up. You take photos of every street, every semi-interesting building, every colonnade, and every Bodhi tree you pass like every one of them will validate your identity as a woman of the twenty-first century.

Standing on the Flag Rock Bastion overlooking the sea, you turn the camera on yourself. You try to get the lighthouse behind you in the frame, but your ocean-frizzed hair whips salt-laced air into your eyes and compromises your motor-skills.

"Shall I take the picture for you?"

You nearly swing your phone into the sea as you pivot. The curator is waiting for your answer at the edge of the empty bastion, by its stone steps. The lab coat is gone. She's wearing a jute hat with a brim that stretches past her shoulders. Its edges flutter in the wind along with her hair and the train of her saree.

You smile sheepishly and hand her your phone. "Yes, thank you."

You find the way she bunches the fabric of her sleeves to sheath her hands from view peculiar, but you're too preoccupied trying to look like you're having the time of your life to question it. Through pressed lips, she tells you how to angle yourself, how much to tilt your head, and how much to smile. When she's satisfied, she hands the phone back to you and wordlessly heads to the farthest edge of the bastion to face the sea.

You consider joining her, making small talk, asking her for recommendations on where to go next, what to eat. But the striking figure she cuts against the darkening grey sky makes you feel you've outstayed your welcome.

As you descend the bastion steps, you wonder how you, from your high vantage point, missed seeing her coming up the empty sand path.

The rain clouds in Galle tail your bus to the outskirts of Colombo. You doze the whole way. A protein and butter-rich lunch has quelled your cramps, and playing with rescued sea turtles at a hatchery near the Galle Fort has lifted your spirits. A thick curtain of rain begins to fall when you arrive at the bus stand, cascading from the roof's ridges in waterfalls.

Your heart stops when you pull out your phone to call an Uber— it's out of battery. You follow the signs to the designated area for taxis— it's empty. One of the security guards points you to a line of tuk tuks across the main road, but you're too alone to haggle with a tuk tuk driver in this weather, and too short on cash to let him swindle you.

You're about to ask the guy at the information desk if he has the Uber app installed on his phone when—

"Where do you need to be dropped?"

There she is, the curator. Miles away from her workplace, with her phone in her sleeve-sheathed hand.

Were you asleep when she got onto your bus?

Startled as you are, you yield the name of your hotel, and follow her to the secluded pick-up point.

"Thank you. Again." You're breathless with relief. "I don't know what I'd have done without you." That ridiculous hat's brim obscures most of her face. You duck your head in an attempt to meet her gaze. "I wish I could make it up to you somehow. Let me get you a coffee. O-or maybe an early dinner."

Yes, dinner.

You don't know why, but the prospect of prolonging this interaction, this proximity to a complete stranger makes your blood thrum. Not so much with excitement about having company, but with hope that someone might *want* your company.

Under her hat's brim, the curator's lips curl in a tight-lipped smirk. "Dinner would be lovely," she hums, "but it wouldn't be wise."

Your heart sinks, yet the inflection of her words has lulled you into a drowsy calm. "No, please, it's the least I can do."

"That's true." You can't hear it over the rain, but you see her draw a long, audible breath, and then gulp. She startles you when she tucks a stray strand of hair behind your ear. A tremor— of dread or pleasure, you cannot say— courses through your body as her fingertips graze the nape of your neck. "I suppose I can snatch a bite."

You don't get a chance to question the intimacy of her touch. Nor do you get a chance to consider her odd choice of words. Your head's been levered to look skyward, and the brim of her hat pushes up against your face. Moist lips press onto the spot over your pulse, and you feel a pinprick. Its sharp sting is flushed out instantly by a surge of ecstasy. It paralyzes you. Gives you wings. Makes you see dimensions and colors you never knew existed. You ought to be terrified, but your body wants more. More, more, more. Until this feeling spills over the brim.

Then it's ripped from you without warning. And you're stumbling back on unsteady legs. Alone. In the middle of nowhere. In a foreign country. Without a charged phone. Heart pounding in your ears, you see her, the curator, now some ten feet away, coolly dabbing her mouth with the flared end of her blouse's sleeve.

"That's the car," she says, nodding towards a white Hyundai pulling in.

You attempt to glare at her in a silent demand for answers.

"You should hurry," is all you get. "Or your pad may leak."

Recoiling at the rude and completely unwarranted reminder you're on your period, you back away across the street, into the waiting car. Your eyes search the bus stand as the car drives out onto the highway—she's nowhere to be seen.

Your skin crawls as your fingertips brush a thin streak of dried blood down the column of your neck. A tightness grips your chest. You think there's something wrong with your bra and try adjusting it discreetly so you don't draw the Uber driver's attention. Out of nowhere, a suffocating heaviness bears down on you. The pain grows sharper and blooms wider, constricting your airways, making you feel like something's broken through your ribcage and wedged into your flesh.

Solitude stretches out like an eternity, a voice not entirely yours echoes in your head. *But an eternity of eternities is something else.*

You try your best to appear calm. Be it a seizure, or a panic attack, under no circumstance can you let the Uber driver know that on top of being alone, you're incapacitated as well.

It takes a while but little by little, the heaviness ebbs like someone is shoveling sand off of you. Only instead of sand, you feel like you're buried under metal pebbles. You have to bite back a scream as the obstruction wedged into your chest is wrenched out. But at least now you can breathe easy again. Be master of your own vessel again.

You're still recouping when you feel it. Hands that aren't your own, grabbing, pinching, stroking. You smell unwashed mouths, feel them pressing into your skin. Your eyes dart about the car. The Uber driver's gaze is trained on the road. There's nobody else in this car but you. Yet your skin burns like it's been bitten by a swarm of mosquitos.

You imagine a dark, swaying room. You imagine lying defenseless under the scrutiny of mangy and entitled, only some of them mildly apprehensive, men. You remember the potent smell of their blood. You remember the incendiary rage coursing through you as you tore them all to shreds, and bathed in the same red blood they, to this day, use to justify their depravities. You remember standing on the prow of the, now unmanned, ship's prow as it sank to its watery grave. You remember diving into the Laccadive and racing the sun to shelter on shore.

You sink into your seat in the car, equal parts astonished and scared. I know where you're staying now, and a stupid part of you hopes I'll come find you. But then you remember the figure on that bastion, confronting the stormy sea with an ancient grudge, and you know I'll drain the life from you if I do.

Allow me to put you at ease, though: I don't prey on the likes of you.

Tempted as I am sometimes.

You said you wished you could make it up to me somehow, and now you have. For when you get to my age, the storyteller's urge to tell stories trumps the predator's predisposition for secrecy and solitude.

You feel me fading from your memory the closer you get to the city. Rest assured, the next time you hesitate to walk another shore like mine, when you feel alone and ill at ease, and question if it's at all worth the risk, you'll vaguely remember the story someone like you made with a silver courtesan, and you'll muster up the gumption to make a few more.

Anjum Noor Choudhury is a speculative fiction author and climate policy researcher from Dhaka, Bangladesh. She is the author of *The Divining Thread* (HarperCollins India, 2022), and her short stories can be found in *Winter in the City* (Ruadán Books, 2024), *Escalators to Hell: Shopping Mall Horrors* (From Beyond Press, 2024), *Tangle & Fen* (Crone Girls Press, 2023), and *Selene Quarterly Magazine: The Complete Series* (Aurelia Leo, 2022).

HOW TO MAKE FRENEMIES AND INFLUENCE PEOPLE

PAULA HAMMOND

M'rami floated on a sea of trash that stretched as far as her compound eyes could see. Her side-eyes gave her a wider field of vision, but with it came overpowering agoraphobia.

Her ancient ancestors had used their side-eyes to help spot prey, or potential predators. Nature had fine-tuned them to detect sudden movements, but she was unused to the additional sensory input they provided— and the effect was unnerving. She felt like danger lurked in every lapis-hued shadow. All she wanted to do was run and hide somewhere dank and comforting. Eventually the feeling became so unbearable that she reverted to her primary eyes. They flickered open like opalescent smoke-bugs and, with a surge of relief, she continued to scan the horizon without the incipient-ache of a stress migraine.

Despite her surroundings, M'rami wasn't rich. She was merely a trash-sitter: employed to keep the claim on someone else's wealth alive, while they were off, doing whatever it was they did.

Her people abhorred waste. Nothing was made that couldn't be unmade, refashioned, or reclaimed. The idea of simply throwing something away because it was no-longer useful or pleasing was anathema, so an excess of waste — or 'Potential' as it was termed— had become the ultimate status symbol.

The authorities only allowed trash-hoards, as long as they weren't left unattended. Which made trash-sitting a sweet gig for someone who had the itchy-soul of youth, desperate for travel, experience and— naturally— money.

The upper-clades mocked Primitives like M'rami. That was part of the reason she'd taken the job. The work paid well enough to have her residual side-eyes and lower arms removed, and with that, a world of opportunities would open to her. Better work, better accommodation, social acceptance.

The piece of flotsam she'd commandeered as a base for her week-long vigil seemed to be made from fungus. It should have shocked her that such a large slab of food-Potential had been taken out of the Wheel but, like most people, M'rami was strangely intrigued by the Hoarders. As a chitling, she'd followed their lives in the glossies with guilty pleasure. Now she was an adult, she felt less pleasure and more guilt, but the fascination remained.

Lying prone, she found that if she fully extended her leg joints, her long, feathered toes brushed up against the rubbish that bobbed around the raft's circumference. The sensitive vibrissae weren't as effective as extra eyes, but they allowed her to detect any unusual motion. She really wasn't expecting trash-pirates but neither was she prepared to forfeit her pay through lack of vigilance.

So far, so good: all quiet.

It was as the third moon was rising— adding its distinctive red-shift to the eerie night sky— that she saw him.

He stood fully upright, both pairs of arms extended, so that his soft torso was exposed. In past times, it had been her people's way of showing that they come in peace— and the gesture still carried weight.

Like her, he had six eyes, two binocular, four residual. In place of the close fitting utility bodysuit she wore, he sported a multi-colored kilt, his chest bare to display the fine, red hair that marked him as one of the Y'maga clade.

Their forebears would have been enemies, and growing up, she'd felt, instinctively, that red was a color to be avoided. She realized that her own yellow trichobothria probably gave him the same fight-or-flight urges.

She tried to push aside her distrust but, it wasn't easy. She was three days from the nearest settlement, in the heart of the Great Mirror Lake, inside a gated compound that could only be accessed using the controller that hung around her neck. She glanced down. The device was still working: an unbroken circle of light that corresponded to the perimeter of the trash-hoard, showed her that there had been no unauthorized incursions.

M'rami swallowed her anxiety and clambered to her feet. Adopting the same upright stance, she stood as still as the bobbing trash-raft allowed, holding her arms rigid, hands, palms-out, to show that she had no hidden weapons. 'Friend' her posture said. Or at least 'frenemy'.

The Y'maga intruder certainly thought so as, with a cheery "hoo", he abandoned his position and began frantically paddling his raft towards hers.

The gentle undulations of the trash-sea turned into stomach-churning waves, and she was forced to sit. The hoard had been chemically treated, of course. It would never rot, but there was no telling how deep it was, and she had no desire to end up drowning in a motile sea of detritus.

By the time her unexpected visitor reached her, she had already discerned two things. First, he wore a controller, the twin of her own. Secondly, he wasn't remotely surprised to see her.

Coming alongside, the Y'maga stopped paddling and hopped across to where M'rami was warily waiting. It was only once she'd tethered the two rafts together, using strands of mycelium as a makeshift rope, that she finally had the chance to look at him.

Y'maga tended to be short and stocky, but he was almost as tall as she was, with slender arms and mischievous eyes flecked with blue and gold. It wasn't unpleasing.

"And you are?" she began, trying not to sound anywhere near as intrigued as she felt.

"D'rarby."

"M'rami" she replied.

"I know," he smiled. "I'm the one that hired you."

"What?!" Her clade were famously volatile and she felt a rush of adrenaline at his words. "I've done nothing wrong!" she bristled. In her mind's eye, there could only be one reason that D'rarby was here — she was about to lose her job, and with it, all her hopes for the future.

D'rarby replied with another infuriating smile. "Unknot your feelers. I've only come to say hello!"

"Hello" M'rami said gruffly. "And when will you be leaving?"

Her aggression only seemed to intensify D'rarby's amusement. He replied in the same irritatingly calm tone: "Well, given that this is my hoard, and you're my employee, I think I'll stay."

If M'rami could have blushed, she would. She hadn't meant to be rude, but D'rarby's sudden appearance caused a confusion of emotions. She was curious, naturally. Excited too. It never occurred to her that she would ever meet a Hoarder. But she was also embarrassed. Embarrassed about the way she looked, the way she spoke. Just being a trash-sitter suddenly seemed impossibly ignominious.

At a loss for what to say, she decided that due-diligence was the best option. Turning her back on her new companion, she went back to scanning the horizon for intruders.

D'rarby's raft was piled high with colorful baskets which he quickly began to transfer to M'rami's. A peek through one of her side-eyes showed him hopping between the two platforms with an easy athleticism.

Eventually the raft stopped rocking and D'rarby began

rummaging through the pile. "Join me, please," he said. "I've brought refreshments."

M'rami's own provisions were little more than dried biscuit and bread-ale. If she was honest with herself, there wasn't enough of either to last the week.

She sat cross-legged and took a plate, which D'rarby began piling with the sort of delicacies she'd only ever seen in the windows of high-end shops. He worked quickly, each pair of arms moving in a graceful ballet of motion. Even Primitives rarely used all of their arms these days— it was considered inelegant— and M'rami was entranced.

"You don't look like any Hoarder I've ever seen," she began, nibbling at the edges of a slice of pie with quiet appreciation.

"Oh, and how many have you seen?" he clicked his tongue in that playful way that her people used to signify humor.

She clicked back, surprised at how at ease he made her feel. "Me and high-society are like that" — she brought her thumb and index fingers within an inch of each other.

"That close?"

"Closer. To be honest, I'm surprised we haven't met at B'lalin's."

"Oh, B'lalin's is so last season," he replied, laughing.

"Seriously, though," M'rami, asked, her curiosity coalescing into boldness, "you haven't had any surgery?"

"No."

"Why?"

"My father would say I was difficult. Head-strong. But, since he's dead, it doesn't really matter what he thinks. Or anyone else for that matter."

"Nice position to be in," M'rami shot back, before immediately regretting the resentful tone she'd injected into the impromptu party.

They ate in silence, M'rami worried that she'd upset her guest while he seemed to be digesting her comments along with the pie.

For the first time since he'd invaded her raft, M'rami had the chance to look at D'rarby. Really look. There was a lightness about him but, beneath that, there was a restlessness — and he carried like a burning brand.

Instead of prying, she leaned over to examine the contents of the top-most basket. There was still plenty of food, but there was nothing like a drink for getting to know someone. She pulled out a tall stoneware vessel with the words 'Red' emblazoned on the side.

"Dangerous?" she asked, eyeing up both D'rarby and the curious bottle.

"It's my own liquor. Something of an acquired taste I've been told."

M'rami poured them both a tumbler-full and downed hers in one. It tasted smooth and sweet with a hint of fire. "I think I could get used to it," she said.

They talked fitfully, at first, aware of the distance between them.

As the liquor flowed, both were excited to find they had more in common than they'd imagined but, when D'rarby casually threw the empty bottle onto the trash-hoard, M'rami's face turned from delight to disgust.

"Really?" D'rarby looked at her, sighed, and before she could stop him, he jumped into the trash to retrieve the bottle.

He was thrashing around on the surface, half-laughing, half-cursing at the silliness of M'rami objecting to one more piece of rubbish being added to an ocean of it. But M'rami wasn't laughing. She'd done her research. Trash-hoards could tangle you up and suck you down. They'd kill you, if you weren't careful.

D'rarby had just reached the stoneware vessel and was swimming back to the raft when his face went pale. He felt a sudden pressure on his lower body, like a vice being tightened, then he began to sink. He stopped-dead— mind racing, limbs tingling as the detritus, below, tugged at him. It was like being stuck in quicksand. He realized, with a sick lurch, that one wrong move could be fatal.

M'rami didn't need to think. She was born for action— and she'd come prepared. In reality it took only a few seconds to find the sand mat she'd stashed in her emergency kit, but it felt like hours. She worked steadily, barking out instructions to D'rarby as she shuffled towards the edge of the raft, and gently rolled out the mat onto the thin skin of the trash sea. It wasn't long enough to reach him, but it would have to do.

The pressure in suck-holes like this could be immense. Enough to crack D'rarby's exoskeleton and liquify his insides. She tried not to think about that. Instead, she fixed her eyes on D'rarby's and began shuffling across the mat. At first all she saw was his fear, but slowly D'rarby's natural optimism resurfaced. He hadn't known her long, but he trusted her— and he was ready.

M'rami's upper hands closed on D'rarby's and with a nod, he steadied himself. To loosen the detritus, M'rami would have to use her lower arms to drum the surface until the rhythm created a sympathetic wave. In theory, that would ease the pressure around his body enough so that she could haul him onto the sand mat.

Her first attempt nearly drowned him. On her second, the mat rippled beneath her, almost pitching her into the mire. Finally she got the rhythm right and was able to use her adrenaline spike to haul D'rarby onto the mat.

Getting back onto the raft wasn't as easy as she'd anticipated. The mat wasn't wide enough for two, so they had to inch their way back, worm-like— she shuffling backwards, hauling him out of the suck, inch by painful inch.

It took most of the night to finally reach safety, and then, all they could do was lie together, hands still entwined, and watch, exhausted, as the moons went down.

Sometime between dawn and first light M'rami fell asleep, waking to the fresh breeze of a new day and the scent of breakfast.

Incredibly D'rarby had managed to conjure up a full-blown feast onboard the tiny raft, which he presented to her with a flourish. "As a thank you for last night."

"Well, if I want to get paid, I could hardly let you drown!" M'rami caught D'rarby's eyes and felt the warmth of their growing friendship.

"Do you know why I came here?" he asked.

M'rami shook her head.

"Because I wanted to meet you. Not you, specifically, of course. But someone like you."

M'rami bristled again. "So, you're on a poverty tour?"

D'rarby sighed. "That's not what I meant. He placed a warm hand on hers. I wanted to meet someone real. Not one of those two-eyed freaks that I've spent my whole life with. I wanted to know what it was like — out here in the world."

"This is hardly the world.'

"It has been for me."

"And what have you learnt? Apart from how not to drown in a trash-ocean?"

He didn't reply immediately, but his eyes took on a far-away look, as though he was having some internal debate. Then he said, abruptly, "All Hoarders own important objects. Bits of history. Culture. A piece of the Cathait Map, buttons from the bodysuit of some famous somebody, 200-year-old bread-ale bottles that no-one will ever drink but that trade for more money than you'll ever make in a lifetime." M'rami balked at that, even if it was true.

D'rarby quietly noted the impact of his words before continuing. "I have a few items, personal to me, that I can't bear to put back into the Wheel. I think we all do?" M'rami nodded as she fingered the thin metal band that spiraled around one of her upper arms. Every time she touched it, she remembered Mom, who had worn it her whole life. If she ever had chitlings, it would be passed on to them. "Then there's this horror," D'rarby gestured at the ocean of trash. "You know what people like me do with hoards like this?" He answered before she could: "Nothing."

The homes of the Hoarders that M'rami had seen in the glossies, were always filled with libraries of carefully curated trash. She knew how some of that was traded on the international market. How dubious organizations employed burglars to steal rarities. She'd read of more than one murder where a hoard was at the heart of it. Surely some of that was true?

"Sure, the rich hoard trash, and some of that trash makes them ever richer, but this? There are less than a thousand families like mine, but we hoard so much that others go without. Now that it's been treated, it can't be recycled. The hungry can't eat it. This whole lake is sterile. The land around it is toxic. Believe me, I've spent a lot of time as a chitling here — and it's not even interesting. It really is trash."

"So why keep it?"

D'rarby shrugged. "Why pluck out your eyes and amputate your arms?"

"Because?" she shrugged.

"Exactly!" D'rarby said it as though M'rami's comment was the most important thing he'd ever heard. "I'm my father's heir. D'rarby Fren-son— about to launch himself into society. Where I go, others will follow, and I'm starting to wonder if it isn't time to rethink some of those becauses."

His words made M'rami strangely uncomfortable. "What are you saying?"

"That changing the world starts with changing your perspective. Come with me. Show me how to be less of this— " He gestured to himself. "— and more of this—" He pressed his hand against hers.

M'rami wanted to laugh, but he seemed so serious. "We don't even know each other."

"Let's change that too."

Now M'rami did laugh. "Look at me!"

"I see nothing wrong with you. And, speaking as one Primitive to another, I can confidently tell you that that this look is about to make a come-back. Pretty soon, everyone who is anyone will want to look like us. And it's going to be fun watching them lose their minds when they realize the horrors they've done to themselves aren't reversible!"

M'rami felt dizzy. She looked at D'rarby's keen, honest face, and sighed. It was tempting, but dreams always are.

They chatted and paddled until the sun began to cast its long fingers over the trash-ocean. By then they had reached the perimeter and were standing on the makeshift pier that led to the exit. "It's time," she said. "Go home and leave me to do my job."

"Come with me," he replied— not for the first time that morning.

"Why?"

"This," he said soberly, gesturing, it seemed to her, not just towards the trash heap but the whole world,"is crazy. It's crazy that families like mine exist. That we have so much. Not just things, but influence. It's crazy, that if we decide that six eyes and four arms are unstylish, people will mutilate themselves to fit in with our passing fancies. We," he said, looking at M'rami with eyes blazing, "are fine, just as we are! It's society that needs to change."

"It's impossible," she said flatly. "Too many becauses."

"Fine," he said, and, with a sudden passion, he clasped the controller that hung around his neck and pressed the device. M'rami stepped back, expecting the gate to swing open. Instead she felt an explosive rush of heat followed by a dull roar. The platform shook, and M'rami fell into D'rarby's arms. Around them, the trash heap burnt.

"What have you done?" she cried, reluctant to untangle herself from his embrace but curious to see the inferno.

"Let's just say, I've taken some of the becauses out of the equation. We can talk about what comes next over lunch."

"B'lalin's?"

"Why not?" he smiled, as the inferno roared behind her. "It's so this season."

Paula Hammond (@writer_paula) is a professional writer & artist based in Wales. She has been published by *Abyss & Apex*, *Third Flat-*

iron, and Air & Nothingness Press, amongst others. Her fiction has been nominated for the Eugie Award, the Pushcart Prize and a BSFA award. Her greatest joy is discovering the things that can be found in the strange, the weird, and the neglected corners of the world. She reads too much, sleeps too little, and firmly believes everything can go in a sandwich. Her new Sherlock Holmes collection, *Eliminate the Impossible,* is out now from MX Publishing.

IN A QUIET SMILE

C. PIVERAL

It's been weeks since Janel interacted with another living soul. She's tried for days to escape her apartment. It seems simple, a turn of the knob, one step over the threshold, but each time—failure. Today she managed to slip her right foot into a shoe.

Janel lives alone.

Exhausted by her call center job in the fluorescent lit basement, where every break was timed and every supervisor made a game out of peacocking their power, avoiding eye contact and avoiding people became a luxury. In the beginning, her new work from home provided solace. The struggle didn't feel so desperate. The loneliness was comforting because she didn't have to live up to anyone's expectations. Except...

Other things began to fill the void.

The silence in the apartment fills the space, her ears, her head. She coughs when she thinks about the quiet— a warm wet blanket pressing across her face. If she listens carefully, from behind her bedroom door she hears whispering, no— whimpering, no—weeping.

She leaves the bedroom behind and heads for the front door.

The apartment is four rooms split down the middle by a narrow hallway: living room, kitchen, bedroom, and bathroom. At the end of the hall, between the bedroom and the bathroom, there's a window. The light that breaks through casts long shadows down the hall until a passing cloud obscures the sun.

In the beginning, it didn't feel so acute, but then the whispers became a voice, and the voice became a warning, and the warning became the visions, and it manifested...

Turns out, Janel has never truly been alone.

Dottie pops up from behind the couch, only her head and shoulders visible. She's grinning. *She's always grinning.* Through her gritted teeth, framed by thin lips, she says, "Stop. Stay inside and save yourself the sadness." The sibilance cuts deep into Janel's ears.

Dottie reminds Janel of those old-fashioned dolls with porcelain heads and soft stuffed bodies holding rigid extremities together. Her cheeks are round and flushed. The sharp scythe of curls that frame her face has a perfectly cartoonish nature. Her abnormally large pupils are full of a deep, intensely familiar void. It disturbs.

"You shouldn't go outside dressed like that!" Dottie says.

Janel sighs. She's wearing mismatched socks, a pair of old sweatpants, and a College Bowl t-shirt inherited from a partner two relationships ago. The faint tolling of a neighbor's cuckoo clock suffocated by the walls murmurs the time. The walk from her bedroom to the front door seems to have taken most of the morning. It's eleven, and Janel hasn't eaten a thing.

Dottie skips exuberantly out from behind the couch. She takes Janel's hand and draws her into the kitchen. "Let's bake some chocolate chip cookies," she says.

Janel's reflection slouches across the mirror as she passes from the living room to the kitchen. Dottie raises a thin, overly manicured eyebrow as if to say, I told you, you're an embarrassment.

Janel looks to her shoeless left foot.

Together, they bake a double batch of chocolate chip cookies. Janel doesn't feel the cold floor beneath her feet. She doesn't feel thirsty. She doesn't feel hungry. Dottie scarfs all of the cookies. The day passes, consumed, one cookie at a time. The windowpane shadows have stretched down the hallway and dissipated in the dying light.

Janel gives up and goes to bed.

In the morning, Janel pulls on a pair of jeans, a clean t-shirt, and a faded purple pullover, the one that hasn't been worn enough for the fabric to pill. Things seem better, more possible.

The window at the end of the hall lines up with another across the courtyard. A flash of movement catches the light. Janel stares at the window, thinking the apartment has a young couple with a new baby. There's a grin and the shine of pearlescent cheeks. Staring back from the other window directly across from Janel is Dottie.

We never leave the apartment!

The bathroom door claps shut, startling Janel out of her observation. Dottie stands just outside, wide-legged and defiant, with her hand resting on the handle.

Janel searches the window across the way, trying to confirm... There is nothing in the window now, just a deep dark shadow like the black inside Dottie's pupils. "But I just saw you..."

"You have your own problems. Don't stick your nose in other people's business."

Janel pulls the window curtain closed against the thoughts of the woman and the baby. "I've my own problems."

Without breaking eye contact, Dottie says, "It wasn't me." It's hard to tell what's behind that constant, exceedingly pleasant grin, but she seems angry.

No matter. I'm dressed. I'm heading out.

"The sink is leaking, and the drain is clogged," Dottie says. "It's just a drip, but if you leave it, it's like to fill up and flood the floor."

Janel averts her eyes and tries to pass. *I can make it out.* She searches for a way to reduce the moment to just a voice in her head, to a whisper, to a passing second-thought of discomfort. The whispers return, the deep sighs, the frustrated thuds of the weeping woman pacing behind the bedroom door.

Dottie doesn't budge.

As she tries to move past, Janel's shoulder brushes the wall. A smudge of grey dust covers her sleeve, but she's heading toward the door.

Dottie's voice solidifies in the air between them. She says, "You know if you brushed your hair like you're supposed to and then wiped out the sink, it wouldn't be clogged with that disgusting tangled clump of—*you*."

Janel slips a foot into a shoe. *I can make it.*

"It's a waste of water," Dottie says. "It will cost you your deposit. Oh, I'm sorry, it will cost you your parent's deposit."

I... Janel slides her foot out of the shoe.

The day is spent cleaning the sink trap, repairing the drip, and brushing her thinning hair over the trash can.

Janel falls into bed, exhausted. Whispers of failure permeate her sleep.

The sunrise glows in the windows of the apartments across the courtyard. They shimmer like the horizon in the end credits of a western movie, pinks, purples, and light blues fronted by golden clouds. The window directly across the way is open, and the curtains are fluttering. Holding her breath, Janel can almost hear the soft billowing sound over the woman weeping in her bedroom.

The mother across the way, still in her nightgown, appears at the window. She's had a bad night; it's reflected in her figure, the way she slumps from fatigue.

An overly large grin peeks from behind the curtains. Janel's heart races.

The woman sees Janel and waves.

Janel, who had forgotten she was not a ghost in this world, tentatively waves back.

Porcelain fingers reach out of the darkness for the wrist of the limp arm hanging at the woman's side. Drawn away from the light, the woman is engulfed again in the dark. Janel can do nothing to stop it. Her mind races for an explanation, a way to help the woman. She frets about her response— it could seem too eager, too weird. *Would the Dottie hurt the baby?*

The weeping behind the bedroom door grows louder.

Janel opens the window wide and listens, for what she can't say. She pulls the bedroom door tight, hoping to hide her footsteps down the hall. *Why?* She doesn't know. Janel lives all alone.

Dottie stands crossed-armed in front of the door— grinning.

The judgment in her eyes will swallow me whole.

Janel slumps once more toward the bedroom but this time stops short. The window's still open. The afternoon breeze blows through her hair, sending a shiver down her back. The sun blazes across the windows. She scans the surrounding courtyard and side street.

A man below, sitting in his car, has his head buried between his arms where they cross over the steering wheel. His face is obscured, and his body convulses as though he's crying. Dottie sits shotgun.

Another? Janel feels like an intruder watching the man in his private moment of grief. She averts her eyes.

On the sidewalk, an elderly lady searches the faces of the people walking past. She tries to talk to them, but they take no notice. They too avert their eyes. Dottie holds the older woman's hand, the grin growing bigger and wider with each passing snub.

They're everywhere. Dotties are everywhere you look— if you bother to notice, if your own Dottie doesn't obscure your view. Janel shakes her head, trying to clear her mind. "That's ridiculous," she says, grinning at the hallucination, but she sees her again and again.

The woman across the way has returned to the window with a writhing, fussy baby on her hip. Her eyes are vacant. She stares not so much out the window but seemingly deep inside herself. Two porcelain pale arms reach out from the darkness. They implore her to give over the baby.

"No," Janel whispers. "Stop it," she says. "No!" Beside her, the bedroom lock clicks open.

"I can't hear you," Dottie hisses, "that's not me." Her teeth shine from the crack in the door. "I'm all yours," she says.

From the darkness behind the woman, arms still outstretched, another Dottie emerges. She locks eyes with Janel while she pulls at the leg of the distraught baby. The mother isn't reacting; she's still lost inside herself, vacant. Her strained lips move almost imperceptibly. *Is she arguing with someone?* There's no one else visible.

A knock against the wall below and Janel jumps. An emergency escape ladder, blowing in the wind, thuds against the wall. Dangling from the window ledge it stops a few feet above the courtyard grass. She punches the screen from the window, and it falls a dizzying two stories to the ground. Clutching the gritty windowsill, she slides one leg out feeling for the first rung.

Emerging from the weeping room, Dottie says, "You're always so dramatic. Don't be ridiculous— someone will see you! Can you imagine the humiliation— if someone sees you?"

There's momentum in the ridiculousness of it all. The decision has been made— she is finally outside the apartment. Her foot gains purchase first on one rung and then another. She's far enough down the ladder that the only part of her still existing in the shadows of the apartment are her hands.

A cold, slick feeling slides across the tops of her fingers. She looks up, expecting to see Dottie, but instead, it's the weeping woman from the bedroom. Her image is warped by Janel's watering eyes, the tightness in her chest, and the shallow gasps that dry her mouth as she descends.

Janel recognizes the weeping woman. *She is me.* Perched on her shoulders like a deranged monkey, Dottie whispers in the weeping woman's ear. She digs her fingernails into the numbness of Janel's hand where it still clutches the sill.

As she jerks her hand free, Janel feels the flesh rip from the talon grip of the nails. In response the ladder swings out from under the eave into the sunlight. Beads of blood speckle the swelling scratches. She descends the rest of the ladder, and drops onto the grass, shaking.

Above, Dottie frowns, nostrils flaring. *The weeping woman is gone.*

The mother is still in her window, leaning cautiously out to gain a better view. From the look on her face, she watched the climb down. *She saw everything.*

Perhaps she's giddied from the adrenaline, but Janel does not feel the promised shame. She glances back over her shoulder up to her window. *No Dottie.*

The sun clears a cloud, and for a moment, Janel closes her eyes, feeling the warmth on her skin and drinking in the passive sounds of a world alive around her.

"Lock's broken, and my phone's dead," Janel yells to the woman. There's no indication she's seen the weeping Janel with the Dottie on her back. "Boy, have I not had enough coffee for this day!"

Competing for the mother's attention, the baby squalls even louder.

"Fussy baby, huh?"

The mother looks at the red-faced, crying baby as though she just remembered it exists. A Dottie pinches a pudgy leg, and flashes Janel a grin.

"Maybe a walk will calm them down," Janel says. "I'm going for a cup of coffee before I call the landlord. You want to walk with me?"

"I'm not dressed," she says. Her shoulders droop further.

"Ah, well, I'm in my socks." Janel holds up a blue-footed toe so the woman can get a better look. In the moment she feels ridiculous — joyfully, bravely, ridiculous. "Just throw on a jacket or overcoat. No one will notice." Janel looks across the courtyard toward the gate. "Trust me, they've all got their own problems."

Behind the woman, the Dottie scrunches up her nose. She looks rabid, like she's about to bite the world.

"Just a second." The woman disappears from the window. The baby still screams. The Dottie glares down at Janel, never blinking, never breaking eye contact. She backs away until the shadows have eclipsed her grin.

A few minutes pass, and the woman appears at a nearby door struggling with a stroller. The baby stops fussing as soon as they cross the threshold.

"Sometimes, I just don't have the energy to go out," she says, pulling the door behind her. "I mean, it feels like something is anchoring me inside that place." She holds out a hand. "I'm Rae."

"Janel."

"Here." She holds out a pair of blue Nike slides. "Until you can get back into your apartment, I thought these might help."

Janel and Rae walk the block in silence for a minute. Conversations take practice. *I'm so out of practice, so awkward. What's the right thing to say?*

"Will you get a break when your husband gets home?" Janel asks.

"Oh," she says, "It's just Samson and me. We live alone."

"Oh, sorry for the assumption." Janel smiles, a genuine smile—no hidden scream straining for release behind a cage of teeth. "Me too."

Rae smiles back— a smile with a hint of relief behind it.

"Hello!" Janel acknowledges the elderly lady from before. The woman smiles at Janel and then the baby—a smile full of warmth. A now grin-less Dottie still clutches the older ladies hand. Janel navigates their group swiftly past and in between grin-less Dotties all along the route. She pretends she can't hear them. Tight-lipped and angry, they're whispering.

Everywhere they go there is a susurrus growing behind porcelain smiles.

C. Piveral's stories combine the dark and whimsical. Her short fiction has appeared in magazines and anthologies such as Flame Tree Press's *Robots & Artificial Intelligence, ZNB Presents: Year One,* Common Deer Press's *Short Tails, Apparition Lit,* and more. A transplant from the American Midwest, she now lives near the Colorado mountains with her rescue dog, Ziggy. For more of her work, visit her website at www.cpiveral.com.

ELEMENTAL GOSSIP

CASS SIMS KNIGHT

It is a well-known fact in certain circles that the key to controlling elemental sway over the perception of reality is not getting caught. Many will swear the best way to derail one scandal is to shift focus with hearsay, the more salacious the better. And this was never more true than the time Morgan High's biology teacher ran off with the nanny.

The rumor mill ground that one down to finer dust than the time the senior class president, David Baumgartner, was arrested for smoking weed. Or when Bryce Hope got drunk with his friends at a strip club in the middle of the day and came back to school afterward to pass out in the senior lounge (apparently not an expulsion-level event when your family paid for the school library). Or the time Chelsea Bradiotti was rushed from the lunchroom to the hospital for open heart surgery, returning a mere week later with a dainty scar peeking out from her famed bosom. In comparison, Mr. Black's infidelity—mere months after the English teacher, Ms. Michel, gave birth to their first child—drove the entire student population to distraction.

The trademark telltale that elemental gossip is at work is that the memory gets mostly sharper with time instead of fading. (Ten years later, the sickening sweetness of the mesmeric gossip about Mr. Black still wafted through the reunion. It was all Hedley could talk about. And Arabella surely would have gone on and on about how Mr. Black had replaced their memories of what really happened with a spell, if she'd bothered to take time out of her busy schedule promoting her latest exposé on occult practices in politics to show up. Only Jake's eyes glazed over as soon as Hedley mentioned the eccentric biology teacher, insisting he couldn't remember even taking biology, an unavoidable side effect. Naturally, there were always risks with memory reassignment.)

A favorite among the lazier students who knew his tendencies toward distractibility, Mr. Black had been the type of teacher who enjoyed a bit of theatrics now and again. It had been practically a school tradition for him to show up as Professor Monarch once a year during the Ecology unit. On that day he sported a bowtie with butterfly wings, matching the ones that poked out the back of his corduroy jacket, folded neatly down his back like a technicolor cloak. His glasses had been replaced with the eeriest contacts outside the movies, and his ears came to a seamless point that didn't resemble prosthetics one bit. He spoke with a strange, unplaceable accent and told strange tales about his ancestors granting wishes to wandering children along their great annual migration.

It wasn't long after the birth of his child that the once-a-year became permanent, and Mr. Black stopped responding to any other name but Professor Monarch. Hedley's mother, the school nurse, claimed he even made the teachers comply with his eccentric requests. It did seem as if a spell had been cast across the school; no one complained or even seemed to think it was strange at all. Hedley hounded her mother for faculty gossip to feed the rest of the group, but that game of telephone only returned vague administrational platitudes about optics and inclusivity.

By comparison, his wife, Ms. Michel, was considered the normal one—when she was anything but. The first day of the fairy tale unit that year, Ms. Michel made the class sign a pledge that under no circumstances would students recount stories without excessive embellishments and superfluous interjections. Bobby Wellington raised his hand.

"Superfluous means extra, unnecessary," Ms. Michel said without waiting for his question. When she tried to continue her lecture on the importance of building narrative threads using three and seven in said embellishments, Bobby thrust his hand into the air harder, like it was meeting resistance.

Ms. Michel sighed. "What is it, Bobby?"

"Would you consider Professor Monarch an excessive embellishment or a superfluous inter-what-tion?" Bobby said with a snigger.

"Interjection," Arabella said under her breath while the rest of the class erupted in howls and shouts. Ms. Michel, on the other hand, looked like she'd been frozen in time. She muttered something under her breath that sounded like a made-up language.

The bell rang.

As Jake and Arabella made their way down the stairs, Arabella asked, "Did that seem weird?"

"What? Signing a declaration to turn the world into a story? You can't expect Ms. Michel to be completely normal, she is married to Professor Monarch."

"No, that class was somehow only a few minutes long."

"What do you mean?" Jake asked, looking over his shoulder at her with a skeptical expression.

"Well, Bobby said something about the Professor and then the bell just rang."

"You feeling okay, Bella? Did you fall asleep for the story structure discussion?"

"No, that was actually the last thing I do remember. I think she fiddled with us."

Jake paused on the landing between the second and third floor. "Fiddled with us?"

"Yeah, so no one asks questions about stuff that is obviously bonkers."

Jake groaned and continued down the stairs.

"No, listen, Jake," Arabella said, putting her hand on his shoulder to stop him in the middle of the stairs. "I've been reading all these old fairytale and occult books and found something about memory spells and natural immunities. How you can't affect large-scale memory replacement without it being ineffective on a small portion of the population."

"Wait," Jake said, turning around as Arabella's hand fell from his shoulder. "Are you saying Ms. Michel put a spell on us because her husband likes to dress up like a butterfly?"

"Not dress up. He *is* some sort of fairytale creature."

Jake chuckled and shook his head. "Did he eat the wrong pie off a magical windowsill? Or is he transfairy?"

Arabella rolled her eyes and walked the remaining steps to the first floor landing. "I think he was born as some sort of mythical butterfly being but became a mild-mannered biology teacher to hide among humans."

"Is he in grimness protection?" Jake asked, holding the door open for his girlfriend with a wicked grin. "Get it? Grimness, like witness but for fairies?"

"If you have to explain it, it's not funny, Jake," Arabella pointed out. "And he's not the big bad wolf."

"Maybe he is," Jake said to a bemused Arabella. "Look, I wouldn't exactly describe him as 'mild mannered'. When I had him, he took a survey of what time of day we all had bowel movements. Used the data to make graphs and charts, the works."

"Whatever he is, he's not what he pretends to be."

"Which part?"

"All of it. He's not to be trusted. And neither is Ms. Michel, for that matter."

It was midway through senior year when rumors of the torrid affair began to spread through the student population and all other chatter fell to the wayside. It all began in what was supposed to be first period English with Ms. Michel, who was a no show. The class waited 15 minutes before they left, as goes the unwritten code of academic conduct. Most of her class went to the computer lab on the first floor of the Fresh Air Building, a dark structure constructed during the 1918 flu pandemic. Like many of the era, it was built for air flow but somehow managed to always smell musty.

Story goes that they heard more than saw Ms. Michel thunder down the stairs and past the door of the FAB computer lab. The patter of her feet sped up, more like rainfall or distant carpet bombing. Her passage created a whoosh that blew the computer lab door shut and temporarily replaced that omnipresent musty smell with the smell of spring, fresh and full of wildflowers. By the time they peeled the door open, there was no sign of anyone. Then there were reports during third period of a "disturbance" in the library, but no one could get any other details and the library remained locked for the rest of the day without so much as a sign on the door. Just before lunch, the lights turned off and on 37 times in seven-second intervals.

Without Arabella there to point out the incongruities, the narrative quickly edited out or revised the uncanny qualities and clung to the simplest explanations. No discussion was required for faulty wiring, after all. And surely Administration was covering up a shouting match in the library. How could it be anything else?

"I heard Professor M is having an affair and Principal Edwards is trying to keep it secret," Jake said.

"Well, I heard the Professor has stage five brain cancer," Hedley said at lunch.

"They only go to four." Arabella, whose father was a surgeon, took a sip from her La Croix.

"Whatever the number," Hedley said with an expression that fell just short of a snort, "it's pressing on the wrong parts of his brain. That's what all the Professor Monarch stuff is about. Apparently, he had some kind of medical incident in the library. That's why Ms. Michel was a no show."

"That doesn't make sense," Arabella said slowly, as if she was explaining the color of the sky to a four-year old. "Why would Ms. Michel miss class first period for something that didn't happen until third?"

Hedley gave her the stink eye. She really hated when people altered course on her narrative. "Then what's your theory, if you know so much?"

"I mean, it's clearly supernatural," Arabella said. "You know the name Michel means 'who is like God', right?"

Everyone burst out laughing. "Everything isn't aliens, Bella," said Hedley, referencing Arabella's most recent deep dive into unexplained aerial phenomenon.

"You send one video to your closest friends about UFOs and alien sightings and suddenly you're the resident crackpot," Arabella grumbled. "I'm not talking about little green men. If I'm so crazy, how about you explain how everyone loses time around the two of them? Or how about the time the Professor went into hypothermic shock after Bryce told him he wished he would chill out? Or the fact that no one remembers reading *The Handmaid's Tale* but me? It's too consistent to be coincidence. Those two are using magic to alter our perceptions of reality."

"You read a ton," Hedley groaned with a wave of her hand. "It's perfectly reasonable to confuse the ones you read outside of class with the ones we read in class."

"I remember reading that book," said Jake.

"See!" said Arabella, "that proves it. Jake has literally never read a book outside of class."

"Hey!" he said, wounded by the charge coming from a bookworm. "But she has a point. Statistically speaking, the simplest explanation can't be true 100% of the time." Hedley ignored him by launching into some pop culture diatribe that had the effect of making them all temporarily deaf.

When they all felt a tremor five minutes later—Rhode Island not exactly being known for its seismic activity—Jake looked over at Arabella with a puzzled look on his face. She nodded knowingly at him and mouthed what looked like the word, "Magic." Everyone else seemed to forget it almost as soon as it happened, without a single peep about it from the chatter in the halls. When Arabella pulled aside Hunter Freeman to ask him about it directly, he got a faraway look in his eyes and mumbled, "Oh yeah," before wandering away in some sort of daze. She looked pointedly at Jake and Hedley.

"Hunter is a ditz," Hedley said, head stuck in her phone.

After lunch when the whole school gathered for assembly in the auditorium, it was a veritable whisper symphony as the Professor took the podium. While the Professor was introducing some zoologist who had come to talk about conservation and environmental degradation, Ms. Michel came storming in. As she moved to center stage, it looked as if a fox tail grew out of the back of her pants, while her head sprouted furry ears.

Apparently, the Professor's theatrics are contagious, the thought echoed through the auditorium, as if someone had said it out loud. Puzzled faces rubbernecked to find the elusive source. The room fell in a hush when Ms. Michel's tail swatted behind her, back and forth. No one made another peep.

Before Ms. Michel could open her mouth, the Professor interjected, "Oh spare me the histrionics, Eloise. Why bother if you're just going to wipe their memories afterwards?"

Ms. Michel's eyes narrowed and her arms went stiff, like a toddler on the edge of a tantrum. "The old ways must be honored," she said simply. "Now do shut up, or you won't find out what I'm replacing their memories with."

The ground under her shook and cracked, sending the flagpole with the school crest over, nearly toppling the guest speaker. The students *ooohed* and *aaahed* like they were on a theme park ride. "In exchange for your freedom from your 'odious' family, General Donal Balefire," she growled, her arms thrown up more to the auditorium of blank faces than to her husband, whose neck had become a peculiar, purplish color, and whose knuckles had gone white from gripping the podium, "I demand a wish, for a wish spoken to a butterfly must always be granted."

Suddenly, the air tasted of metal, a static spark almost visible. Ms. Michel's hair stood on end as she continued, "I wish to banish you back to your homeland, Tirnanog, never to return. Separated from your precious humans for eternity, and held accountable for the crimes you fled from."

Ms. Michel's hair fell, along with her husband's face, the Professor fading from memory. Usurped by elemental gossip.

The next day, Mr. Black's affair was all anyone could talk about. Word was, he had run off in the night with the nanny. Ms. Michel was so upset, she quit and took their baby back home, which was supposedly in one of the northern Canadian territories.

"Does anyone else feel like there is more to this story?" Arabella asked at lunch. She had the same far-off expression on her face as when she tried to recall her dreams, trying to force the bits and pieces to poke through and trigger more details. Meanwhile, Hedley and Jake scoured the internet looking for the social media of the nanny, who reportedly wasn't much older than any of them. Word had it she was some distant cousin of a recent alum, but no one had been able to find either hide or hair of her.

"Can't get much juicier than this," Hedley replied, not raising her eyes from her phone.

Jake raised his, trying to search his brain. "It does seem like something is off."

"Yeah," Hedley replied, snickering, "like how did Mr. Black convince anyone to run away with him?"

"And who is he going to be now? Mr. Black, Professor Monarch, or General Balefire?" Arabella said.

"Who's Professor Monarch?" Hedley asked, still glued to the screen.

"And who's General Balefire?" asked Jake, the queasy feeling of inexplicable fear and déjà vu landing like a brick in the pit of his stomach.

Cass Sims Knight lives in Portland, OR with her pets, who are not pulling their weight on social media. Her fiction has appeared in several magazines, including *Penumbric Speculative Fiction*, *Stupefying Stories*, *Luna Station Quarterly*, and *Drunk Monkeys*. You can find her at cassandrasimsknight.com.

WINKS & PINKS

SARAH TOTTON

It all started when the Edwardian fancier's boyfriend walked in. Our storefront sign said *Unfair Exchange*, *Winks & Pinks*, *Lost & Found*, or sometimes *Daisy & Mick's*, depending on the day and Mick's sense of humor. The shop's front door wouldn't open for just anyone; potential customers needed to get a pass first, and you could only get a pass from someone who'd been in the shop before. Whoever gave you a pass was supposed to explain how the shop worked: you gave us something to lose for you and we lost it, or you came in asking for something and we found it for you. Simple. But some people had a hard time grasping the concept. Like the Edwardian fancier's boyfriend.

It was Wednesday. Wednesdays were stressful because on Wednesday we had to balance the till. Correction. *I* had to balance the till. And it had to be done perfectly because Bax dropped in to check, and heaven forfend if it didn't balance. All that was left of the two guys who ran the shop before Mick and I were a few scrag-ends of beard hair and the echoes of tortured screams. (Mick claimed this was just background music piped in from the Fourth Circle of Hell.)

This particular Wednesday wasn't typical. Mick burst into the shop at 8:00 a.m. with what looked like a bundle of blankets under his arm. He went past me and disappeared into the break room. So I was manning the shop alone when the Edwardian fancier's boyfriend turned up: young guy, straw hat, striped suit, cringing like he thought I was going to clobber him. And me, just an innocent slip of a girl. Ahem.

He sidled up to the counter. "Excuse me, young lady. Could you..." He leaned in close and whispered, "...lose my girlfriend for me?"

"Losing people," I said, "is against store policy."

At this point, Mick came sauntering out to the shop floor, crunching a biscuit, and reading a magazine called *Little Devils*.

"Where have you been?" I asked.

Mick ignored me and said to the man. "Does your girlfriend make you dance the turkey trot?"

"All the time!" said the man with great fervor. "And she calls me Bertie. Only my name's Doug."

"I think we can help you," said Mick.

"Actually," I said, "we're not supposed to—"

"Come with me," said Mick, putting a comradely arm around Doug's shoulders and leading him to the back of the shop. Mick came back two minutes later. Alone. "And that," he said, brushing the biscuit crumbs off his hands, "is the end of that."

"What did you do?"

"Relax, Daisy. I sent him into the First Circle of Hell. Should be a cakewalk compared to his girlfriend."

"Are you crazy?! You can't send people to other dimensions. You'll throw the till off. Bax will kill us."

"I'm kidding. I just locked him in the futility closet."

"We don't have a futility closet."

"That's the irony. Don't worry. I'll let the guy out in a few hours. Go see what's for lunch, huh?"

I thought of Mick as the brother I'd never had. Which was to say there were times when I loved him, and other times when I just wanted to give him a noogie. My actual family were nothing to write home about—so I hadn't ever since I'd left.

I went to the back of the shop. *Lost* shelves on the left. *Found* shelves on the right. On the shelves lay duffel bags, sealed plastic containers, and smoked glass jars. There was a piggy bank for petty cash on the *Found* shelf. We couldn't access the cash without breaking it open, and we only did that once a week, because that was how long it took the porcelain Oink to heal itself and start excreting money internally again.

"You're not balancing the till yet, are you?" Mick yelled from the break room.

"No." *What does he care? He never balances the till.* "Just checking what's for lunch."

Lunch was in the big rubber tub under the bottom shelf at the back of the room. The back wall of the shop sported five wooden doors. Being completely sane, I had never ventured to open any of them. The lunch tub, on the other hand, I opened daily.

Mick yelled from the break room, "What do we got?"

"Sardines. And a Danish."

"What flavor?"

I sniffed. "Blue cheese."

"Pass!"

I picked up the tub and took it to the break room. Mick was doing something behind the breakfast bar of the kitchenette. When he heard me come in, he straightened up, all flustered.

I set the tub on the table and opened the tin of sardines. We took turns fishing them out of the tin.

Mick set a mug of coffee on the table in front of me.

I took a sip. "Wow. This is amazing."

"Just make sure none of what you drink leaves the shop, if you know what I mean."

"Is this leprechaun coffee?"

Rumor had it, for every bean that went into a cup of leprechaun coffee, seventy leprechauns lost their lives picking it. Rumor also had it the only way to get it was to go to Hell.

"Um...," said Mick.

"Are you out of your freaking mind going through the doors? You don't know what's back there."

"Actually, I do. I made a map."

He showed it to me. It looked like a target. The outside ring (which was purple) read:

Fifth Circle of Hell (hoo boy, do not *go there again).*

The green ring inside it read: *Fourth Circle of Hell (great coffee, watch out for leprechauns).*

The blue ring read:

Third Circle of Hell (Cindy).

"Who's Cindy?" I asked.

"Mind your business." He snatched the paper away.

Someone screamed in the hallway.

"What was that?" I said.

"Nothing." Mick bolted out of the room.

It sounded like the Edwardian fancier's boyfriend.

I went into the hallway. Almost immediately, I heard another ungodly howl, only this time it was higher-pitched and emanating from the break room. I traced it to the cupboard under the sink. I opened the cupboard and got the shock of my life; Mick had brought his kid in. I knew about his kid. Not because he talked about her or showed me any photos—but he seemed to have a perpetually harassed look and periodically he'd drop comments like *joint custody* and *my ex.*

The kid was small and egg-shaped (like Mick), and she was wearing a weird bonnet with two dome-shaped white mounds on the top, tied under her chin with an enormous bow.

Her bow had come undone so I pulled off the bonnet. She had two horns peeking out from her blond curls. Now, I didn't know much about kids, but I always thought the term *little devil* was figurative.

"Why do you have horns?"

"They're *horts*!" she said with enormous dignity.

"Oh well, never mind then. I'm sure that's perfectly normal."

"My mommy's indisposable."

"Of course she is." The conversation was becoming unmanageable. "Mick? Mick!"

Mick came up behind me all flustered.

"Cute bonnet," I said. "Didn't know you crocheted."

"Ha, ha," said Mick.

"What's her name?"

"Punkin."

"You sadist. What's she doing here?"

"I couldn't find a sitter."

"And her mom is?"

"Indisposed," said Mick.

"What's going on with the Edwardian fancier's boyfriend?"

"He escaped out the front door."

"Then it's time for me to balance the till."

"Um, about that..." Mick looked decidedly uncomfortable.

"Something you want to share, Mick?"

Mick laughed nervously. "Me? No, I'm just— Punkin, put that down!" He started to wrestle a can of cleanser out of the kid's fist.

"I can see you're busy. I'm going to balance the till."

Whenever anyone asked me what I did for a living, I told them I was in distribution. Like Robin Hood, only without the glamour or the righteous striving against the unfairness of life. I knew that fairness was out of my control. I did my job and went home to my empty apartment above the laundromat, because what else was I going to do? I had no skills and no prospects.

I retrieved the scales and brought them to the main shop floor. I bolted the front door. Then I started taking things off the shelves.

Lost from the left. Found from the right. On a good week, the bins, duffle bags, and containers were all empty because the turnover was so good. On slow weeks like this, the bags and bins were full. The pans could only hold so many objects so I had to keep emptying them. One in the *Found* pan, one in the *Lost* pan. I put a set of keys to a house that had burned down in the *Lost* pan and Guy de Maupassant's necklace (faux of course) in the *Found* pan. One compromising photo from a clandestine affair, one odd sock—odd socks were always turning up on the *Found* shelves.

The most important rule of the shop was that the till had to balance. The contents of the *Lost* shelves had to equal the contents of the *Found* shelves. In other words, however many objects transported themselves from our dimension to one of the Circles of Hell, an equal number of objects had to be transferred from one of the Circles of Hell to our dimension. For every item someone turned in for us to lose, one would appear on the *Found* shelves for us to give to a customer coming in. That's how it had been for the three years I'd worked here. Today was different.

I went to the break room. "Mick? Our numbers are out: the till doesn't balance."

"Maybe you counted wrong."

"I checked six times. We're up by one *Found* item."

Which meant we had one extra object in the store we couldn't account for.

Mick didn't look as surprised as I thought he would. "We'll worry about it tomorrow."

"Bax is coming in half an hour, Mick. He'll think we've pocketed something we were supposed to lose. We're in deep trouble. I suggest we search the store. I'll start with the shelves. It might have fallen out of a bag and rolled somewhere."

"Daddeeeee!!!!" Punkin wailed.

"Relax, Punkin."

"Mick, this is serious." But I was talking to myself. Mick was talking Punkin down from her hysterics.

I looked under the *Lost* shelves. It had to be there; if it wasn't, then it might have been our fault for closing the shop too long for lunch—if someone had turned up to give us something to lose and the shop had been locked...

Maybe I could chuck a *Found* object through one of the back doors. But then what if I found the extra object afterward, and I couldn't get the one I'd thrown away back?

Ever had one of those moments when the penny drops? I had mine face down on a floor covered with dust bunnies.

"Mick, I think I've figured out what our extra object is."

Mick at least had the grace to look guilty. "Look, normally I send her back to her mom on Tuesday nights. But this week, she's..."

"Indisposed?"

"Yeah."

"Your kid can't be here when Bax comes. She's throwing off the balance."

"I can't send her back through the Door alone," said Mick. "It isn't safe."

"Then go with her."

"Then the numbers are still going to be off. Except we'll be *down* by one."

"Thought about this already, have you? What do you suggest?"

"I tried to balance things out with the Edwardian fancier's boyfriend, but he broke out of the Door."

"Of course he did, Mick. It's called *free will.*"

Just then, there was a rattle at the Fifth Door. Mick and I looked at each other. Bax.

"Mick, if you stay here, Bax is going to take Punkin to level things out. I don't even want to think about what he'll do to us. What if we stow Punkin somewhere where she'll be good and quiet. Then you go and meet Bax. I'll sort out the till problem. Okay?"

Mick thought about it. "What are you—?"

"If it works out, I'll see you in a bit." I left before he could stop me.

There was only one option. It wasn't fair to send a kid through a Door alone. So I'd go through myself. I heard Bax's key rattling in the lock of Door Number Five. I figured where I was going couldn't be as dangerous as an angry Bax. And the only way to balance the till was to put one thing back where the other one had come from.

It wasn't like it was a permanent trip. I'd just step out long enough for Bax to see the till balanced, then I'd come back out again once Bax left.

I hesitated. The doors were all numbered, but I'd forgotten what Mick had written on his color-coded map. Definitely not Door Number Five. I chose one at random: Door Number Three. It was unlocked. I heard Door Number Five open as I stepped through.

So, Third Circle of Hell.

Not what I'd pictured. Room full of cubicles, people hunched over, tapping at keyboards. I approached one of them and cleared my throat. He kept typing.

"Excuse me," I said.

Nothing. I tried this with a few more people. Same thing. The movies make being invisible look fun. It isn't.

I watched one of the workers typing. He was sweating, dishevelled, and kept glancing at the clock on the wall. I felt sorry for him. He reminded me of me. Stuck in a rut at the shop, totally stressed, totally freaking miserable. But it was the only job I'd ever worked. The only job I knew how to do.

Then it occurred to me that if this guy couldn't see me...I could pretty much get away with anything.

Mick was always telling me to loosen up. Now was a good time. I picked up a full coffee cup and proceeded to empty it over the guy's keyboard.

He went right on typing. I read what he was typing. It said:

Oh, how little you know, my sweet innocent fairy child. Tra-la-la.

I stuck my tongue in his ear. Ew! Earwax. I spat on the carpet.

"May I help you?" said someone behind me.

Oh crap.

An older woman stood there looking at me. Too much lipstick, eyeglasses with pointy magenta frames and long chains hanging down from the arms. And horns.

"Um," I said. "I was just..."

"Visitors to this dimension must report to reception."

"How do you know I'm a visitor?"

"Because you are so insignificant as to be virtually insubstantial." She demonstrated her point by poking me with her pen, which went through me.

"Do you have an appointment? Or should I call security?"

"I'm here about Mick and his kid, Punkin."

She went all flamy. Her eyes turned bright red. "That no-good, cheating son of a silver birch!"

"Pardon?"

She pointed at me. "So *you're* the other woman he's been seeing."

"Other woman? He's old enough to be my *brother*!"

"Don't deny it!"

"Are you Cindy?" I said.

"I'm her assistant. Ms. Harridan is currently indisposed."

"Indisposed doing what?" I asked.

"She happens to be playing in an extremely important troll-bridge tournament." A wisp of smoke puffed out of the assistant's left ear.

"Tell her she's got to pick up her kid, or Mick is going to be in huge trouble."

The assistant picked up a phone from the nearby desk and spoke into it. "Security to Hell. Circle Three, please."

At this point the elevator doors opened and in walked Bax. Which made me, at that point, wish I really *was* invisible.

"Would you care to explain yourself?" he said.

"Um."

"You and Mick were entrusted with preserving the balance of the universe. You're fired. I've demoted two staff members from the Fourth Circle of Hell to replace you."

I thought about what that meant. No more showing up at the shop, losing a wedding ring for a bitterly divorced woman, losing evidence of a murder, finding a set of keys to a new SUV for some cheating husband...no more responsibility, no stressing over the till balancing, no more freaking rules... No more reason to get up in the morning.

But everything had to balance. Everything that came *out* of Hell had to be balanced by a thing going *into* it. So if two people were leaving the Fourth Circle of Hell it meant that two other people had to...

"You should have just let me handle it," said Mick.

"Right, because you can talk your way out of anything," I said.

"Thanks, by the way."

"Don't thank me. I went to Hell for the leprechaun coffee. I stayed for the atmo."

Mick pushed the shopping cart along. Punkin rode inside. It was already full of stuff. Some of it tinkled as the cart rattled over the sidewalk. He picked up a stuffed teddy bear from the gutter and gave it to Punkin. The gutters of Hell were full of interesting things, things we thought we'd lost. I always wondered how the shop worked, where the lost stuff all went, who decided what turned up on the Found shelves. Now I knew. It was arbitrary. Like life. It was so nice having a job that wasn't in customer service.

"We looking for anything in particular?" I asked.

Mick shrugged. "Whatever turns up."

I looked at the tall buildings, the glittering broken glass and rubble, the fish thrashing in the gutters, Punkin riding in the cart, and something occurred to me.

"Mick, what exactly are *horts*?"

"Well, they're..." Mick glanced at Punkin. "They're kind of like..."

"Horns?"

"No," said Mick. "Horts are delicate things beautiful little girls have. Horns are what big, smelly, lady demons have."

"Like Cindy?"

"Ahem," said Mick.

"You know, Mick," I said. "Some parents might consider it good manners to teach their kids nonsense names for certain anatomical parts. But you're not being fair to the kid. Say my parents had done that to me...what's a guy going to think if I tell him to keep his hands off my barts?"

Mick looked at me seriously. "Has someone tried to touch your barts?"

"It was just an example."

"'Cause if someone did—"

"You'd kick him in the tarticles?"

"Daddy, what's tarticles?" said Punkin.

Halfway into Mick's explanation, I started laughing. I had to grab hold of the cart to keep myself upright.

"What?" he said.

"I'm just so...damned... happy," I said.

He rolled his eyes. "Whatever gets you through the day, Daisy."

Sarah Totton's short fiction has appeared at *The Walrus, Room Magazine, Nature: Futures, On Spec*, and in her short story collection, *Animythical Tales*. Her humor has appeared at *McSweeney's, The New Yorker*, and where no man has gone before, namely, the Funny Women section of *The Rumpus*. Her debut humor collection, *Quirks & Super-Quirks*, is out now.

PART THREE

TRANSFORMATION

You're kinda buzzed as you sway to the heavy sound of industrial techno fused with the haunting, mournful drone of a hurdy gurdy. It reverberates throughout your entire being. *Soul music,* you think dryly. The pounding in your ear drums, the crush of the ravers, it's all... well; you're a bit woozy again. You make your way past villagers, weekenders, sightseers in flip-flops, starlets in club kid boots, and fighters in bright linen gambesons, all dancing wildly to the music. There's even a few leather-clad Goth elves, their near translucent skin shimmering in the half dark. Emerald and amaranthine lasers sweep across the crowd, lighting up the side of the mountain so that it looks like a dollar-store snow globe.

You fucking love it.

"Woooohoooo!" Daria throws a hand around your waist, her other hand sloppily holding onto her tankard, the wine spilling down her tunic. "You're the best! You know that, right? Our new best friend!" She laughs, bleary eyed.

Drinks are on you because you did rather well on the battlefield today; far better than you expected. Far better than anyone expected, you remind yourself bitterly.

It seems two tankards is your limit, however, because your head is swimming. You find a table and sit as several influencers walk by, staring. You're sure you've seen the blonde one on the cover of some magazine or other. There's always magazines staring at you when you're on duty at the checkout at work. You know you look like shit from fighting, not put together like they are, and your face turns beet red as you glance down at your mug.

Daria pats your back. "Don't you worry, you're sexy too. Piotr, tell her she's sexy. What? You're sexy."

Piotr, looking silly with a glow choker and binky round his neck, joins you both at the table, accompanied by a fricken behemoth of a man named Otto, a sellsword you all met at the tourney.

"I'll tell you what's sexy," Piotr starts.

"Oh, here it is." Daria sighs.

"Those moves you pulled at the mêlée. That was freaking amazing! Who taught you to fight like that?"

All eyes are on you.

"My grandmother," you say. Piotr snorts.

Otto cuffs him on the shoulder. "Don't you mock her *Baba*!"

"I wasn't!" Piotr winces, rubbing at where Otto hit him. "I was blown away, actually. I have absolute respect for our elders. Babas fucking rock, except mine; she hit me with a wooden spoon all the time..." Everyone laughs.

An odd wind picks up, and a strange woman moves through the crowd carrying a golden cup before her in both hands. Barefoot, a crown of flowers in her copper hair, her golden dress is made of the finest chain mail yet flows like silk.

"Ahh!" Otto pronounces. "The Dreamseller!"

As the Dreamseller makes her way amongst the attendees, several give her coins, and she in turn graces each of them with a sip from her cup. They immediately fall into fits of giggling, or whirling away to dance, or breaking out into song. One fellow strips down completely and runs out of the Gather bare-assed.

"Some can't handle it." Otto nods, signalling to the Dreamseller. She approaches, smiling, but you shiver when she stares at you with her golden cat's eyes. Up close it looks as if her copper curls are covered in a mist of gold dust. Otto pays her to sip from the cup, and then starts spinning with his arms out, his face turned up to the sky.

"Quick! Catch the snowflakes on your tongue!" He laughs.

But there's no snow.

A couple dance provocatively not too far off, clearly in the effects of the Dreamseller's cup, and you feel another stab as you're reminded you're not here dancing with anyone; you've been left behind. Suddenly, you're not feeling as festive as the others, and when the Dreamseller offers you a turn, you shake your head, unable to meet her gaze.

A short while later you resign yourself to wearing the mantle of chaperone as you sit with Daria, doing your very best to ease her upset, her mascara streaking as she sobs uncontrollably. She's having a hard trip.

"I don't think Piotr really loves me." She sniffs.

You want to tell her he looks devoted, but your own heartache has made you jaded. You just hug her harder.

"I came here 'cause I knew it would make him happy. I hate fighting. But his *true* love has flaxen hair."

Don't they all, you grimace. At least it certainly feels that way to you right now.

Daria points accusingly up at the mountain. "Did you know, he has posters of the princess up on his wall? He even once told me he had a huge crush on her. I laughed. I'm so *stupid*! I hope she's freezing her ass off up there. Princess my *ass*!" she yells at the sky.

You give her your water because it's clear she's the weepy kind of drunk, and you really hope it's not going to be a long night; the *Climb* is early in the morning, and you all wanted to watch. She shivers, and you wrap your coat around her.

"You're an eldest, aren't you?" she says, patting your arm.

"What?"

"You're an eldest child, a caretaker. Youngests have horseshoes up their ass, but middles don't get shit. Piotr's a middle. I'm a middle, too. You... you're an eldest. I can tell."

You're an only, but you don't correct her.

"I bet most people here for the Climb are middles. How else do we make our mark? Piotr thinks he'll make his mark here. It's dangerous, but... how could I say no?"

The drum beats alter, and the mountain's now the colour of blue ice.

"I think when I grow up, I'm going to be a therapist for middles."

"You *are* a grown up," you remind her.

"Shut up." She grins, shoving you playfully.

MAYBE SHE'S MADE WITH IT

M. H. BAVLSIK

Every morning, I sat on the toilet seat and watched my mother put on her face. She didn't have one of her own, you see.

She'd paint on a mouth for parent teacher conferences with *MAC's Honey Love Matte Lipstick*, dutifully carving out demure eyes in *Clinique's Quickliner for Eyes* (shade *Intense Clove*). She made herself look soft, welcoming, nurturing—like some kind of nutritional baked good.

For work, she'd smooth on *Nars Natural Radiant Longwear Foundation* in *Tahoe*. The cream reminded me of a peanut butter sandwich, a resemblance made more acute when she would cut out a mouth in *Velvet Cherry Lip Color Matte by Tom Ford*. A few swipes of *Lancôme Monsieur Big Mascara* and then she'd peer at me, out from under long dark lashes she'd separate with a pin. When she was frustrated, they'd quiver like the anxious legs of a spider.

She used to have a face, I think. I've seen pictures of her, tucked away in plastic photo albums shedding memories out the seams. When she was a girl, she had bright eyes and lashes that looked like dandelion puffs.

Once, when I was much younger, I picked a clumsy bouquet of dandelions and gave them to her as a present. The flowers were already drooping when I offered them, but my mother hugged me so tightly in return. She pressed them into a plastic sheaf and stood it up against the mirror. Sometimes they made me feel foolish, drab little splotches of yellow nestled between her crystal bottles and golden tubes of cosmetics. Like an egg yolk cracked over a jewelry box.

She wouldn't let me try any of her makeup. Well, not for real at least. She'd sometimes let me streak *Armani Beauty Lip Maestro Liquid Matte Lipstick Four Hundred Red* across my own mouth. It made my lips look like a wound, bloody and raw. My mother would laugh and call me her little fangs. Then she'd dab it off with *Neutrogena Fragrance-Free Compostable Makeup Remover Cleansing Wipes.*

When she'd go to dinner with my father at the club, she would draw smoldering eyes from smudges of *Urban Decay 24/7 Glide-On Eye Pencil* (the deepest black shade, *Perversion*) and chisel cheek bones from *Nars Blush* in peachy *Deep Throat.* After she drew on her mouth with *Charlotte Tilbury Pillow Talk,* she'd blot her lips with a tissue, then toss her kiss in the trash can. Sometimes I thought of retrieving them for myself, covering myself in her soft remnants.

She'd always complain about the club after going. She didn't like that they let people smoke indoors and that the food wasn't any good. But she'd always smile when she did, white teeth agleam between the *Hush Hush Henna Buxom Power Line™ Plumping Lip Liner.* I think she loved going to the club because she could complain about how much she hated it afterwards. She loved having things she could pretend she didn't want.

After, she'd creep into my room so I could read her a story, to practice my French. I'd tell her about poor Donkeyskin and the dirty shepherdess while she peeled off her *Velour Whispie Me Away* false eyelashes. After she'd dabbed off all her creams and powders, my mother would press her bare skin to my hands, chuckling at my pronunciation of *âne* and correcting the shape of my mouth when I said *poilleuse.*

For the gym, my mother would tap beads of *Glossier Perfecting Skin Tint for Dewy Sheer Coverage,* the color only an unmemorable number, a strange simplification of her constantly changing complexion. A fluffy tarantula leg applicator from *Too Faced's Better Than Sex* (edited to *Better than Love* in some countries) *Volumizing and Lengthening Mascara* would let my mother see out of watery eyes. I can't recall their color, though I must have seen them countless times. No lipstick for the gym, only *Dior Addict Lip Balm,* color *Rose Nude.* It would only give her the impression of soft, kissable lips. I guess she didn't need to smile too much at pilates.

She never wore makeup when it was just the two of us, in the small hours between work and school and my father coming home. She'd nuzzle her face against mine with skin as soft as a peach. Once, I asked her how she could talk without putting on a mouth and she chuckled without amusement.

"You can hear me, can't you?"

"Well, how can you see without any eyes?" I tried again.

She smiled, and I knew she was smiling even though the skin where her lips should have been was pale and puckered.

"You remember the pictures of the orcas? With their big white eyes?"

I nodded, thinking back to the whales. "But those weren't really their eyes. Their eyes were underneath."

"Those aren't really my eyes either." She kissed my cheek.

I tried to look at her more closely, searching her face for her real eyes. The orcas' eyes were deep and black, beady afterthoughts to the bright streak of white on their heads. My mother didn't have any onyx beads embedded in her face. I gave up looking and wrapped my arms around her neck. I loved her without eyes.

Other times, I would watch my mother concoct the perfect face, her jars and bottles of skin creams and elixirs twinkling, like liquor bottles behind the bar. *Tatcha The Dewy Skin Cream Plumping and*

Hydrating Moisturizer would sit beneath *Sunday Riley CEO Glow Vitamin C + Tumeric Face Oil* during the day. At night, *Shiseido Benefiance NutriPerfect Night Cream* shimmered on her cheeks after a cleanse, courtesy *Peter Thomas Roth* and his *Irish Moor Mud Purifying Black Mask.* I liked to dip my fingers into the pots and rub the sparkling creams and gels between my fingers. Then my mother would take a towel and wipe the slipperiness from my skin.

"You don't need any of these," she'd tell me, soft-spoken without a mouth made up. "You're perfect all by yourself." And I would always know that she meant it.

One day I stole a black eye pencil from my mother's collection. The other girls in school had them. I drew dark lines across my lids with wobbly fingers, using the *Smashbox Always Sharp Longwear Waterproof Kôhl Eyeliner Pencil* in *Raven Black.* The line on my left eye looked slightly thicker, so I deepened the line on my right until it was too much and I had to return to the left to even them out again. I skipped the mascara. (Later, I would cringe at the memory of my spikey brown lashes sticking out from smudgy raccoon eyes.) And yet, when I looked at myself in the mirror then, I couldn't quite understand how I looked different. Did my eyes protrude less? Did they look bigger? Something inscrutable had happened to them and after my clumsy makeup, I looked prettier. Not beautiful like my mother, but with a certain pulchritude creeping from my eyes like a bloom of mistletoe in a host tree.

The results startled me.

A boy held the gym door open for me. One of the popular girls asked me for a stick of gum. She remembered my name. In the locker room, I was included in a raunchy joke, and the other swimmers laughed when I responded in kind. A teacher called on me when I raised my hand with the answer, even though I sat all the way in the back. Most memorably, the boy I had liked all semester asked me if I knew the answers to the homework.

I stole a tube of lipstick next. Not the *Armani Lip Maestro,* but a more demure shade of rose with the *Color Sensational Ultimatte Slim*

Lipstick by Maybelline. I liked the brand's slogan. With the shade *More Stone* smoothed across my mouth, I found that more people noticed me. Teachers whose eyes had glazed over in boredom before suggested I run for student office. The girls in my gym class exchanged phone numbers with me and texted me after school. I found that suddenly I had friends, suitors, boyfriends, even a simpering crony or two. It was as if I had painted a door of opportunity with my pilfered cosmetics.

When my mother discovered my lacquered face, she wasn't angry, as I had feared. She tilted my chin up to hers and examined the *Covergirl Clean Fresh Skin Milk Foundation* I had shellacked over my pimples. Her full lips, wet with *Chanel's Rouge CoCo Gloss Moisturizing Glossimer (Rose Naif)* pursed briefly and she sighed.

"Don't forget to wash your face at night. You don't want an infection."

She bought me an eyelash curler later that week. I pulled out a hank of spiky mascara-clumped hairs and never touched it again.

I continued experimenting with makeup, though after reading a gory magazine article, I avoided pinching any more of my mother's. I slathered shimmery *ColorPop Jelly Much Gel Eyeshadow (Big Ego)* paired with *Essence Holo Bomb Shiny Lipgloss (Iced Gloss)*. I dabbed tarte *Shape Tape* concealer and green *e.l.f. Camo Color Corrector* to hide the red blemishes that sprouted across my face. The more makeup I piled on, the more products I needed to make it stay: *Benefit's The POREfessional Pore Minimizing Primer* to make my face a flat and even canvas; *Wet n Wild MegaGlo Contouring Palette* to add back shadows and depth to my features; *Urban Decay All Nighter Waterproof Makeup Setting Spray* to make it all stay put.

One evening, shortly after I'd graduated college, I was cleaning the makeup off my face. I'd switched to more durable stuff after I'd joined a consulting firm, formulations that wouldn't crack under pressure or break down with tears. I swiped *Jaclyn Cosmetic's Pout Off Nourishing Lipstick Remover* across my lips and when I pulled the *Makeup Eraser* away, my mouth had come off with the *Stila Stay All*

Day Long Wear Liquid Lipstick (shade *Patina*). I stared at my reflection in the mirror. Where I had cleansed lay only raw pink skin, a corner of my bottom lip peeking out. I looked at the microfiber cloth in my hand, searching for my mouth. The cloth held no trace of myself, just a smudge of mauve. I put my finger to my lip, gingerly probing the area. It didn't hurt, but it had that stiff soreness of flesh scrubbed clean. I cleaned the rest of my face more gently, trying to preserve the last parts of my lips. I tried dabbing softly at the crust of black gel on my eyes, but no matter how I went about it, where the makeup came off, my features did too.

I cried myself to sleep that night, tears leaking from blank skin. My only consolation was that my face now looked just like my mother's. That, and I wasn't quite sure exactly what it was that I'd lost.

The next day, not knowing what else to do, I painted on my face just like any other day. I found that I needed more of my *Nyx Slim Eye Pencil Long-Lasting Eyeliner* to define my eyelids. And that without my *Anastasia Beverly Hills Rosewood Lip Liner* my mouth blurred into my chin. But otherwise, I hardly looked any different. Or not any more different than I usually did with my chameleon's toolkit. And when no one noticed the blankness under the makeup, I didn't know if I was disappointed or relieved.

I simply carried on, perpetually made-up. Such a funny way to say it, I suppose. Made up. Like it wasn't real. Like I was only a series of convenient truths and pleasant fictions glued together like a band of *Flirtatious Lilly Lashes*. It didn't seem to matter though. So long as I looked the part, I had a job, promotions, friends, and dates. Eventually, even a baby—delivered through streams of *Estée Lauder Sumptuous Extreme Lash Multiplying Volume Mascara*-stained sweat.

The first night at home with her, she woke me in the middle of the night with a ratty cry. I went to draw on some eyes to avoid upsetting her with my featureless face, but her screaming grew louder and my hands shook too much. I wrapped a scarf around my head instead and picked her up. She stopped wailing and I could have wept with relief. I rocked her against my chest, trying to soothe her back to sleep, but her grabby little hands caught my scarf and pulled it down, revealing the empty skin of my face. My heart thudded and I tried to nuzzle the fabric back up, to hide the horrible blankness, but the baby jerked the scarf further down. I'd thought that I could simply continue as I had, and maybe one day—one day in the vague and distant future—I would explain to her why I had no eyes or lips. Gently, I'd show her my monstrousness, when she was old enough to understand. Instead, my child was only days old, and I'd exposed her to this. It felt as wrong as exposing my vulva.

Her tiny fingers reached up to my face, grabbing at blank flesh. She smiled. Her damp little palms slapped lightly against my cheeks, and, slowly, the numbness of my terror receded. She babbled, and I pressed my face against her hands. How strange, to be loved unconditionally.

My daughter is six now. Every morning, she sits on the toilet seat and watches me paint on my face. I see her eyes flit from me to the shimmering powders and sparkling creams. I want to warn her away from them, tell her that lipstick is crimson poison and eyeshadow, slivers of razors. I love to trace her too-wide-eyes and pouty cupid's bow mouth. I know they'll be gone someday, worn away by the same tools that generate attention, power. One day she'll lift an inky black brush and paint the world her own. And I will love her as I loved my own faceless mother: without ever quite knowing the person behind the palimpsest.

M. H. Bavlsik works in software and IT by day to support her bossy corgi. By night, she prefers dark lipstick and darker stories.

DISSOCIATIVE BODY DISORDER

CHRISTINA ARDIZZONE

Body maintenance is hard without Mother's help but Enola manages. Only her favorite, Two, needs to eat full meals. The rest survive on protein bars. Wearing Two, she's just finished consuming a pear, five crackers, and a sip of wine. Now she retrieves the nail clippers from a kitchen drawer and heads to the Body Room. She ignores her stomachache, which follows her no matter who she wears.

The wallpaper is robin's egg blue like the lavatory in her childhood home, where she would take bubble baths so full of bubbles that only her feet were visible over mounds of lavender foam.

The bodies are squeezed together on small cots she bought in bulk at Costco using Mother's membership. It's been half a year since she last saw Mother and today she is coming over. Enola's right hand twitches towards the phone in her pocket. She could text the support group an update. Something like, "She's not even here yet and I want to dissociate." She knows the group leader, Nya, would come right away. Enola doesn't, though. She can handle things herself.

Enola walks past One and stops at Three to touch her cheek.

She's always been impressed by the beauty in Three's face. Maybe it's that her dimples are less creased than One's, or that her lips are infinitesimally fuller than Two's? Still, it's disingenuous to wear her too often.

Enola clips nails off with quick, efficient grace, the nails dropping into a small plastic cup she carries for that purpose. In only a few minutes she's done with seven pairs of nails. She tries not to think about how odd it is that she only feels her touch in the body she wears. If she thinks about it too hard she gets dizzy, the logistics of her current hands not being her only hands echoing through her rattled brain. What does it mean that she can't stop producing bodies? She knows what Claire, her trauma and dissociation specialist would say. Something about how the bodies are created to protect her, even if they are unsuccessful. It's hard to be grateful when she barely has time to sleep.

The doorbell rings.

"Shit." She rises from her criss-cross applesauce and stretches her back. She's tempted to switch to Seven because mom always thinks Seven is skinnier than the others, but decides Mother needs to accept her for who she is. Still, the elastic snapping of her nerves intensifies. Her left hand itches and she absent-mindedly scratches the palm.

Once in the hallway the smell of baking apples wafts from the kitchen. Enola congratulates herself for timing her apple chips well for visitors.

She opens the front door. Mother stands there holding a package of processed chocolate chip cookies. Her grey eyes brighten when she sees her daughter.

"Sorry I'm so early, honey." Mother enters, puts her Kate Spade purse down on the couch. Her apartment is small for the amount of people in it, even if only one is conscious at a time. Hopefully her landlord never notices.

"You cleaned! I'm so proud of you. I'm glad you're finally out of that funk since you left the hospital."

Oof. The self-harm scars are on Six. It's painful for Enola to look at them. She half expected them to appear on all the bodies, but she knows that isn't how her disorder works.

"How is everyone?" Mother swipes over-long bangs from her eyes and sits down next to her bag.

This is a nosy question, and anger bubbles into Enola's chest, but she tries not to react. Instead she takes the blue package of cookies to the kitchen. She turns off the oven even though the apple chips aren't done. By the way her body is reacting to seeing Mother she knows there is no way she'll remember to take them out in time, even if the buzzer was taped to her head. Why did she agree to let her visit? Oh yeah, guilt at never wanting to see her. She was such a bad daughter.

"I'm not sure who you mean. I'm not back at the library yet." She lines the cookies on a plate and brings them back to the living room.

Mother avoids her eyes. "Oh, honey, I just miss you. I haven't seen them since you left home."

Deep breath in. "I'd rather not."

She nods but Enola notices her eyes are glassy with tears. "I took care of them for you when you were younger."

"The first three."

"Yes, and I was proud to help. My friend Gale from the post office was just telling me that her niece has DBD and her parents are very involved in their upkeep. She has twenty! Can you imagine?"

Enola can imagine. She's read all the literature on Dissociative Body Disorder, the scientific journals, all of it since she was diagnosed three years ago. Acute childhood trauma causes it. What had Gales' niece been through? Funny that her mom finds it so entertaining. Enola's anxiety is now palpitating behind her eyes.

"Did you know that famous musician, oh what's his name? Bumpkin? He has DBD. He brings them out on stage and sings through each of them. He only has five, but it's still pretty impressive. They all have the same voice qualities, with very minor differences."

"Them?" It's hard enough for Enola to feel like a complete person without her own mother calling a person like her a *them*. All the bodies are her, and she is responsible for their actions. Why did her mother have to emphasize how many there were? Enola was fine with her bodies remaining separate (though the upkeep was always a chore) but fusion was nice, too. Since she started therapy she's had Nine and Ten fuse into one body. The experience was trippy and not something she wants to think about right then.

Mother gasps. "You know I didn't mean it like that! Just–the other hims." She looks down. "I've always been more understanding than your father—"

Pain flares in Enola's stomach and travels to her head. Just like that she leaves body Two. Mother's words are muffled. She takes deep breaths in Nine/Ten.

Enola loves Two and instantly misses wearing her. Up until college she hid One and had hoped that two bodies would be it, that her case wouldn't be so bad. Then Three came after that debilitating breakup junior year. And Four. But Two was with her when she first got her period, and when she'd flown over the handlebars at age eight and needed stitches on her chin. Two had scars she wasn't ashamed of, and she wasn't so perfect looking as One or Seven or Twelve.

Enola's back in Two, and Mother is crying and trying to hug her. A desperate, tangled love wraps around Enola's heart. As a child not old enough to tie her shoes, read a street sign, or write her name, Mother had offered some safety and consistency, even if her hugs were cold and her words crisp. Now, though, every moment in her presence is both comforting in its familiarity and terrifying in its unpredictability. Mother can't stop herself from rambling, and during those rambles Enola usually feels less than human.

Deep breaths.

Mother's lips quiver as she stares at Enola, clearly waiting for a response. What had she said? Enola hadn't heard a word. Suddenly the plate of cookies drops and Enola can't tell if the body did it on purpose. The plate is fine but the cookies shatter, crumbs all over the white carpet.

"Sorry," Enola says softly, and bends to pick them up. Her stomach lurches and a familiar panic floods her body. "Excuse me." Enola holds a hand to her mouth and runs to the bathroom. She shuts the door and leans over the sink.

She floats away from Two but doesn't enter any of the other bodies. Instead she is stuck, fixed in position above the head of Two. She watches as Two vomits up a large, round ball of phlegm into the sink. Two picks up the ball without Enola's help, putting it in the shower. She then turns on the shower spigot and the ball of phlegm grows.

A loud knock hits the door. "Enola, honey? It's happening again isn't it? Do you need help?"

Mother keeps knocking and Enola keeps floating, not a part of herself but not quite separate, either.

Finally the knocking stops. Enola's view is fixed, but as time passes–and Enola isn't sure how much time that is–her bubble drifts toward the forming body in the tub. Now it has arms and legs peeking out of the middle, and the new body resembles a Cabbage Patch Kid. Then it's stretching and stretching, and Enola feels that stretching like an itch, and that itching intensifies the closer her bubble is to the body. Then, finally, all she can see is the back of her own head, and then she's in the newly formed Eighteen.

Her muscles burn and her skin is damp, so when she tries to lift Eighteen's arms she immediately slips back into the tub. She sighs, and would love to go out in Two again, but she has no control over body switches when a new one has formed. She's stuck in Eighteen until the body decides to let her go. Sometimes that takes a few hours, sometimes days. Enola was stuck in Sixteen for three days, and Seventeen for a week right after she formed.

She grabs the towel hanging by the sink and wraps it around her body. Then she steps over Two, who is slumped against the wall with her eyes closed. She'll drag her back to the closet, but that will have to wait.

Enola stumbles out of the bathroom and for a moment she thinks Mother has left, but as she rounds the corner she sees that Mother is sitting on the couch reading a book on her phone. Always crappy romance novels. Mother rises.

"Honey! Do you need help?"

Enola steps back and shakes her head. Mother tries to go around her. "Enola, let me get your other body back in the room. It's going to be hard for you to carry."

Enola shakes her head again. She's mute until her vocal chords adjust to existence, too.

She watches Mother crumple inside as her shoulders drop and her eyes cast downward. "I'm always here, Enola. Don't forget that." Mother grabs her purse off the couch and leaves.

A deep sigh exits Eighteen's lungs.

She slides down the wall and flops on the floor. She begins tracing the woodgrain of a floorboard with her fingers, lost to the world.

Later there is a knock at the door. Enola startles. Who could it be?

Her phone is by her hand on the floor, and reading the screen she realizes Eighteen must have texted Nya from the DBD support group while she zoned out. Great. Enola gets up slowly, using the wall for support. She opens the door to a young woman with short brown hair and a plain, angular face.

"Hey. It's good you reached out. Can I come in?"

Yes. She wants to shake her head emphatically, to leap forward and hug Nya and, using hand gestures and a white board, tell her everything that is bothering her. Instead she remains in place. She manages to shake her head no, though the body tries hard to resist her.

Nya smiles, and Enola again almost hugs her.

"Well, you can always call my number again if you need something." She reaches into her messenger bag. "I thought you could use some chocolate. Lindt is my favorite so I brought you some truffles."

Nya hands them to Enola, and tears stream down Enola's face.

"It's always hard when a parent visits. You might try low contact? Regardless, you should know that you're doing great."

Enola can see her hesitating, like she wants to come in and help even though Enola shook her head no. Instead she smiles, then leaves. Warmth floods Enola's body as she shuts the door and unwraps a Lindt truffle. She pops it into her mouth, and, wrapped in the momentary pleasure of the chocolate, she closes her eyes. She'd always been too embarrassed to call for help. She's glad that her new body made that decision for her. She slides back to the floor.

She knows she needs to go back to the bathroom and spend several minutes dragging Two back to the closet. Then she'll have to get Eighteen her own cot. She also needs to transfer into each of the bodies and go to the bathroom. Then she needs to chew a peanut butter flavored protein bar in seventeen different mouths. She used to vary the flavors but gave up when it got too hard. She should do all those things and she should start now. Instead she savors the aftertaste of the truffle, leaning her back on the recently closed door. She holds this pleasure and accepts the reality that even with all the support in the world her disorder will always be hard.

She sighs, puts her head against the door, and closes her eyes again. She'll rest for just a few more moments.

Christina Ardizzone is a writer and mother living in New Jersey. She is a graduate of the Odyssey Writing Workshop as well as the MFA writing program at Sarah Lawrence College. Her work has appeared in *Dragon Gems* under the last name Ardizzone and various publications under the name Christina Scott.

VENUS

JACQUELINE PEREZ

Leyla knocked lightly on the door of her sister's apartment, no longer feeling comfortable enough to use her spare key. She gripped the plastic bag of live mealworms in her left palm, suddenly flush with shame at the inadequacy of her gift. The vendor at her local farmer's market had proudly marketed the yield and quality of his tiered-colony mealworm farm, pointing a stubby finger at the garish, red "Gourmet-Style" sticker slapped on the front of each plastic bag. Leyla glanced down at the bag in her fist and saw the writhing mass of brown sludge, each mealworm barely discernible as it struggled against the confines of the plastic.

"Coming!" She heard her sister's muffled shout from inside the apartment. The door seemed to fly open as her sister appeared on the other side of it, frantic and disheveled. Sections of hair had fallen out of her bun and became glued to the side of her face with sweat. "You could have let yourself in," her sister said, catching her breath. Leyla noticed that her sister's eyes veered over her shoulder every few seconds, looking to the back corner of her kitchen.

"These are for you," Leyla offered, presenting the grubby bag from her fist, as though it were a bottle of wine at a housewarming party. Her sister broke eye contact with the kitchen corner to examine the offering. “Well, for you– and your Venus,” Leyla added, softly smiling to convey support for her sister. Her sister smiled and accepted the bag, but Leyla saw the momentary slip. Her sister’s lips pursed in disgust— or was it disapproval?— just for a brief flash before regaining composure and smiling.

“Thank you,” her sister said. “Come with me to the kitchen. I’ll introduce you.”

Leyla followed her sister, her concern growing with each step. The apartment, which once had the distinct smell of cinnamon and oranges from her sister’s signature simmer pots, now oozed with the dingy mix of home compost-based soil and the rusty tang of copper. The baseboards were lined with buckets containing food scraps: egg shells, coffee grounds, apple peels. Every surface seemed to be covered in yellow notebook pages, ripped from their coil binds, her sister’s once neat cursive reduced to a manic scrawl. An iodine antiseptic bottle was left on the kitchen table, uncapped, emitting a noxious odor into the room. All around it lay hundreds of cotton balls.

“There’s tea in the kettle, help yourself,” her sister said. Leyla was thankful for the distraction from the state of her sister’s home. She opened the cupboard and smiled as she selected the light pink mug that her sister had made in one of their pottery classes. Her anxiety soon returned as she poured tea from the kettle and realized that it was cold, likely having been sitting out for hours if not longer.

“Here she is,” her sister squealed proudly. Leyla returned her attention to her sister and saw her. There, in the corner of the kitchen, illuminated in the violet glow of a grow light hung from the ceiling, was the object of her sister’s unwavering attention. A small Venus Flytrap, with just three open traps and one closed bud, perched on the counter next to the sink. Its pot was set in water a few inches deep inside the bowl her sister used when serving Caesar salads in the summertime. She recognized the pot immediately. After spending hours working on it in the pottery studio, Leyla had decided to gift it to her sister for her birthday. While the clay was still wet, she stuck her pointer finger through the bottom of the pot to create a drainage hole, thinking that her sister would use it to propagate her pothos plant. She looked at the pothos now, hanging from the curtain rod above the window, its leaves shriveled, dying of thirst. Fading from green, to yellow, to brown.

"Is there something wrong with the mealworms? I saw on the news that live mealworms are supposed to be nutritious for Venuses," Leyla said, nervously inspecting the disarray throughout her sister's home.

Her sister sighed. "I appreciate the gift, really. It was very thoughtful," she said, digging through the piles of cotton balls on the table. She pulled out a miniature sewing kit from beneath the pile, which Leyla had not seen before. She doused a cotton ball in iodine before extracting a sewing needle from the kit and wiping it down. "It's just that... I've decided I would prefer to feed her with my blood before moving onto something larger like insects," her sister explained. "It's much better for the plant. There is a study that indicates that Venuses fed with blood for the first three months of life have thicker stems and more traps than those who grow up on bugs." Leyla watched as her sister carefully sliced her thumb with a sewing needle and squeezed a few droplets of blood into the eager mouths of her Venus. The traps snapped shut, hungrily accepting her sister's offering. Her sister sliced once more and rubbed the closed bud, seemingly willing it open. She drew her thumb down each thin stalk and rubbed each leaf, until the plant emitted a hazy crimson sheen.

Leyla knew the study her sister was referencing. It had caused a media frenzy as clickbait articles descended upon social media the week before. She had regrettably opened the comment section of one article and witnessed one Venus-owner calling another an "attention-seeking narcissist intent on starving her Venus for clout" for suggesting that live insects were a viable alternative to blood.

"Right," she sighed, not wanting to draw further divides between herself and her sister. "You are so wonderful to your Venus. She is lucky to have you."

Her sister looked up at her, eyes bright with tears, and smiled. It was the first time she managed to peel her eyes away from the Venus since Leyla arrived. "Thank you so much for saying that. It has been a harder adjustment than I expected, but I love her so much already. I can't imagine my life without her anymore."

Leyla sipped tea from her ceramic mug and felt the loneliness slipping down her throat, cold and bitter. The realization dawned on her that they would never again work next to each other at a potter's wheel, giggling as their overworked bowls became lumpy and misshapen. She ran her thumb over the grooves of her sister's fingerprint, accidentally preserved on the side of the mug as a result of her gripping the clay too tightly before baking it in the kiln. Now it served as a stark reminder of who she was before. Leyla felt the smooth, uninterrupted lines, knowing that the indentation could no longer be matched to her sister. Her thumb was now thick with scars.

"Joe, I hardly recognized her. She was a mess. This kind of crazed look about her. Remember how clean she used to keep her apartment? She used to scold me if I forgot to use a coaster! Now the whole place is covered in grime from her homemade compost and loose pages of notes on plant care. I mean, she looks like she has lost her mind," Leyla said, sinking into the cushions of her couch. She looked to her husband, desperate for validation that her sister was in fact slipping away. As much as the thought terrified Leyla, and as much as she didn't want to admit it, she was more afraid of the possibility that her sister was actually the normal one. That maybe she had overreacted to the change in her sister's behavior.

Joe gave her a pitying look as he rolled up the sleeve of his button-down shirt. He reached for the wine opener on the coffee table in front of them and started to uncork a bottle of Malbec. A shiver ran down Leyla's spine as she watched him pour the deep red liquid into their mismatched thrift store wine glasses, thinking of her sister's blood dripping into the greedy traps of her Venus.

"Look, of course she's consumed with the Venus right now. Who knows what causes someone to wake up and decide that they need a Venus. But we both know that once that thought is in their head, they won't stop until they have one," Joe said, handing one of the glasses to her. Leyla lifted the glass to her mouth and drank deeply. It was a Sunday night – the first Sunday in years that her sister wouldn't be joining them for dinner. She imagined what her sister was doing in that moment, perhaps hunched over an open textbook scribbling notes like a madman or stirring a foul mix of food scraps to be used for soil.

"I just don't get it. Everyone seems to want a Venus eventually, but I don't understand the appeal. I never have." Leyla was happy with her life, satisfied. Free to seek out her own pleasures and follow whims, and she treasured the spontaneity of it. But occasionally, in dark moments, she found herself wishing that she truly wanted a Venus. There is such comfort to be found in conformity.

She had first met Joe at his garden shop three years prior, when she mistakenly went shopping on Venus arrival day. Everybody knew about Venus arrival day, since the plants were so rare, and only becoming more rare each year. Leyla usually checked the Venus arrival schedule on the garden center's website before going to shop, since it would be so chaotic on those days. But it had slipped her mind.

On this day at the shop, Leyla was browsing the seed aisle, looking for some herbs for her patio garden. She didn't have much space in her apartment, but she found some hanging pots that she could string up to her balcony to grow some herbs. It made her feel mature to pluck some leaves from her basil plant to sprinkle over her pasta with canned tomato sauce. It was something.

As she reached for a packet, she was hit with an abrupt force from behind, sending her flying into the seed racks. Hundreds of packets fell from their shelves to the ground, bursting and sending seeds flying as a group of people stampeded through the aisle.

"I've been here since 6 a.m. waiting for the Venuses to arrive! Give it to me!" Leyla saw a young woman scream as she tried to claw a little Venus pot out of the tight grasp of an older woman.

"Please," the older woman rasped. "I've been coming here for months trying to get a Venus. I don't know how much more fight I have left in me." The young woman stumbled back as she let go of the pot.

Leyla grabbed a handful of seed packets from the ground, not caring which herbs they were anymore. She walked briskly to the register, glancing over her shoulder, worried she would be trampled in another feral charge.

The man at the register rang up her seed packets and placed them into a small brown bag. As Leyla thanked him, she looked into his warm brown eyes and could tell that he sensed her nervousness. Her irregularity.

"Hey, take my card," he said, handing her an index card. It read simply, "Joe's Garden Center" and a phone number in black text. On the back was a black and white outline of a Venus Flytrap. "If you text me, I'll add you to my alert list. I send out warnings before Venus arrival day to anyone who wants to avoid the madness. I got you," he said with a wink.

"I have a surprise for you," Joe whispered as he slowly opened the door to their bedroom, hoping Leyla was still awake. A new shipment of Venuses arrived that afternoon, which kept him at work late into the night, sorting inventory to prepare for the next morning. He reeked of soil and felt it all over his hands and face, seeping into his pores. His shirt was covered in streaks of dirt from wiping his hands on it throughout the day.

Leyla was in bed, reading by the warm yellow glow of her bedside lamp. "You do?" She smiled, placing her bookmark on the page, and setting the book on her nightstand.

Joe walked in and perched on the edge of the bed, careful not to dirty their comforter. He reached into his pocket and presented her with a crumpled beige packet. To her shock, it was unmarked except for one small icon drawn sloppily in black pen: a tooth.

"How did you get this?" Leyla asked, unsure how she was supposed to react.

"My Venus supplier slipped it to me today. I couldn't believe it either - maybe they're not real," he said.

Leyla knew the value of the packet in her palm. Virtually all new Venuses were created through propagation these days, as they were easier to guarantee growth and survival. Although the seeds were risky, they also provided the owner with something priceless: time. They could be planted when the owner was ready. Leyla had seen stories on the news of people being robbed at knifepoint for Venus seeds.

"I don't know what to say," Leyla said. It was true - she was dumbfounded. She had thought that she and Joe had an understanding. That Venuses required a level of work and sacrifice that they were not ready for. She thought of her sister's mangled fingers.

"I know but hear me out. These seeds might not even grow. They might be all dried out already. Or they might be some herb that someone passed off as a Venus to make some quick cash. We won't know unless we try," Joe said, placing his palm over hers, cradling the packet between their hands.

Leyla saw the hope in his eyes, in his soft smile as he looked up at her. She thought of her sister's slight grimace before she corrected herself, smiling as she accepted the bag of mealworms. Did her sister already have some understanding that Leyla lacked? Some universal truth that only became clear through bloodletting for the sake of a parasitic plant? It was hard for her to imagine. Her life had felt so full. Spontaneous after-work dinners with friends at their favorite wine bar, pottery classes with her sister, vacations with her husband all over the world.

Looking back, she realized how these once-frequent activities had dwindled as friends became infatuated with their Venuses. Her sister was just the latest, and most painful, casualty.

Her eyes returned to her husband. She rested her forehead in the crook of his neck, breathing in his earthy scent. It killed her to think of disappointing him, of being the barrier between him and an opportunity for happiness, fulfillment. Already, she felt this version of herself start to slip out of her body as she exhaled, riding the wave of her warm breath, dissipating in the air around them. “All right,” she said.

Jacqueline Perez is a new writer, publishing her first short story, *Venus.* When not writing, she enjoys browsing for used books, collecting vinyl records, and propagating her many houseplants. She lives in Boston, MA with her husband, Iván.

CURSEBREAKER

CARLY MIDGLEY

The deal is done. It's time to go.

Before I'm five steps from the cursebreaker's stall, my eyes are roaming the crowd, looking for monsters. The market is everything I imagined and worse: stale air, pitch-black rock, creatures packed together tight enough to feel each other's heartbeats. The insignia of a skull grins from hundreds of booths offering spells, treasures, wishes, bones.

I shove my way to the less-trafficked eastern edge, right shoulder first—my last human limb. Here I have a better view of the tunnels that lead to the labyrinth, and of the creatures approaching them.

I avoid the first one that tries to lock eyes with me: a magpie at least twice my size. Strings of jewels in aqua and scarlet and vivid violet wink like eyes from its feathers.

The merchant who shook my hand warned me away from such creatures.

"This isn't the safest place," he added, "for a man in your condition."

Again, I tell myself I imagined the laugh in his voice. Again, I consider: just how stupid am I willing to be?

Getting here was easy enough, just as the stories say: one step through a dark portal, summoned with the flip of a coin coated in my blood. Getting home, on the other hand, will be...difficult.

The market nests at the heart of a labyrinth. Thousands of branching tunnels twist off into the darkness, leading to dead ends or other worlds or deeper into the earth. There is one true path up to the surface.

One.

In my pocket, my fingers clink against the marble-shaped spell the cursebreaker gave me. There's an ache in my core where he took his payment—a precious memory of my father's final words—but it aches less when the spell is in my hand. My fingers tick along the raised letters that mark it as mine: PROPERTY OF LUCIEN ALABASTER.

It will not work, the merchant said, until I've found my way back out.

The magpie dives into the tunnel, oddly at home in this subterranean world. I avert my eyes again from what comes after it: a man made of yellowing bones, his fingers carved into sword-sharp points.

The merchant isn't wrong. I don't belong here. This is a place for the strong, those whose bodies can be relied upon. I can't trust myself to survive here, not for long, so at any cost, I must be swift to reach the surface. Navigating the tunnels would take too long, as would joining the miners digging a path straight up. Word is they're still ten years out.

That leaves one option: hitch a ride.

Some monsters lair in these tunnels; others use them as a familiar thoroughfare between the market and their homes on the surface or in other worlds. They know these tunnels with an intimacy I could never hope for, and they fly, crawl, slither far faster than humans.

Most, they say, will take passengers.

So I watch the tunnels, biting back impatience. I don't approach the fire-eyed horse made of clay, or the woman who—like my cursebreaker—smiles with too many teeth. I want nothing too wild, nothing too human.

I finally settle on something that's visibly neither: a sinuous worm gleaming slick brown in the ever-present torchlight. I hurry toward it. "Ho! Are you bound for the surface?"

One end of its body lifts, swiveling to face me. Though its head is as featureless as the rest of it, I shiver with the sense of a gaze upon me.

Its voice hisses like steam. "Toward it, yes."

"Will you take a passenger? As far along the true path as you're bound?"

It pauses, interminably long.

"I can pay," I snap, and finally it answers me.

"For the truth of why you came here," it hisses, "and for the deepest of your fears, I will allow you to travel with me."

It's a steep price, nearly as steep as I paid for the spell. I'm not eager to air my weaknesses here, trapped below the earth in the company of desperate strangers. But all I've paid will be for nothing if I fail to bring the spell to the surface, and I came here prepared to lose what I must.

So I tell it: "I came for the antidote to a family curse."

I do not say I inherited the curse from my father and his father, that I feel smaller every time it claims a piece of me. I do not confess how weak it makes me feel, to know that time is the only barrier between me and the loss of every sensation of being alive.

"A curse," the creature sighs. "What curse?"

In answer, I lift the hems of my pants and pull my left glove free.

Glass flashes in the torchlight. Glass legs, feet, ankles; glass fingers, palm, wrist, and arm. The glass that makes me is pristine, not even cracked: the fruit of too many years spent in hiding, in soft beds and safe houses, away from such things as rocky cave walls.

I show only as much as I must, then cover myself. Still I can sense staring eyes, and a silence around me that I like not at all.

"As for fear," I say, too loudly, "I fear dying as my father did."

Around the hole left by his final words, I remember only images. My father's body catching sunlight like an ornament, a solid mass of cold, slick glass. My father in bed—always in bed, never walking the woods or splashing in the water as he did when I was small. It seemed maddening, to simply lie like that, locked away from the world by a deadened body that could do nothing but shatter.

The curse had taken little of me then: a foot, my left hand. But I hadn't hugged him, reached for his hand, in years. What would be the point, when he could not feel my touch?

"I fear the curse will take every piece of me away," I tell the worm, because I can sense it is hungry for more. "That I will die empty and unfeeling."

Without waiting for a reply, I step forward.

Take me, I think. *Remake me. I'm losing myself anyway.*

The worm does.

It's terrifying.

We snake together through the tunnels, my arms and legs tight around the worm's damp body. It's breathlessly fast, undulating under me, a new shape every second. It takes all I have to stay upright as it sways and weaves, to wrench myself away when we skim too close to walls. I'm exhausted already, my focus wavering like a muscle held taut too long.

It happens fast. Accidents always do.

Rounding a corner, the worm jerks sharply to the left. The spell in my pocket leaps with the movement, out into the air, and the wall to my right rushes toward me too fast, and I have a choice: twist away from the wall or lean toward it to save the spell.

I take a sharp breath. This is no choice at all.

I lean right hard, snatching the spell with a desperate hand. My right leg hits the wall.

A crack splits the cavern. Pain splinters through me, surprising: I expected to feel nothing, familiar undying nothing. The worm jerks away from the wall, and again we're riding, but all I can feel is the pulsing sting in my right leg, burning like a real wound.

The monster stops not long after. A small mercy, I suppose, though it doesn't feel that way when I slide from its back and my leg buckles beneath me. I'm lucky to catch myself with my good hand.

"There are others nearby," the worm says. It slithers back into the darkness, down and away.

I allow myself five slow breaths before I yank up my pant leg and survey the damage. I am, again, lucky: the leg is still in one piece, though lined with hairline cracks that splinter the light. The fractures web outward from a froth-white patch on the outer side of my shin, where I was struck. Tiny daggers of glass sprinkle onto the rock.

It hurts, I think, stunned and sluggish. *Why does it hurt?*

The curse is a conqueror. What it touches becomes an unfeeling object, no longer a part of me. After all, I cannot feel caresses there, cannot feel warmth.

Yet these cracks sting like shredded skin.

Of course this is all that's left to me. Bitterness wells, suffocating, in my chest. *Of course the curse takes every sensation but pain.*

But it's still sensation, and I didn't believe that was possible, and my muddled brain can't make sense of what that means to me. Something lurks below my anger, too big for me to hold, threatening to crush the air from my lungs.

I shake my head, holding tight to the spell as a distraction.

I force myself to walk.

It doesn't take long to find the "others" the monster promised. Just up the tunnel is a wider cavern, and inside a smattering of strangers, all human. I can tell they're tracking my limp as I stumble to a wall and settle against it, though they pretend not to look. Some are sure to be hitchers like me, ready to scrap over the next monster that passes.

Still, three of them are gathered in a group, talking loudly. A place like this breeds both friends and enemies quickly.

"So," says one young man. He's feigning nonchalance, but not very well. "What did you get from the market?"

The woman he's asking gives him a grin that's all teeth. "Glory."

They erupt into cheerful bickering and whooping, teasing and taunts. Despite myself, I watch them. They kick at each other, toss rocks, slam hands emphatically against the earth. They're so at home in their bodies, so confident their flesh will remain predictably whole, predictably theirs.

Then comes a flutter of wings, just down the tunnel.

I haul myself up, but I know I can't outrun the strangers. The three who were talking are sprinting toward the sound already, while the best I manage is a halting hobble. Every step wakes the pain in my leg.

But when I step into the tunnel, my guts knot, because the creature that's come is a giant magpie.

The vendor who sold me the cursebreaking spell, who cautioned me against riding the magpies, told me one important thing:

These creatures have a weakness for anything that sparkles.

The young woman and the bird are haggling, offers snapping back and forth. Perhaps I should wait, let her have her chance, but I have an advantage, and if I have to sit with this pain and these thoughts a moment longer, something in me will break.

So I rip off my glove and shout, "I'll give you my left hand!"

The bird's obsidian eyes slide to me. In them, hunger gleams.

Emboldened, I step closer, dropping my glove to the ground.

"If you're bound for the surface," I say, "if you take me as far as you're going, I'll give you my hand."

My fingers glow gold in the torchlight. The three humans stare at me.

The magpie chuckles, throaty and soft.

"Yes," it says sweetly.

Then it snaps off my hand.

My scream and the smash hit my ears together, the loudest thing I've ever heard. The pain comes in blackening waves, pulsing with my racing heart.

The tunnel snaps out of focus.

I am a child, crying over a turned ankle still made of flesh and bone. My father is beside me.

"Don't be so careless, Lucien!" he snaps. "You're precious."

In the memory, he helps me up. His glass fingers graze mine: a sound like a bell, a vibration humming through my glimmering hand.

I smile at him, and—

I suck in a rasping breath, ground myself back in the dim labyrinth.

Something is unfurling inside me. I am falling, heart thrilling and fearful, as something foundational slips out of my grasp.

The magpie uses a deft talon to knot my severed hand to a chain on its back. It sweeps a broad black wing around my body, ushering me closer.

I have lost something, my brain hums, nonsensical, as I slump between its wings. *Something precious.*

I feel the edge of something like panic.

But too late: the magpie sweeps away into the darkness of the tunnel. Beneath the pain, I try to place this pulsing sense of emptiness. The hand was a burden, too fragile to do what a hand is meant to do. I should be glad to be rid of it.

Still, the tinkle of the chains behind me makes me ill. I keep thinking of my leg, shattered and aching.

I keep remembering vibration in my fingers, telling me of my father's touch.

It's a small memory, something I would certainly never have dredged up if not for the rattle of the rocks against me, the jolt of the magpie's beak. Yet suddenly it feels important, vital in a way I can't understand.

What does it mean?

Why must it mean anything?

But it must. It *must.*

Despite the tight quarters, the bird flies fast. The tunnels flash by, blurs of grey and brown. Soon we're in a high-ceilinged passage, double or even triple my height, and I'm surprised to find my shoulders relaxing. This is the least confined I've felt since the market.

I am almost afraid of the lightness in my chest. I am still underground, still made of glass. I still have plenty of reason to be afraid.

And yet...

Carefully, I shift my uninjured leg so that it brushes against one of the treasures dangling from the magpie's chains. I hear the chime of it. I feel the impact buzz through my glass. I'm surprised by the joy that bursts in my chest.

It's not touch, not exactly, but still.

I *feel.*

All those years hiding and hating, and all along I could *feel.*

Then the bird flips and I am falling.

It's so fast, surprise swallows my scream. For a moment, I can't understand why the magpie is high above me, why there's such glee in its eyes, why I can't stop staring at the trinkets still secure on its back.

The magpie dives. Its talons snag my shirt, just below the chin, and I dangle: ten feet above the earth, perhaps fifteen. Just high enough to shatter.

The magpie says: "Everyone's talking. The little man with glass limbs. How you *sparkle.*"

I find myself bargaining silently: it will be all right, even if it drops me; perhaps I won't break, or not all of me will. Perhaps I can offer it something else, something that hurts less—

"This isn't what we agreed to," I manage. I do not sound brave.

The magpie chuckles. "You never said to take you up *safe.*"

"But—"

"Smashed glass is glitter," the magpie whispers. "My feathers will glow."

I'm not afraid. I shouldn't be afraid.

But I am. I remember the pain of my leg hitting stone, the pain of my wrist in the magpie's beak. This will hurt, and despite myself, I care.

Despite myself, I feel. Guilt and fear and anger and joy, still joy, senseless and stupid and refusing to die.

I am not dead, I think. *Not dying. Not yet.*

These legs bore me through the market. This hand shook the cursebreaker's, held my father's. They are weak, they are fragile and flawed, but they're alive—they're *me.* The proof is the pain that pulses through me even now, from my splintered leg and my jagged stump of a wrist.

The proof is the hum that I felt in my fingers. Something of the world travelled through them to me.

"The glass is a weakness," my father said. "It will destroy us both."

Except my shattered wrist glints as sharp as any dagger, and for one fierce moment, it feels like no weakness at all.

With my right hand, I grab for one of the bird's jeweled chains. With my left, I stab.

Blood bursts dark over my forearm. The magpie shrieks. For a moment, I dangle from the chain while the bird twists, sagging toward the earth, but its wingbeats are faltering, and then they stop.

We fall.

Five feet. Perhaps ten. Not enough to kill, but enough that, when my right side hits the earth, my injured leg explodes.

The crash is terrific, the pain blinding. Sparkling pieces of me fly across the tunnel, littering the ground with ice-clear radiance. Some end up in the dead magpie's feathers after all, and this strikes me as funny, but my lungs are too empty to laugh.

For many long minutes, breathing is all I can manage. In. Out.

Feelings leak back to me slowly. The surge of protectiveness I felt for my body. The rush of piercing the magpie's heart. Strange sadness for my shattered leg.

What now? I ask myself. *What now?*

I'm still in the labyrinth: no place for a man in my condition. Here, the spell is still useless. In the tunnels around me, unseen, a thousand monsters wend their way. They'll take a passenger, if I'm willing to trade more of myself away. If I'm willing to be reckless, putting myself—whatever I am—at their mercy.

On the rocky ground, the magpie's treasures glitter. My eyes land on a sceptre: clear as glass, tall enough to reach my shoulder. No sturdier than the leg I've lost, surely—but enough, I think, to bear my weight.

I can't bring myself to love the curse that eats at me, the glass that turns me brittle. But the pain and hope pulsing through me resound with a single thought: at least until I return to the surface, we are one and the same. My flawed body has carried me here, and I will carry it—as best I can—back out.

With my right hand, I grip the uneven wall, hauling myself upright.

Take me, I think: to myself, or to the labyrinth.

But I don't ask to be remade.

Carly Midgley is a writer, freelance editor, and library program planner based near Toronto. Her work has been published in outlets including *The Huffington Post*, *Litmospher*e, and *Working Title*. When not writing, she can be found drinking too much tea and overanalyzing books and video games. You can find her on Instagram @carlymidgleywrites or online at carlymidgley.com.

SVALKA

AGGIE NOVAK

Svalka is not a good place for dreams, but Annoushka can't help it. Her favourite dream is a tattered and grubby book about a magic stove. She can't read the words, but the pictures tell the story. A sad girl, just like Annoushka, sleeps by her stove. Then one day it awakens and carries her off. It takes her far away to a handsome prince, and happiness. Annoushka's stove isn't warm or made of brick, it's just a broken electric hob sitting on a plank that stretches between two old wooden crates. So she wishes extra hard to make up for it.

"Stop flying in the clouds." Mama slurs from her pallet of scrunched-up newspapers. "You'll float away."

But Annoushka won't stop, even if she learns how to help it. Without dreams she fears—she knows—she'd be just like her mother. Her mother doesn't dream. She doesn't do much of anything, leaving the work of survival to Annoushka.

In the day, Annoushka skips through Svalka. She clambers, light-footed, up sliding towers of burst black bags and plastic bottles. She picks, sharp-eyed, through mounds of stinking scraps. She sorts, nimble-fingered, the useful from the useless. Recyclables, metal, old electronics. People discard all sorts of wonderful things, and Annoushka is good at finding them.

Those she can sell, must sell, to the men-in-charge. Sometimes they give food, but mostly a stinging not-real vodka that Mama drinks. To keep away the cold, she says.

In winter Annoushka has less time to find dream-things. Instead she looks for sheets of plastic to keep out the wind, and cardboard to keep in the heat.

Every morning there are people who don't wake up. After three days of heavy snow, when the air is so cold it hurts to breathe, Annoushka's Mama is one of them.

She sits by Mama for a long time, waiting for her to wake. Annoushka knows from the blue of her lips and the stillness of her chest that she won't, but she waits anyway. There are lots of not-so-good things about Mama. The way she drinks and sleeps for hours while Annoushka works. The way she tells Annoushka not to read so much, not to hope for better things. To accept what she has. But there are lots of not-so-bad things too. Mama never hits her, not like some of the other Mama's or the big men-in-charge. And she knows everyone in Svalka. Because of Mama, Annoushka knows who is kind and can be relied upon for help when she really needs, she knows who to bribe, and which men to stay away from no matter what.

Best of all, Annoushka knows Mama cares about her and wants to keep her safe, because she says so. Now, there's no one left who cares at all.

She hides in the cramped gap under her stove while some of the others take the body away. Babushka Vera says Annoushka can move to her shelter, if she likes. She thinks Babushka Vera is nice, and could maybe care about her too, but she lives with her son. He's one of the men Mama warned about, and Annoushka doesn't like the way his eyes follow her everywhere. Besides, she is ten years old now, and old enough to survive by herself.

The next morning, when she wakes up, Mama's body is long

gone. But standing on her newspaper bed is a very small, very strange woman. She's no bigger than a cat, with a cloud of puffy white hair and leathery skin that makes her look at least a hundred years old; long, sharp fingers; chicken feet; and a pointed nose like a pencil tip. And Mama's watery grey eyes.

"What are you?" Annoushka manages in a quiet rush of words. "Did you kill Mama?"

"I am Svalkitsa, I am kikimora." She *does* look like a little Svalka with a skirt of paper scraps, a top of old bottle caps, and rotting fruit peel in her hair. "I don't kill."

"Kikimora?" Annoushka nibbles her lip and glances again to where Mama's body had been. Babushka Vera always tells her if she's too messy or dirty, a kikimora will come and strangle her in the night, or snatch her away to a stinky swamp. "Please don't hurt me. And if you're going to break my things, please leave my pictures alone."

Svalkitsa sniffs. "I'm not going to break you or your things, child. You care for this house, so I'll care for you." She crosses her tiny arms.

Annoushka likes the idea of having her own real house. A pretty dream. "Just so you know, I don't have any extra food for you."

But to that Svalkitsa just smiles with a mouth full of needle teeth. "I don't need your food."

Instead, she thrives on small offerings of dream-things, delighting in pictures as much as Annoushka. Best of all, Svalkitsa is warm. Just like the stove she wished for, the strange little creature keeps the winter out.

"You want to go far away?" Svalkitsa asks one night as they lay curled together. "Like in your pictures?"

Annoushka nods, clutching her book about the princess and the walking stove. "Can you carry me out of here like the stove?" Not wanting to push her luck, she adds, "But I don't need a prince. I can share my new home with you."

The kikimora lets out a giggle that grates like scraping metal.

"My arms are a bit small for carrying, Lisichka." Annoushka's heart glows every time Svalkitsa calls her little fox, but sinks at the kikimora's refusal. "But if you want to leave, I can help you."

"How? Magic?"

Svalkitsa winks. "Maybe a little."

After that, Svalkitsa reveals her affinity for warmth extends to finding still-working lighters and matches with an ease that can indeed only be magic.

At night, huddled around a tiny flickering light, the kikimora teaches Annoushka to read.

"Words will carry you away from here better than a silly old stove could," Svalkitsa promises. "Words are like a train ticket. They can take you wherever you want to go."

So Annoushka learns.

Reading isn't as hard as Annoushka expected, but even more magical than she hoped. Soon the damaged books dug out of the dump aren't enough to satisfy her. Their torn and missing pages frustrate her: she wants every word. So Svalkitsa works her magic, disappearing for a few hours or a night and returning, first with picture books, then novels, with creased spines and dog-eared pages. None of their pages are missing.

Svalkitsa sits beside Annoushka as she reads, keeping her warm and helping her with the difficult words. The kikimora isn't good at everything though—she is entirely dreadful at maths, for one.

"I want to go to school," Annouska announces one morning.

When she was littler, Babushka Vera tried to teach her sums, scratching the letters into the muddy ground with a stick. But since her knees started bothering her more and her fingers turned nobbly and stiff even those brief classes stopped.

Svalkitsa smiles, her wispy eyebrows quivering in excitement.

"Of course, Lisichka." As if that's what she wanted Annoushka to do all along.

Annoushka frowns, thinking of the school girls in her stories. "I don't have the right clothes, though. Or the right books." A heaviness settles in her chest. "Will it cost a lot of money?"

"Don't worry, Lisichka. We will both be clever as foxes."

She disappears off into the magic space between homes where only house spirits can go.

When her kikimora returns almost two days later, she clutches a bright blue backpack as big as she is. The fabric is clean and doesn't have a single hole in it.

Svalkitsa deposits the gift at her feet. "Go on!" She clacks her bony hands together. "Open it!"

The bag is already the nicest gift Annoushka has ever received. She crouches and unzips it to reveal notebooks—brand new ones no one else has ever written in—and a small case of pens and pencils. Best of all, there's an outfit folded at the bottom. The smart white blouse and dark grey skirt smell of soap and flowers. She brushes her fingers across the soft fabric, but doesn't try them on yet. She'll have to wash herself first. Under the folded clothes sits a pair of polished black shoes so shiny Annoushka could almost use them as a mirror.

"Do you like them?"

Annoushka pulls Svalkitsa into a tight hug—it's like cuddling a bundle of sticks.

The kikimora scratches one of her clawed feet against the floor, and Annoushka releases her. "I'll take that as a yes."

Annoushka nods and they both wipe tears from wet eyes.

It's not just clothes and exercise books that Annoushka needs, but Svalkitsa thinks of everything. She gives Annoushka an address to write on enrolment forms, and when she admits she never knew her father's name or even her own surname, the kikimora helps her think up a new one.

Anna Ivanovna Kniga. She writes it on the forms and on the front of all her new books in careful, neat letters. *Kniga*—the word for book—suits her better than anything her mother could have given her.

On her first day, Svalkitsa braids her hair into two long plaits, just like the soon-to-be-princess carried away by her stove.

The new clothes are only slightly too big.

"Room to grow," says Svalkitsa, stretching to the tips of her talons and straightening Annoushka's collar. "You look perfect, Lisichka."

But the other kids at school don't think so.

Despite how thoroughly she scrubbed the stink of Svalka from her skin, how neatly Svalkitsa did her hair, and how clean her clothes are, when she steps into her new classroom the other girls stare at her and scrunch up their noses.

"Who are *you*?" One of them asks, her mouth twisted.

"A-Anna."

Another girl frowns at her outfit. "Your clothes look funny."

A third girl, with a smile and a kind voice asks, "Where did you go to school before?"

"I d-didn't."

They all raise their eyebrows at each other, but before they can say anything the teacher comes in and orders them all to their seats.

School is hard.

"What year did Tsar Nikolai II die?" The grey-haired, pursed-lips teacher, Galina Alexandrovna, asks her.

"I-I don't know.

"What is twelve divided by four?"

"I don't know."

The teacher draws her brows into an angry line and moves to loom over Annoushka's desk.

"What about three times six?"

Not wanting to repeat herself, Annoushka begins counting on her fingers.

"Enough of that. Is there anything you *do* know?"

"I know how to read," she says with relief.

But the class titters behind her and the teacher just scowls harder, her face a web of wrinkles. "No talking back!"

"I'm sorry, Galina Alexandrovna."

Annoushka doesn't get called on again.

"How was school?" Svalkitsa asks when Annoushka makes it home, her route involving several buses and a walk.

"Good."

The kikimora's raised eyebrows disappear behind her dandelion-puff hair, but she combs out Annoushka's braids without pressing further.

Every day that week, Svalkitsa asks about school, and every day she gives the same answer.

It's only at the end of the week that she finally admits, "School is harder than I thought it would be."

"It will get easier, Lisichka." The kikimora prods her nose with a pointy fingertip. "You're the smartest girl I know."

"The other girls don't like me. And neither does Galina Alexandrovna."

Svalkitsa narrows her grey eyes, making her look more like the malevolent spirit the kikimora in stories always are. "They don't know you."

Annoushka supposes that is true. "Even Russian class is hard," she adds. "I thought I'd be good at it."

"It's very hard to be good at things the first time." Svalkitsa shrugs and her bottle cap shirt rattles. "Are you sad you tried?"

Annoushka considers and then shakes her head. "I learned about multiplication. And we get a hot lunch."

"Really?"

She nods enthusiastically. "Soup and kasha and pork *kotleti*. There was even *syrok* for dessert."

"See," said the kikimora, showing off all her narrow teeth, "soon you will be the best student in the school."

So Annoushka keeps going to school. Around class and homework, and on her days off she still has to pick through the rubbish heaps of Svalka, digging up whatever meagre treasures she can find. Svalkitsa stays by her side, helping however she can.

When the lessons are so hard she can barely follow them, Annoushka stares out the window and makes shapes in the clouds, or invents adventures for the pigeons cooing on the sill. She still dreams as much as she breathes. But Annoushka is not ten anymore, and even a girl who floats in the clouds learns things about the world below. Things like the fact that no one wants to be friends with a trash-girl. Her out-of-fashion clothes, a lingering whiff of garbage, her lack of previous schooling, and her reluctance to talk about her home: all of it adds up to something undesirable that Annoushka can't seem to separate herself from.

She never becomes the best student, but she becomes a better one. She decides she wants to become a teacher—a kinder one than those at her school. Maybe she will work in the library and find the perfect book for each child to read. She will never have to scavenge for the greedy men-in-charge again. The little girl who needed a magical stove to carry her away is gone. Now, Annoushka dreams of carrying herself.

"You'll be wonderful, Lisichka." Svalkitsa scrutinises her appearance one last time.

Annoushka's clothes fit perfectly, and her hair is pulled back into a sleek ponytail.

"Thank you." Annoushka chews at her lip. "But will I be wonderful enough?"

The answer was no.

She knows she did well enough on the exams, but to ensure a scholarship and stipend for university she still needs to pass an interview.

The stern-faced woman behind the desk reminds Annoushka so strongly of Galina Alexandrovna that her palms slicken with sweat. The woman's desk is piled with bouquets of flowers and boxes of chocolate. Gifts, she realises, from other students. But Annoushka is empty-handed.

"Good morning, Anna Ivanovna."

When Annoushka tries to speak, her tongue is heavy and dry in her mouth. "G-good morning."

She can't recover from her initial nervousness, stumbling over all her answers, and saying as few words as possible.

At home, Svalkitsa asks her how it went, and she just shakes her head. The rejection letter arrives a few weeks later. If Annoushka wishes to attend university, she'll need to pay for it herself.

"I am stuck here," she tells Svalkitsa. "I have the ticket, but they won't let me on the train."

"We will find another way, Lisichka. Clever foxes always do."

She will have to save as much as she can and dream of more.

"At least I don't have to move into a student dormitory without you," Annoushka says.

Instead she finds a job working at the desk of a hostel. The shifts go for a full day and night, with Annoushka catching sleep around the arrival of guests. The salary is small, but it is enough to keep filling her belly with hot meals, cover her in a thick winter coat that keeps her truly warm, and buy a proper battery powered light for her home. Home is still Svalka, for apartments are impossibly expensive. She still has to spend days between shifts picking through junk for the men-in-charge, their demands growing now that she's an adult.

She still has to worry about the thinness of her walls in winter and how to hide what she has from the neighbours.

Slowly, Annoushka stops dreaming.

The days melt together in an unchanging, hopeless blur. Boring as her job is, the long hours leave her too exhausted for proper scavenging. She doesn't read late at night, Svalkitsa at her side. She doesn't leave her offerings anymore, and the kikimora visits less and less.

Annoushka falls behind on her quota, and begs for time to catch it up. She takes a day off work and spends it sifting through trash until her fingers bleed. But the knack she had as a child is gone, and it isn't enough. She doesn't meet her quota and the men-in-charge come to her home. They beat her and discover her scant savings. Finding what she held back only makes them beat her harder.

Bruised and aching, Annoushka lies on the cold floor, head tucked under her makeshift stove. For the first time in years, she dreams of it coming to life and carrying her away—anywhere will do, as long as it's better than here.

Svalkitsa appears beside her, now faded like a ghost. Annoushka looks into her pale grey eyes—Mama's eyes—and wonders if her mother had ever lain here, wishing for someone to take her away. Mama had been trapped here too.

"You can go, if you like," says Annoushka. "I don't think I will ever have the right ticket."

Svalkitsa grabs her wrist with bony fingers, no less strong for being transparent. "There is one place I can carry you, if you want. You can come with me."

"To become a kikimora?"

"If you wish."

She nods. "Please." She picks up the book about the princess and the stove. "I'm ready."

Annoushka, now tiny herself, lets Svalkitsa carry her away.

Aggie Novak lives with her wife by the beach in Australia, where she spends most of her time hiding from the sun and heat. She writes around studying for her pharmacy degree and entertaining her three dogs. She loves all kinds of speculative fiction and often draws inspiration from Slavic folklore and mythology. When not writing she can be found drinking tea and reading everything in sight. Her published works can be found in *Hexagon*, Flash Fiction Online and more! For the full list see aggienovak.com

PART FOUR

WARLINE

Up close, the mountain is beyond imposing; it's terrifying. Your first experience watching the actual *Climb*, and you're not quite sure what to expect. You've heard the stories, all quite gruesome, and you wonder yet again what kind of person would choose this course. You're not that kind of idiot. Bright pennants snap in the wind, displaying the crests of all the noble houses of the kingdom; the loyal ones, anyway. Hussars ride past with their cuirasses brightly gleaming, the horses, their manes plaited with blue and gold twine, high stepping as they *passage* and foaming at their polished bits. It gives you goosebumps to watch it.

The stands are full, but there are no bad seats as the risers ascend up alongside the mountain, so you all have a perfect view of the warm-up arena as well as the main ring. You don't mind being squished between Otto and Daria on the hard wooden bench as there's an unusual chill in the air, and you gratefully sip your steaming coffee.

Huge snowflakes drift down, soft and slushy. "Otto. You're psychic!" says Piotr, but the big man gives him a blank look. "It's snowing. You'd said it would snow. I thought you were nuts."

"That's going to screw people over." Daria frowns, and you nod in agreement.

The crowd watches in reverential silence as expert mountain climbers, MMA fighters, the hussars, mercenaries, foreign knights, and even some tech bros all kneel, arms open wide, awaiting the touch on the forehead from the priests as they wield bunches of holly and rowan in benediction.

Drums beat in unison, echoing across the stadium and announcing the start, and one by one the candidates each make their attempt. The mountain climbers throw their ropes high, but partway up it grows steeper, and their spikes and their cleats barely make a chip in the glass. They plunge back down, their skin sloughing off from the friction as they tumult to the arena floor, where they then lay broken and still. The crows fight one another to reach them, but the priests wave them off, at least for now. Then the tech bros with their crypto-bought gadgets, all fail too, plummeting faster than their safety gear can deploy. Mangled, their bodies at odd angles, you observe darkly, *what's the world with a few less ethereum chasers*? Unkind, you know. But if you step back for more than a minute, the horror takes your breath away. Best to stay numb.

The knights gallop past on their chargers, hoping momentum, and the evil-long studs on the shoes of their horses will aid them. Otto snickers at the colourful plumage on their helms, shaking his head. The snow adds to the slipping, and attempt after attempt, hope after hope fades as they all crash back down. It's absolutely horrific, but the crowd roars in appreciation. You realize they don't care if the candidates win or lose.

Later, as the sun sets and the crows swoop from body to body, you stand alone by the ring-side staring at what's left of the candidates strewn across the field, all piled in heaps at the base of the mountain. The carnage is madness. What a waste. Otto joins you, leaning over the fence.

He looks up at the mountain top, now blurred by swirling snow. "That bitch is up there laughing at us. I hope she enjoyed the show."

It's a good thing you're winning at a lot of the skirmishes, because you're pretty sure you've lost your job at the grocery. Messages show up on your phone (*fucking store)* but you've been leaving your boss's texts on read. Otto's won his fair share as well, but Piotr and Daria? Not so much, and it's causing discord. You offer to front them some of your winnings, but Piotr refuses. That's not why he's come.

"The Gather is for glory," he reminds you, despondent.

Daria apologizes, watching him as he stalks off back to the inn. "He thinks he's a nothing, a *middle*. He's convinced the Climb is the only way to redeem himself."

"That makes zero sense," you tell her. "He's done nothing wrong." Daria shrugs, dejected.

Piotr and Daria argue more and more frequently, and he's taken to leaving her alone the last two nights. You try to sleep, but you can hear bitter words through the wall. *If you think middles are so fucking low, what are you doing with me?* I'm *a middle!* Daria shouts. You hear the door to their room slam, and then running down the stairs. *Daria. Daria!* Piotr calls. You close your eyes in sympathy. This part of coupledom you do not miss.

At breakfast, both you and Otto try to cheer Daria up, but she's withdrawn, and you can feel she's planning something.

You're still taken aback when, at the next Climb, Daria isn't seated beside you in the stands. It's clear Piotr's worried when he asks if either you or Otto have seen her. You haven't. When the candidates enter the field, however, your heart jumps out of your chest.

Daria's among them.

"Daria!" Piotr shouts, but she refuses to look up. You all rush to the in-gate, but the priests block you from entering. Piotr's beside himself, frantic as they drag him back to the stands, shouting for her to get the hell out of the ring. You can't watch the next part. You know it's over when you hear Otto let out a sob.

HOUSE OF JADE LIONS

Y. M. PANG

Eldest Sister dangles from the awning of the south balcony. She swings back and forth, back and forth, though no wind blows. Her white-clothed feet thump against the grey railing. Death has leached her skin ivory-pale and frozen her face in an eternal grimace.

I watch her from the first-floor veranda, the furthest I can go before the barrier stops me. During the initial days of the haunting, I'd liked lingering on the balcony with her, tracing the silver thread on her red robes with my fingertips, marvelling at how the shining silks contrasted the washed grey of the House of Jade Lions. Nowadays I can barely reach the soles of her swinging feet, no matter how I stretch my shrunken arms and jump.

In the largest bedchamber, Mother kills Father every evening. He'd be the first to rise, but wouldn't manage a single step before she swings the axe, sending rivulets of blood bursting from his neck. The red turns to grey to match the rest of the floor. They would lie there for the next twelve *shichen*, immobile, before resuming the routine the following evening. I probably could climb over them in the interval, an adventurer scaling the bodies of two sleeping giants. But I don't dare. Who knows when Father wouldn't wait until evening to rise. Who knows when Mother wouldn't wait until then to kill him.

Eldest Brother kneels by their bedchamber, stone still, an ineffectual guardian statue. I was once taller than him, but now my entire body is barely the length of his forearm.

In the sitting room, Second Sister and Third Brother play an endless game of Army. They move their chariots and generals and foot soldiers as I enter, but when I leave and return, their pieces are back in the same places on the board.

I cannot tell how much time has passed. Sometimes I stare out the wax paper windows at the moving halls and palaces. Occasionally I glimpse a man in gold robes etched with dragons: the Emperor. But his face is unfamiliar; he is not my Emperor.

I glance up at the ceiling of the dining room. The jade lions dangle from braided red cords. Unlike Eldest Sister, they do not move from a nonexistent breeze. I stretch out a hand like a child catching snow—I'm so small now, it's only a matter of time before I'm no bigger than a jade lion. No rusty fluid drips from the lions' sleek bodies into my palm, though one of them appears to smile.

I stormed into my bedchamber. Eldest Sister rushed in after me.

"Please, won't you at least—"

"No!" My voice burst out as a scream, even as I tried to take deep breaths, to calm down.

Eldest Sister stopped before me, took my hands in hers. I tried to pull away but her grip remained firm.

She leaned close enough for me to count her eyelashes. "Brother, you know this is no use. Whether you like it or not, they will force you to marry her. If they must strip you and pull your limbs into the wedding robes, if they must force the wine down your throat... they will do it."

"Then let me choke on it," I said, and she shook her head.

"Come," she said, "it will not be so bad. Her family is suitable, and she is an accomplished painter. Even if you have no particular feelings toward her, you can still do your duty."

Duty. Because we were no different from the other families in the Palace City, no matter how I pretended otherwise.

"Why do you resist so much?" Eldest Sister asked. "Have you fallen in love with another woman?"

I shook my head.

"A man?"

"No."

"You can tell me. I will take the secret to the waters of oblivion."

I sank to my knees. Tears gathered behind my eyes, and I lowered my head, hoping she wouldn't notice. Her arms encircled me. She smelled of jasmine and incense.

"I just want everything to stay the same," I said. "As it has always been."

"I know," she murmured. "I felt that way too, once. But time does not stand still."

She didn't understand what I wanted, couldn't understand what I wanted. With my head still resting on her shoulder, I met the eyes of the jade lion on my nightstand. *Can you understand?* I wondered. *You're the guardian of this house. Surely you understand, even if you cannot help me.*

The jade lion did not reply, but for a brief moment its eyes gleamed red.

I always look forward to dinnertime. We dine together at a table of smooth, dark wood, chatting about Chancellor Gu's latest Flower Country policy, and the Empress' exquisite mid-autumn feast. Wax paper covers the doors and windows, letting in light but not vision, so I can pretend the Palace City around us does not exist.

Eldest Sister sits on my left. Third Brother is on my right, always hitting his chopsticks a little too audibly against his bowl, which Mother nags him about. Father sits to Mother's left, and to his left are Eldest Brother and Second Sister, completing the circle.

One by one, they fade.

Mother goes first. One of the jade lions falls from the ceiling and lands in her pork bone broth. It must have shrunk when it hit her bowl, because she scoops it up in her next spoonful and chokes on it. She coughs, and continues coughing for a long time. Father reaches for her, but she pushes him aside, sending him crashing to the floor. Finally she wheezes, her mouth open, her eyes rolling back.

She falls still. She becomes translucent like the wax paper windows, then fades away. Her afterglow is red, like sunset.

Father does not rise. He lies in a lifeless heap, turning grey, then becoming ashes that drift away.

Eldest Brother stands, his body suddenly covered with studded armour. He turns, and noise hits me like one of his training ground blows. The clang of swords, the thunder of hoofbeats, the cries of the dying. Churning dust and shadowy riders surround him, whisk him away to the Southern Campaigns.

Second Sister follows. Cloying petals encircle her, and she rides off on them like they are boats and the world is her stream. Mother has emphasized how much of an honour this is, for Second Sister to be chosen as a companion to the Princess of the Flower Country. But my well wishes die in my throat.

Third Brother is married off to a lady with a different name each time, but it's the same length of red wedding silk that strangles him. His afterglow is shadow, is negative space.

Eldest Sister and I remain. I know what comes next. The ghostly form of Chancellor Gu will stride up to her, wrap his spindly arms around her. Gu, the son of a weaver, the man with common blood, whose only claim to greatness is being principal graduate on the Imperial Exams. I scream until my throat is raw. I snatch at Eldest Sister, but she becomes as transparent as her new husband, and slips from my fingers. Her afterglow is gold as the Emperor's robes.

But this time, Gu doesn't come and Eldest Sister doesn't fade. Instead she leaps up and slams her fist into my throat. I tip backward in my chair, gasp for air as Mother had done. I brace myself for impact against the hard, unforgiving floor, wondering if it'll finally shatter me, but the crash never comes.

Instead, I wake in my own bed. The green silk sheets are stained with sweat, though the patch is smaller than I expect. The beaded curtain swings, though no wind blows. My left hand rests on the jade lion on my nightstand. I'd once been able to hold it in my palm, but now it's half my size, so this feels like petting a large guard dog. A large, cold guard dog whose coat is hard as armour.

I try to withdraw my hand but find I cannot. My hand is welded to the jade lion. My fingers have turned greenish-white.

I grab the jade lion with my free hand, shove it with my foot. Finally I succeed at prying it off. It skitters across the nightstand and smashes against the floor. Its seven pieces scatter in different directions, but still one reddish-brown eye stares up at me.

"So *now* you break," I mutter. After all those times I'd smashed it without making a dent.

I raise my left hand. I try to curl my fingers, but cannot. Running my other hand over my palm, I find my skin as smooth and hard as jade.

I sit up. The drop from bed to floor looks precipitous in my miniature body, but I don't hesitate. I do not know if this latest ailment will spread, but I cannot take chances. It's time to pay Eldest Sister a visit while I still can.

Her eyes were wide, dark, hooded with long lashes that looked almost iridescent. Her black hair knotted in elaborate braids, and her lips curved in a mysterious smile. Her hand, as she extended it, was deft, long-fingered. Her father had brought her paintings before he'd brought her, and they were indeed beautiful.

I did not want to marry her at all.

Mother shoved me. I stumbled back, tripped over a chair, and fell. Sprawled on the dining room floor, head throbbing, I stared up at the jade lions suspended from the ceiling.

"You *will* marry her!"

Mother didn't look like herself. Her hair fell from its combs and pins, and her eyes glared wide. I could scarcely believe she was the same woman who'd taught me my characters, her hand closed around mine on the brush. Her calligraphy could equal anyone's, even the head tutor's.

"You are a son of imperial blood!" Mother yelled. "Your marriage has never been negotiable."

"I—"

"General Chen has agreed to let you marry his eldest daughter, even though you are merely the second son. It is the best match we can hope for."

"But I don't want to."

"Can't you think about your family for once? Or do you only care about yourself?"

"But it's because..." The words died in my throat. *It's because I love you, all of you, that I want things to stay the same. I want what Eldest Sister promised: that we would always stay together.*

Mother steadied herself on the table. Her other hand reached for her cup of tea. I could smell the greed on her, like rust and old stone.

She raised the cup. "You will do your duty to this house. I am the daughter of the Huawu Emperor, may his soul rest among the stars, and you will listen to me."

No, I thought. *Please. Let me remain in this house. Let all of us remain. Even if I must give up my body and become a ghost, a doll at Eldest Sister's side...*

The jade lions on the ceiling must have truly felt sorry for me, for not only did their eyes turn red this time. They cried, too, tears of blood dripping down their pale green bodies.

A droplet fell and landed in Mother's tea.

That night, Mother unearthed the old axe from the storage room and swung it at Father. Blood gushed from his neck like fluttering wedding silk. Mother's eyes were rust-red, like the transformed lions dangling from our ceilings.

Eldest Brother and I stood in the doorway, shaking and helpless. Father slipped to the ground, his head not quite severed, still connected by some flesh and sinew. The axe clattered from Mother's hands and she collapsed on top of Father, washing her face in his blood.

Eldest Brother clutched the jade lion pendant around his neck. His nails dug into his palm, drawing blood. Then he swayed, fell. I caught him, placed him gently on the floor, away from the growing pool of blood. But already the red was turning into grey.

I found Second Sister and Third Brother in the sitting room. They played a game of Army, red and black pieces on the lined board. The room smelled like incense, and they breathed heavily. The rich brown wood of the table faded. The only colour came from the jade lions, and they were now more red than green.

My siblings' breaths laboured, faltered. I waited until they stopped breathing before I searched for Eldest Sister.

I found her in my room, sitting on my bed. She looked up from her scroll when I entered, her eyes holding nothing but hatred. "You!"

The jade lion on my nightstand, scarlet eyes glowing, reached out and raked a claw across her neck. The lightest of touches, barely drawing blood. Then it reared up on its hind legs, poised to strike again—harder, deeper.

I lunged across the room and closed my hand around its strangely warm body. I smashed it against the nightstand. Then I cried out in pain.

The lion was whole, but the fingers of my left hand felt broken. I tried to move them, but when I did I realized they weren't wrapped around the jade lion at all, but around Eldest Sister's throat. Her pulse fluttered beneath my hands. She gasped and twisted beneath me and I wanted to let go, but I couldn't, I couldn't.

She dug a nail into the second joint of my index finger, where my hand felt most broken. Pain shot through my bones and I released her. She raced from my room, loose hair flying behind her. Not screaming, not crying, just silent. I lay there, my hand throbbing. The jade lion stood upright on my nightstand, as if I'd never grabbed it.

Eldest Sister donned her red wedding gown and hung herself by the light of dawn. Colour bled out from the House of Jade Lions, until the only things that were not grey were my parents, my siblings, myself, and the lions. *They'd* returned to pale green.

I pushed open the front doors and stepped onto the veranda. Dizziness swept over me. The halls, the houses, the gardens of the Palace City were moving. Or maybe the House of Jade Lions was moving, moving through them, dragging me on a journey with no rest or escape.

I hit a barrier when I reached the bottom step. My still-aching hand brushed what felt like jade.

I was shrinking.

Or, I woke up one morning and I was suddenly smaller. That was a less problematic thing to believe. Because if I were shrinking, then one day I wouldn't be able to push open the front doors. One day I'd disappear.

I padded over to Mother's bedroom, because she had the biggest mirror. At least her room was on the same floor, though the journey still took forever on my shortened legs. I scurried around Mother and Father's prone bodies and gazed into the bronze.

I was the size of a doll, not even reaching a human's knees. My face looked different, too, like someone had carved my likeness into a dough figurine. Intricate, a little short of human, but a little too human to be devoured.

I inhaled. The scent of blood and rust and stone was gone. I walked back to the dining room, gazed up at the jade lions. "You didn't want us to leave either, did you?" I whispered.

I heave myself up the stairs to the second floor. It's been a while since I've done this. Standing on one step, I find the next one as tall as my chest. I grab the lip of the stair, haul myself up. Repeat. My right hand does most of the work. My left hand—a cold, hard stump of jade—refuses to make a fist, refuses to move at all. I can only shove it ineffectually against the steps, which are so grey that only the smell tells me it's not stone.

When I reach the top, my chin, chest, and forearms are covered in scrapes and bruises. I plod past the bedrooms of Second Sister and Third Brother, their furniture dusted with cobwebs. I stop before the double doors of the balcony, and push at the left one.

For a moment it doesn't open. Then it groans, and I stumble forward as the door rips from its hinges. It smashes against the balcony floor, a crack appearing across its middle.

Ears ringing, I stare up at Eldest Sister's swinging body. "Hello," I say, still panting from my climb. "I've come to visit you."

I reach up. Her foot dangles far above my functional hand, big enough to obscure a third of my vision. "Those damned lions," I whisper. "Who would've guessed they could do this?"

A creaking sound. I assume it's the right door, still attached to its hinges, though I don't feel any wind.

"It's Mother's fault too," I say. "She shouldn't have angered the lions by trying to send us all away."

More creaking. I follow the silver thread of Eldest Sister's robes, up to her collar. A jade shard rests in the folds of silk, so sharp I worry it would cut her skin. My eyes drift up to where the rope bites into her throat.

I frown. The rope is frayed.

I experience one moment of blank incomprehension before the rope snaps, and Eldest Sister crashes down on me. The impact slams the breath from my lungs, sends me tumbling across the balcony floor. I land hard on my side, and when I stretch out my left hand, I find a spiderweb of cracks in the jade.

The balcony groans beneath Eldest Sister's weight. Its wooden floor cracks, as if echoing my broken hand. The cracks lengthen, spread, branch off—until the balcony breaks apart beneath us.

We fall, wooden pieces scattered around us. I gaze down but cannot see the Palace City below, just grey emptiness. I twist my head around just in time to see the second floor collapse onto the first, beams and stairwell crushed to dust. Objects fly out as if ripped away by a violent wind. Here, the bronze mirror in Mother's room. There, a porcelain bowl we used for dinner, still emitting high-pitched rings though Third Brother isn't hitting his chopsticks on it. The House of Jade Lions disintegrates.

I grab a piece of red silk—the collar of Eldest Sister's robe. I cling on, reaching for her throat with my other hand. My jade fingers break off as I brush them over the red-black mark left by the rope, but I cannot feel anything.

I look out at the scattering pieces of the House of Jade Lions and muster a smile. "At least we're still together," I say.

Eldest Sister tilts her head. More likely, a wooden plank just jostled her. Unlike the others, Eldest Sister never moved after the haunting, after she'd hung herself.

But, unmistakably, her hand rises. Her mouth twists like a sword slash and she says, "This is all your fault."

Her hand closes around the back of my neck. She plucks my tiny body off her and dangles me in the air for a moment, examining me as a bride would an unwelcome wedding guest. Then she tosses me away.

I scream. I claw at her receding figure as more pieces of the house fall around me. The old axe. An Army piece. A teacup spotted with red. But somehow, through it all, I do not see a single jade lion.

Y.M. Pang spent her childhood pacing around her grandfather's bedroom, telling him stories of magic, swords, and bears. Her work has appeared in *The Magazine of Fantasy & Science Fiction*, *Beneath Ceaseless Skies*, and *The Dark*, among other venues. She is a finalist for the Aurora Award and the WSFA Small Press Award. She dabbles in photography and often contemplates the merits of hermitism. Despite this, you can find her online at www.ympang.com or on Twitter / X as @YMPangWriter.

THE DEAD PATCH

MADELEINE GIBSON

It was a bitch and a half to get the tractor around without hitting the dead patch, which is why I was the one breaking ground for planting today instead of Leah. I'd say she was trying to get out of working — which don't get me wrong, she was — but I'd also had to dig the back wheel out of the rotting mucky soil more than once when she'd miscalculated and that was worse no matter how parched and crackly my skin got in the sun.

Way back when we thought this was going to be a solvable problem, Mrs. Haversham from three doors down had told us to try natural remediation, otherwise known as sticking some plants in the ground and letting them do the hard work. It had been too good to be true, but I was sure Mrs. Haversham was still lurking in the back of the university library a few towns over and poking through the stacks for one more plant we hadn't tried. The alternative was being wrong, and Mrs. Haversham hadn't been wrong for a solid decade and a half, not since I was a couple feet shorter and a hell of a lot dumber.

Well. It was possible she'd never been wrong at all and my

mother had only *told* me she had been wrong about something, but either way the dead patch lay smugly undefeated.

Anyway, we'd tried the remediation, but all the vegetables came up with the skins peeling and something that might have once been a pumpkin had spread questing, decaying vines towards the clean ground. We'd had to go all scorched-earth with a weed torch to get it under control and Leah still hadn't gone into town to replace the propane tank. I loved my sister, but she was very seventeen. I didn't begrudge her a childhood, or at least, I didn't *want* to begrudge her one. It was just that I needed the help—I wasn't yet used to planning farm chores around two people instead of three. When Leah deigned to show up, it wasn't too different, but damn if I didn't hate that the answer was being patient.

My tea was sulking on the counter the next morning when I finally made it downstairs. Leah had fucked off in the car to god-knows-where, but I could still feel her eyes burning into the back of my head. "Yeah, yeah," I told my cold mug of tea, and microwaved it. If Leah wanted me to drink her precisely-steeped tea while it was still warm, then she should give in and admit my sleeping schedule was at best unreliable. It was hard to get out of bed some days, and the trip out to the dead patch yesterday meant today was one of the hard ones.

In my favourite kitchen chair, I watched the first rain of the season fall on our fields and drank my subpar tea.

Later, when the clouds had blown away, I went to weed the dead patch. I was pulling up grass from the edge of the dead spot because I didn't want a repeat on scorched-earth, and for a while it was all fine and normal as it could get, vis à vis having a dead patch of land out back. Until the next hank of grass was followed by a chalk-white hand.

I shrieked and fell on my ass. The hand planted itself on the edge of the dead patch where the solid ground started and *pulled.* I was crab walking back before I even thought to start escaping– old habits coming in handy at the weirdest times– and *fuck,* there were two hands now. Faster than anything should have been able to, the monster hauled itself out of the dead patch into the still-moist air.

"Absolutely not," I squeaked. I was still on the ground, my mouth hanging open, palms planted in the rich farm mud. April showers bring walking corpses.

It was dry as a bone and whiter than one too, like it hadn't come right out of a pit of muck. The salt-zombie turned to me, and my stomach dropped sheer through my feet. Shit, I hadn't thought of that. Salt and water, I hadn't–

The monster exploded into sodden chunks with a wet *crack* that thudded against my ribs. I screamed again, then clapped a hand over my mouth. The sudden mouthful of dirt was enough of a shock to send me staggering to my feet spitting and sputtering. Leah stood behind where I'd been, the farmhouse shotgun levelled over my shoulder at where the salt-thing had been. In the light of the setting sun, she was all but glowing, pasty as moonstone. I gaped, shocked beyond words, and out came: "Could you have picked a *louder* gun? It's not deer season anymore! Someone's going to–"

Leah lowered the gun enough that she'd only shoot me if it was on purpose and spat, "Oh, sure, I'll let you get–"

"We have a *crossbow.*"

Leah made an incoherent noise, just like she always did when she was bluffing, and that was when I saw her hands were shaking. "Look down," she said, "and tell me you want to have only a crossbow on your side."

I did look down, and she was right. Salt had sprayed out in a wide arc reaching almost back to the now-disturbed dead patch. It looked like we'd forgotten which way our driveway was and also what season it was and tried to salt away some black ice. Other than the body. The body was really a fly in the ointment. A stick in the mud. The dead spot nightmare, back to haunt us again.

Yeah. I didn't know if an arrow would have helped much. The salt-body wasn't moving, which was good, and probably related to the massive hole Leah had blown in its chest. It *had* been moving, which was bad. I looked at Leah instead — which was worse because she was seventeen again instead of badass — and she was worrying at her bottom lip. She'd lowered the gun completely now, but her grip was tight enough to make her fingers blotchy red and white. I lowered my voice and tried to file all the screaming away for later, when I had time. If I had time. "Hey. Leah. It's okay."

"Yeah?" She could have sounded more unconvinced, but only if she'd tried. It worried me she wasn't trying. "You'll..."

"I'll take care of it," I promised. I didn't know what to do, but I was the older sister, so. Not the time to think about myself. I made little shooing motions, and said, "Go get cleaned up. I'll be in soon." To prove it, I bent to toss the first handful of salt back into the hole. If I left to go get a shovel, I wasn't going to come back. I smiled at Leah with muddy teeth. "Go on. I'll be okay."

At dinner, my hand was halfway to the saltshaker before it clicked. I stared down at my mashed potatoes and wished it had been Leah's turn to make dinner because even her godawful peanut butter sandwiches were better than— How was I supposed to eat bland potatoes if—

"Pass the salt if you're not going to use it," Leah said, exasperated. She knocked my hand aside to get at the salt, sending the pepper flying in the process. The clatter of the pepper shaker hitting the floor wasn't anything like a gunshot but all I could hear was a bang and an echo and then everything tipped sideways.

From behind fogged glass, I watched myself shove my chair back from the table. It took two tries to get the doorknob to turn because I was suddenly too small within my body. The gravel under my bare feet felt like static, my shirt hot sandpaper against my skin.

When I was a baby, before I knew better, I used to think that tears meant something special. I would cry on the gnarled old apple tree in the back of the grove and imagine this was what comfort felt like, its branches and leaves wrapping me up in the good kind of hug. Nobody was going to reassure me now but I pressed my forehead to the pitted bark and tried very hard to exist anyway. My back was aching and the cuffs of my flannel were twisted but I knew if I tried to make things better this would turn into screaming and if I started screaming then Leah would come find me and that would be the wave that drowned me.

In the tree, I stared straight ahead at my hand around the branch. The dark furrows of the bark were more familiar than the back of my hand. I wasn't feeling anything yet, but I thought I might be getting close to it. I breathed because I had to and told the tree, "Sorry." It was the closest thing I was ever going to get to a more-adult adult in my life and that was heavier than its branches should have to bear. "Sorry about the hell pit. Dead... thing. All that salt." I closed my eyes, breathed in the smell of lichen and wet leaves and apples young enough they hadn't started worrying yet. It helped. Maybe. I felt distant from myself; a horizon and a telescope, two opposing magnetic fields, the sort of thing that wasn't meant to be in one piece.

I stayed in the cradle of my tree past sunset. Then I went to bed, because the tree wasn't an adult but I was. I had to be. Not like anyone else wanted the job.

The next time it rained, Leah stayed with a friend in town and I slept with one hand on the shotgun. Nothing happened. Leah came back with curtains for the window looking out over the dead patch and made me tea when I was awake and neither of us said anything about anything.

The second time it rained after the dead patch catastrophe, I stayed awake for seventy-two hours in a row. Leah stopped making tea at the sixty-hour mark and started threatening to sell the apples from my favourite tree to hipsters at the farmers market. I slept, eventually.

The third time, I was determined to be chill. Zombies rising from the dead was fine and dandy and day-ruining, but they never rose twice on TV and that was going to have to be good enough for me. I rattled the tractor up to the Havershams with a bushel of apples, because Leah had stolen the car again, and promised Mrs. Haversham I was definitely going to try mushrooms on the dead patch next. It was a lie, but I was good at those. She told me that she was saving for a trip to her namesake village in England and I told her we were saving for a trip to the sea to try and find our extended family. It was normal, which should have been the first sign that something was going to go wrong.

The second sign was more obvious.

"Babygirl," the salt monster said when I opened the front door. "Where have you *been*?"

She was more solid than last time, more composed. Maybe she had been waiting, biding her time like always. I said, more exhausted than I knew existed: "Can't you stay *down*?"

My mother ignored me. Her arms were crossed, her sea-salt-skin shimmering in the late-day sun Leah's conspicuously absent curtains weren't blocking. The salt-monster sat at the table in my chair like she had never left at all. Like we had never buried her out back where nobody would ever have to look at her again. "No car?" she said. "No Leah?"

I didn't say anything.

She sighed, like I was the unreasonable one. Her lips were cracked as parched earth, our few rains a paltry substitute for the ocean we were supposed to be living in. "If you wanted your sister dead, you should have done it yourself, it's not as though you don't know how." A nod to the shotgun, untouched by the umbrellas. "At least if you did it, it'd be quick. You didn't go with her, don't you *know* what kind of area this is?"

Leah.

Leah had dug the hole the first time. I'd never seen her committed to anything with that furious fervour before or since. She hadn't done the deed, but she had sobbed into my arms on her late-fall birthday and I hadn't known how to hold her together while she shattered. I had combed my hands through her hair, felt her salt-tears on my shirt and known: enough.

That was why it had been easy then. Even easier, now. I'd chosen Leah and I wouldn't take that back for anything.

I'd chosen this place too. My home. Even when I dreamt of the ocean, I woke up here. I was salt on potatoes, not salt of the sea. Our people, wherever they were and whoever they were, would want us back if they knew of our landlocked existence. Our mother wanted us for herself, and had dragged us inland to make that a reality. She wanted us to belong to *her*, not a people, not a culture, not a family. I didn't even want the sea back, to be honest, even if that's where I was originally supposed to be. I just wanted tea in the mornings, cold rain, good apples, and to be able to wrap Leah in a hug without either of us flinching at an unexpected touch.

"You know," I said, and thought of how far away the Havershams were and how Leah was right and nobody paid much attention to deer season anyway. "I *do* know what kind of area this is."

This time, I buried her in the empty propane tank where the rain couldn't get in and her crocodile tears couldn't get out.

This time, I didn't think she was coming back.

Madeleine Gibson is a writer and collector of hobbies. She can be found wherever there is wool or perhaps a piece of terrible media that needs pondering.

THE THUNDER MUTTERS

KERRY RYAN

You go to sleep one night and wake up in a completely different bed in a completely different house. You have no idea where you are or how you got there.

When they first started living together, Romy would come out with this kind of thing late at night just as Emma was about to fall asleep. Romy thought it was cute. 'Well, what would you do, Ems?'

'Stop with the spooky shit,' Emma would say. Or when she still had a job: 'Come on, darling. I've got work in the morning.' Then she'd roll over, pulling the pillow over her head. 'I love you,' Emma would mumble into the goose feathers. If Romy didn't say it back, well, she had a lot on. And that was before the baby.

Romy edits the *Journal of Horror and Supernatural Studies* and, every year, she curates their film festival. She has grown that festival from a nothing to a something, she often says. Romy mostly programs films that explore hauntings or monstrous entities in suburban environments. They are linked to capitalism and sex in a way that Emma can't quite grasp.

'We as women are consumed and regurgitated by monsters,' Romy said on their first date. 'Every single day.'

'Yes,' Emma had nodded. 'That's right.'

Close to Christmas, Romy has to go all the way to Canada for work and Emma is left behind in their small flat with the baby. When Romy is away Emma is supposed to be looking for a part-time job because money is tight. But the good jobs aren't posted until January anyway. This is what she tells herself.

You wake in the middle of the night and hear the baby crying over the monitor. When you go into check, your baby is fast asleep, but you can still hear crying.

Romy sends photographs from Montreal of street signs up to their necks in snow. *I feel the same,* Emma texts back but there is always a delay before Romy replies and when she does it's as if Emma had sent a different text altogether. *They're killing me. Food is good though. Love French food.*

The Montreal job is for a big tech company. Romy has been brought on as a Consultant Conference Producer. 'It's a lot,' she said after they offered it to her. 'But the money is like, wow, and I can't say no because...'

Because of you, Emma, though this wasn't said out loud. That was when Emma had stood up and asked in a voice that was not her own whether Romy would like a cup of chamomile before bed. Or anything. Anything at all. It was really no trouble.

Get some sleep, Romy texts from Montreal. Every book and post Emma reads says you should sleep when the baby sleeps. But what if the baby hardly sleeps and when she does, you are jerked instantly awake by any kind of sound—feet slapping up the concrete stairwell outside; a souped-up boy racer reversing into the estate; a dog's whine that sounds just like a baby whimpering.

You leave the nursery and walk to the hall. You pass the mirror and see a shadow following you but when you turn, nothing is there.

The thing to do is count to ten. You are not your thoughts. Thoughts are not facts. Notice the colours around you in the living room. Really notice, take your time. Examine the red blanket Romy's mum knitted; the dark green ficus in the brass pot; the orange rug you bought from Habitat without using your credit card. But make sure to bypass the Dr Caligari poster above the fireplace. No, don't look too closely at that. Instead, walk over to the sofa and feel the red blanket Romy's mum made. Feel its soft intricacies. Feel the love that made it. Believe that a mother can love a daughter to this extent. That she can spend months creating something with care in every stitch. Breathe in slow, steady. Smell the coffee that waits for you in the kitchen. And if you haven't already, peel off your socks so the soles of your feet meet with the cool floorboards you sanded and varnished yourself. Here. Now. You. This home. This moment.

If none of this works: sing.

Sing to the baby all the songs you wish your mother had sung to you.

You stumble out of bed and go to the mirror, but the person looking back at you is not you.

Fresh air always helps. The sky has snapped to a clean blue. The sun is weak, yes, but warmer than usual at this time of year. Emma pushes the pram along the canal path as the morning mist lifts from the rippling water. But when she gets to the copse, the trees close-knit and gloomy, she stands at the edge of the woods, wondering what she's doing. The branches creak and groan. The gloom seems to hang between the bare trees. She can hear the baby's soft breath, in then out.

You are walking through the woods when you come across a clearing. In the middle of the clearing is a house. The walls are made of flesh, the roof is made of bone, and the—

Emma turns and heads back home. The sky has darkened. In the distance, thunder mutters. It's going to rain and rain hard, yes, but maybe not quite yet and, besides, the baby needs fresh air. Then she will sleep and sleep and sleep. Maybe. Perhaps.

Emma pushes the pram against the wind around the small green in the middle of the estate. The playground is fenced off, though the wind and the kids have battered down most of the fencing. The swings are swingless, and where the slide once was, there is a patch of upturned earth. A poster in the community centre claims the new playground will open very soon. Someone has scrawled a cock and balls over the photograph of the smiling construction worker with his thumbs up.

The estate was built 70 years ago for local workers but now a lot of the flats are owned by people who are definitely not local. The For Sale signs go up then down and Emma watches from her balcony as the council kitchens are torn out and thrown into skips. The cabinets smashed up, the guts of all those cheap MDF dreams exposed.

'I like them,' Romy said of their new next-door neighbours.

It's true that they always smile and wave on their way to the train station and jobs in the city. Yet with their navy duffel coats and neat Scandinavian shoes, they're the most likely suspects for the estate newsletter with the interesting typeface. A clean graphic design, yes, but the usual dirty business of noise complaints and anti-social behaviour: kids banging footballs against the bin shed when it clearly states NO BALL GAMES that kind of diabolical behaviour. The text tries for friendly, but the subtext is that those making hay with Thatcher's legacy want the estate to become akin to the Sycamore Avenue they grew up in; gardens neat and tidy; no cars with exhaust modifications; and absolutely no children playing along the walkways.

'This place is coming up at last,' Romy said when she read the newsletter. Emma said nothing.

But it will be handy when the playground is reopened. When the baby is older, Emma can sit on the bench and watch her daughter play and be the kind of mother she has seen in films and on TV.

Where the path forks to Londis, the old woman who lives somewhere in the Samuel Mathews block wants to peer in and coo at the baby, but Emma pulls the pram hood down.

'Sorry,' Emma says, moving past her. 'Sorry, I'm in a rush.'

She can't cope with any more germs and the woman does not look clean. Her nails are filthy. She smells turnipy as if she's been pulled up from the earth.

Emma walks briskly on though the woman's hurt expression hovers before her all the way around the green and back. But the baby must sleep. Then everything will be better. Everything will be brighter.

Emma's mum used to sing a hymn about things getting brighter.

In the morning it will be brighter,
In the morning it will be glory,
For the Second Coming is at hand.

Because the New Light Church had their Army of God planning meetings in the same community centre as Brownies had their meetings, Emma was allowed to attend with other girls from school. How she loved that uniform: the yellow sweatshirt, the brown skirt. She sewed every badge on herself—the few she had. *I Promise To Do My Best.* But the church didn't last so neither did Brownies.

One time, Emma was telling her mum about something funny Brown Owl had said and her mum yawned right in Emma's face. She didn't just yawn; she shouted yawn, yawn, yawn then crossed her arms and said: 'I am so bored. I am so bored I could die.' Not long after, Emma's little sister was born, and everything got worse.

After walking around the green three times, Emma is close to the playground once more when she glances up at her flat.

A dark shadow is standing at your bedroom window. The shadow reaches out towards you...

Emma stops dead. Someone is in their house, in their bedroom. She grips the pram, ready to run, to scream, but the clouds part, the sun comes out, and it's plain that no one is there. Just the folds of the curtain and what must be the edge of their wardrobe against the wall.

Jesus Christ, Emma.

Still, when she finally is inside their dark and silent flat, after bumping the pram softly up the stairwell for an eternity, she checks all the cupboards, the shower, the wardrobe and even under their bed.

Just in case.

Your wife comes home. She looks the same, she sounds the same, but she is someone else. No one believes you.

No, it is Romy. It is beautiful Romy with the half-moon scar on her left eyebrow and three piercings glinting on her right ear. It is Romy who smells the same, who is the same but thinner or as she says: so thin she could slip down a drain.

'I missed your cooking, Emma. I just don't like French food. I can't stand it.'

Romy doesn't say that she missed her little family, but people just have different ways of expressing love. Romy has brought presents. She is good at giving gifts. This is Romy's love language.

The first present Emma opens is a mug with the conference name and date on it. The next is a conference t-shirt and the last is a tiny keyring with a map of Montreal. The metal sits cold on Emma's palm.

'Aren't they good? Really cool design on the t-shirt especially.'

Emma nods but she is listening out for the baby. Each nerve stretched taut for that first whimper.

'It was mad over there, Ems. I can't tell you how busy I've been. I am so so exhausted.' Has Romy's voice always been this loud? It fills up the room, demanding attention. 'But anyway, how are you managing?' She cocks her head. 'Tell me the truth.'

'I'm ok. Just tired.'

'Still tired?' She frowns. 'What did the doctor say?'

'I've not gone yet. The baby's cold has thrown everything off.'

'Baby? What baby?' Romy is standing. She is looming. 'What baby, Emma?'

Kerry Ryan has won the Spilling Ink Short Story Prize, the Hachette GYOS Prize 2024, and has been shortlisted for the Myriad First Editions Prize, the Writers & Artists Prize 2023, and the HG Wells Prize 2023. Her writing has appeared in The *Manchester Review, The Kenyon Review*, the *Telegraph*, the *Guardian*, the *Evening Standard* and others. She is the founder of *Write like a Grrrl* and her courses and workshops are taught all over the world.

THE PRISONS THAT HOLD YOU

HANNAH MCLAUGHLIN

You stand at the doorway to the holding cell, the corridor behind you dark and comfortable, the door ahead just a thick slab of stone, crooked and insistent, sweltering where it touches your cracked gray-green skin.

Hands shove, and you're inside the cell, boots crunching on sludge and chipped ogre teeth and tiny animal bones the core hounds left behind. You crouch, eyes pinched shut, because the wizard orb mounted to the cell entrance is as bright as the core's innermost layer, utterly blinding to your full-moon pupils.

This will be your third pit fight, so you know what to expect.

Always, the wait is the hardest. You have a minute, maybe two, to find a weapon in your cell before that inner oval slab slides open like the unfolding of a tomb, when all the prisoners will stampede feverishly into open space.

Only one will survive.

You keep your eyes closed so that the blindness is yours to command, hands darting, featherlight, searching for a weapon. *Don't panic, there's time,* you tell yourself, but the feeling is right there beneath your collarbone, pinching your trachea like a tiny fist.

Fingers move like lightning, skittering over a stretch of curved bone —a bow and quiver, too unpredictable for close quarter combat— and a line of equally useless objects: halberd, spear, war hammer. All taller than you. You snatch the bow, useless thing that it is, slinging it and the quiver over your shoulder.

You picture the arena, the one time the orbs dimmed enough to see it, that swell of rough gneiss all around, steep walls streaked yellow and slate gray, the bottom layers marred by those perfectly oval slabs that mark the cell entrances. You tried counting holding cells once, stopped at fifty. Goblin-made, obviously. If the place wasn't designed to kill you, it'd be gorgeous, really, except for that crack in the center of the arena floor, right where the orbs glow brightest.

The slab begins to groan.

Frantic, you fumble, heel striking an object slammed deep into the sludge. *Yes.* Finally, *finally*, something of real worth: a sapphire pickaxe, the kind of tool your mother and grandmother and great-grandmother have pressed into your thick calloused palms since birth, a thing only those in the down-deep understand. Perhaps your captors left it just for you, a taunt against you and every other goblin they've enslaved in this hellhole. But you know the damage a well-timed throw of gemstone into stone can do, how it can shatter even lava-hewn basalt.

Here we go.

Stone grinds stone. A deep rumble, a war cry. Not from you. Some idiot pounds forward, desperate to prove himself, eager to kill. A high-pitched whistle like the beginning of a scream shocks the air—a dagger, thrown from the cell beside you—and a grunt quickly follows.

One down.

A drum pounds—*thud, thud, thud*—rhythmic and surreal, then two, three, four join the chorus, a call to battle reverberating through the mountain so that pebbles tumble like snow down the sheer gneiss walls, every wight and dwarf within miles spilling eagerly over the arena's rim to watch. Shouting and goading and whistling, a thousand sounds assault your sensitive ears, making you momentarily deaf and blind. Then one sound separates from the rest: your cell door closing, rolling across a buried dwarven track that runs below the doors. Anyone too scared to fight will be left inside, a snack for the core hounds. Clutching the pickaxe tight, you slip through the door, eyes closed, the cacophony a physical pain, but not comparable to the hovering wizard lights, brutal and blinding.

Your neighbor sets upon you immediately, confident and overeager. You can't see him, of course, but the hairs on your ears measure the tempo of his pulse. Metal rings.

You don't wait for the dagger in the chest; you duck, the blade whistling through the air, missing you entirely, then you launch yourself at him, ears guiding your steps. Forward, forward, forward, you swing that pickaxe with each step, aiming high since you can't locate the target. Pain slices your arm, quick and burning, but adrenaline masks it. You don't need eyes to see, not when your ears are better, proven as the pickaxe pounds into flesh, finding its mark.

And then there's no beat at all.

High above, the audience jeers when they see you, their reaction so different from that first victory. The dwarves had meant for you to be food for the big champs, those ageless giants and the ice trolls, just an easy, forgettable mark, so they'd been happily surprised, that first time, when you'd proved them wrong and made a handful a small fortune. *Zhiljek, Zhiljek, Zhiljek,* they'd chanted, as coins exchanged hands and slipped over the walls, your name on their lips another sort of drum.

"Dirty gobber!"

"Die, already!"

Groans and battle shouts echo all around. If the spectators are still jeering, you can't hear now; there is nothing beyond the roar of adrenaline and the pain of death and the occasional victory shout. You slip from shadow to shadow, finding the spots where the gneiss is coolest and crouching low.

A troll roars in pain. Close, too close. Every hair in your ear sings.

Still, you pause. The trolls are your kin, those great oafish cousins, the kind you don't invite to a party unless you want it to be a *really* good time. Unbidden, you're moving forward, the call of kinship too great to ignore. You listen to the music their duel makes, the rhythm of metal against bone, the troll's long-armed swing a slow howl against the assailant's stab-lunge-stab staccato.

You wait for the rush of air that passes when the troll steps back, and then you jump forward, aiming the pickaxe for the spot where his opponent's feet send shockwaves toward your toes, swinging upwards with all your strength, which is surprising, given that you're likely a quarter the size of these fools.

Another grunt, then you're tumbling, you and the nameless body tangled together, rolling across the floor. The body—gargoyle, you think, judging by the thick-skinned scales and rancid breath—lands on top of you, horns pinching your thigh, your waist.

Keep moving—the most important rule. But you can't, because you've got the world's biggest gargoyle on top of you. Dead, you think. Or close to it. Like you will be, if you don't get moving.

The troll speaks to you in Gnomish, its rock-salt timber a surprise. "You fight well, little rat."

"Goblin," you snort.

"Ah, I can't see," he says, the words an apology.

"Me either."

"They took your eyes, too?"

"Oh. *Oh.*" You pause, surprised that sadness can still touch you. "No. It's the lights. Too bright."

The last words come out as a sigh, the gargoyle's deadweight unbearable, pinching a nerve in your lower thigh. A creak and a groan, then, just as sudden, the pressure is gone.

"Thanks," you murmur to the troll, standing on shaking legs. "What, uh, weapons do you have?"

He laughs, all throat. "Do not think that this help will keep me from killing you. But I will save you for the end."

"I have an idea, you great lout. But I need to know what weapons you have."

"Sledgehammer."

You think of the bow on your back. Wonder if it's broken. "There's a crack in the gneiss. Three-quarter thick, grade seven."

You speak quick; there's no telling when the dwarven guardians will notice that you're talking instead of hacking each other. A pause, and you wonder if the troll is still debating your demise or merely dumb. Grade seven—a code used for deep mines to describe the place where two shafts converge, usually created along a fault line.

"And you think—what? To pierce it with your little hands?"

"And your hammer." You breathe the words, something like hope expanding your chest. You can't break through the gneiss alone, not unless you had a full day and night to chip away, but with a troll's strength—well. It might be possible.

"They'll kill us."

A shriek, high and ethereal, signaling another death.

You shrug. "We're already dead."

Not true. If it were, you wouldn't be fighting so hard. But the best lies are the ones tucked deep. And you're tired. Of digging through ogre teeth, of fighting to the death. Escape is the only means to life.

Spin, clash, dodge.

A cool breeze tickles the hairs of your inner ear. You press forward as the battles around you separate into single combat clashes. You spear for the middle, opening your eyes to orient yourself and regretting it instantly. Pain like the core itself as fire scorches your pupils, the shock rocketing you to your knees.

A hand hauls you up. The troll. "Move."

But how? You listen for the music to tell you where you are, but there's only the dimming moans of the fallen, the rush of relieved exhales from the victorious. You can't tell which way is toward the arena's center and which way leads back to the cell. There is only the heat of the light above you and a slight throbbing in your arm, and—

"The orb lights," you breathe. "Follow me."

It doesn't matter that you can't see; you follow the lights, the heat, right toward where the orbs shine brightest, where they singe your green skin and make it feel baked and blistered. No hiding in the cool shadows, now. You sprint for the place that feels like Hell itself, kicking off your boots as you run, because you'll need your feet to find the crack since you can't see it.

"Here," you say, unable to keep the grin from splitting across your face. Your toes curl over the lip of the crack. You repeat it louder, when the troll doesn't answer. "Here. Where my voice is."

But he doesn't answer. Did you lose him? Blazing stone, there's so much *noise*. The punch of a blade into flesh, the clang of sharp iron. Creatures dying and groaning and battling for their life. And above all that, there's the crowd, still screaming.

You crouch over the seam, lifting the pickaxe. Pound, pound, pound. Stone flecks away, nipping at your arms. Not near enough.

"Move," says the troll, winded from some scuffle you didn't witness. "My turn."

A whisper of wind from his upraised arms, then you're leaping out of the way. *Boom.* A shockwave rocks the ground beneath your feet. *Boom. Boom.*

Metal tickles your throat, and a female voice speaks into your ear. "Impressive, to find a goblin that can last so long under these orbs." You freeze, silently cursing. Keep moving—but you'd forgotten that rule, hadn't you? It's always the blade you don't see that gets you. Blood trickles down your neck. Or maybe it's sweat. Hard to tell.

Oblivious, the troll pounds on the gneiss floor. *Boom. Boom.* The gneiss is strong. As it should be. Goblins don't make things cheap. But is it too thick? What if you misjudged the grade of the crack?

"What is your friend doing?" asks the female behind you.

"Not a friend," you croak. "Ally. Breaking us free."

"Little fool. You think to carve your way from stone?"

Boom. Boom. Boom.

"Grade seven," you whisper, not sure if the words will mean anything to her. But you hold them in your heart like a promise. You know what you saw, that day the orb lights flickered. Grade seven fault line. A doomsday statement for any mine shaft, an incurable weak spot. In the deep-down mines, the dig would stop immediately, lest you collapse the tunnel completely.

Boom.

The blade presses into your throat. Your lungs constrict. *Not like this.* "Better to die this way, I think," whispers that female voice. She almost sounds sorry.

BOOM.

The sound of thunder. The floor shifts underneath, a thousand splinters running like spiderwebs under your bare feet. A gasp of surprise, then the blade at your throat falls away.

You fall.

Sweet darkness.

Cursing, fumbling. Somewhere in the dark, someone moans softly, either crushed by fractured gneiss or impaled by some weapon. There is panic, as creatures figure out if they want to flee or fight, but of course, they can't see without the lights, so they're also bumping into each other, fighting to breathe.

But not you.

No, for the first time all day, you can *see.*

The troll slumps across from you, dazed, his blood streaking the patchwork gray-blue of its marble skin, recognizable as *your* troll because of the hollow pits where the eyes should've been. He groans, and you shake his shoulder. The arena feels like another world, but you've got to move. Now. The dwarves won't like their playthings leaving, not when they've paid so prettily for them to be here.

"Get up," you hiss.

Creatures bay in the distance, the hairs on your ears tingling a dire warning. You kick the troll, but he doesn't move, just moans, slumped against the fallen gneiss. Already, panic sets in among the rabble. Some fight, clawing their way forward; others dead-sprint down the tunnel like you want to do. There's no telling where it leads, but the promise of escape is too great to ignore.

The baying grows nearer. Core hounds. They mean to wipe out the arena. Start fresh with a new batch.

Frantic hands shove you against the tunnel wall. Creatures blur as they pass, stampeding down either end of the tunnel, an arsenal of weaponry forgotten at your feet. You kick the troll in the side. "Get up! Get up!"

But he doesn't, and in a choice between you and this oaf, you'll choose yourself every time. You flee into the dark.

The last of the prisoners scampers ahead of you, a loping six-legged gait, then disappears into the long, narrow stretch of tunnel, dark and beautiful like a promise, the core hounds so close you can smell them behind you. One howls, long and low, and you picture it finding the troll, feasting on its slumped form.

Keep moving, eyes ahead. Home, home. The dark calls to you. You've your axe and your sight and a path forward through the stone. If you can last the next few minutes, you'll tunnel so deep and so far that the dwarves won't be able to breathe for the heat of where you're going.

You glance back. A rookie mistake. The troll's on his feet now, back against the wall, swinging that sledgehammer while three core hounds crouch and snarl around him. Above the lip of the newly formed hole, dwarf guards peer over the edge.

The dark sings to you. Home, home. This is it, the distraction you need

The troll bellows, a core hound getting through his defense. You take one last look at the dark. Adjust the pick. He saved your life, this great ugly thing that broke through the weak point when you'd only dented it.

There's no choice. You go back.

A core hound's got its teeth around the sledgehammer, and the other two haven't figured out that the troll can't see yet, that its throws are wild and random. A sickening crack, and the pack drops back, hunching, waiting for an opening. One sees you coming and yelps, high and excited.

Above, a dwarf's face leans over the demolished floor's rim, squinting into the tunnel. As you run, you scoop up a rope spear someone's forgotten in their haste to escape and hurl it at the dwarf. The throw goes wide, but the dwarf doesn't realize, only catches sight of something hurtling toward him from the dark. He twists and rolls, dangling above the tunnel.

As one, the core hounds lunge for him, a starving, excited mass, frenzied in a way they weren't before. This new, easier target is far preferable over the difficult one, and the guard disappears under a flash of fur and fang.

"Let's go, you great brute," you gasp at the troll. The troll swings his head, and you grip his arm to steer him toward you. "This way. Hold onto me."

Together, you head down the tunnel, an absurd sight if anyone was around to watch, your steps tiny and quick compared to the troll's lumbering ones. The baying picks up again.

The troll grunts. "Shoulda left me, little gob."

You nod. You should have.

There's no sense in trying to outrun a core hound, so you slow, spinning toward the way you'd come. As you do, you smell sulfur, that telltale sign of a deep dig, the kind no dwarf would dare undertake. You laugh, the pressure in your chest subsiding, tears stinging your cheeks.

"Have you gone mad?"

"A goblin mine," you say, adjusting your grip on the pickaxe. "After we kill these hounds, I can get us home."

"Huh," grunts the troll, less impressed. "You ever killed a core hound?"

"No, but I'd never killed an ogre or a banshee or a wyrm, and they died by my blade just the same." The hounds rush toward you, their teeth the only pieces of light, their muzzles drenched red from a fresh kill.

"Just another fight," you whisper, reminding yourself and the troll, even though fear spikes your chest. "The arena's just smaller. Fight's the same. Doesn't change much for me, but one swing and you can clear the width of this place. Just keep on swinging that hammer of yours, and I'll get the ones that make it through."

"And then?"

You smile. Raise the axe.

"Home."

Hannah McLaughlin teaches creative writing and composition to both high school and college students. She lives in Oklahoma with her husband of fourteen years and their three kids. When she isn't working, she loves nerding-out about games and fictional worlds, and she gets most of her inspiration from her experiences as a military brat.

THE WORD THIEF

SILVINA PALMIERO (TRANSLATED BY MONICA LOUZON)

At first, it was just a feeling—the vague suspicion that, in certain moments, words were vanishing into thin air. I noticed it for the first time at the foot of the Andes, while I was trying to spot the point where the mountain peaks touched the sky. Surrounded by centuries of rock that presaged me and would survive all my descendants, I could feel the enormity of the nature around me, with its eternal clouds, unscalable heights, and intense cold. I found it impossible to fully comprehend all the sensations I felt at once, or to summarize them in just a few words. I was very young then. At that age, I still didn't have the slightest interest in figuring out the precisely right way to describe everything.

Time passed, and I became obsessed with words. Words became my cult. I studied them with determination and devotion, but the more I dug into the mysteries of language, the more evident it became that I would never understand them all. The more I read or wrote, the fewer words I found to express certain sublime moments accurately, as if I were trying to grasp something that was always evading me.

What was the precise word for watching a sunset over the

Tyrrhenian Sea from the heights of Guardia Piamontese, standing just below the Porta del Sangue? What was the word for how death still impregnated that soil, how the sounds of a massacre still echoed off these rock walls? How could one describe the heartbeat still throbbing among the ruins of a civilization, beating beneath sands mixed with ashes of gladiators, slaves, and warriors? What word could capture the cold, the solitude, the despair still inhabiting the remaining walls of a prison at the end of the world?

What turn of phrase could describe the palette, pulse, paint-brush, and creator's breath behind every artwork? What was the term alluding to the miracle of life emerging between a woman's legs, the joy breaking through the pain?

What word could ever be immense enough to describe that perfect love from the fairy tales, that completeness, that one place in the world where you know you belong for sure? What did one call the exact point in the sky where two souls collide, then vibrate in unison?

How could you verbalize losing love, its absence marked and dominated by the hole in your chest through which all air somehow escapes, forcing you to inhale with all your strength so you don't die of asphyxia?

How could I explain the color of the sea from my childhood, or the aroma of the first jasmine blossom announcing the imminent summer?

The harder I fought to express certain things, the fewer words I could find to do so. Each time this happened, I despaired a little more. My therapist attributed it to my natural anxiety and high standards: he advised me to relax and to stop putting so much pressure on myself. My boss assured me that my verbiage was intact and that my alleged lack of words was only a figment of my imagination—but he still made funding available for me to enroll in a public speaking class. I felt the situation was most comparable to writer's block, so I enrolled in a writing workshop, and in a new book club.

Nothing worked. I still was missing words in key moments. I

knew the words were there, but they simply would not come when I needed them. I started wondering if I was going crazy.

That's where things stood when one day—by chance, if such a thing exists—I walked into an old bookstore on the Avenida Corrientes that was selling off its stock before closing its blinds forever. Nothing saddens me more than a bookstore shutting down.

I selected a pair of philosophy tomes I'd been looking for ages and, as I looked at the shelves full of compact treasures—who knew where they'd end up—the bookstore owner recounted the same story that I'd heard many times before. Chain bookstores had finished liquidating small businesses like his, which had already been hit hard because nobody was interested in reading anything other than the hottest bestseller these days.

What was the word for shipwrecked dreams?

I confided in him the truth: for quite some time, I'd been looking for the right words to name specific things, and I'd begun to suspect that I was losing the words forever. The shopkeeper studied me for a few seconds, then smiled.

"That's because of the Word Thief," he said.

At first, I thought it was just a pretty metaphor, but the man seemed to be talking about something more tangible. He claimed that all the words just on the tip of your tongue, all the words that never came to your lips when you needed them—the ones playing hide-and-seek in your brain—all of them had been taken away and hidden in a secret place by the Word Thief. According to the bookstore owner, there were debates about whether the man was an impassioned linguist, a compulsive collector, a crossword creator, or a serial hoarder. But the point, he said, was that the Word Thief had kidnapped all the missing words—all my missing words. The shopkeeper had never seen this Word Thief before, but everything he'd just shared with me had come firsthand from a very reliable source.

"And where can I find this guy?" I asked, with some skepticism. I half-expected him to reveal that the Word Thief was Santa Claus's neighbor at the North Pole, or that the being lived in a parallel dimension that could be entered through the back of a wardrobe.

"He lives in the basement of the Biblioteca Nacional," the store owner replied without hesitation. "In a little room, near the janitor's closet. You have to be creative if you want to get down there, because it's not a publicly-accessible floor, but once you reach it, you'll find him easily enough."

That said, the shopkeeper wrapped my books with the same care one would use to clothe a baby. He charged me a laughably-low sum that wouldn't even pay for the cost of printing their covers, then gave them to me and shook my hand.

"Good luck," he said as a goodbye. "I hope you find all your missing words."

What would you call the story I'd just heard?

This time, I didn't even try searching for the term. I was sure I wouldn't find a word that would satisfy me completely and, in any event, I had something much more important to think about.

There aren't many people who go to libraries anymore, but the Biblioteca Nacional is still an exception, drawing them in with its never-ending catalog of books—some of which are the only remaining copies—as well as its thorough newspaper archive and busy calendar of art shows and cultural activities. I'd always been attracted to this place by its delightful mixture of classic and vanguard aesthetics, so I already had the advantage of knowing the entire building's layout by heart.

I chose to visit the Biblioteca Nacional on opening day for a traveling exhibition of Antonio Berni's works. With all eyes on the creations of the celebrated painter from Rosario, I had no difficulties slipping into the staircase that led to the basement. If anyone asked, I planned to tell them that I'd gotten lost looking for a bathroom, but no one did.

I reached the place where cleaning supplies were kept and there it was: the door to the Word Thief's room. It was tiny, without a latch, and it bore a little sign that said,

Silence.
Enough words already rest within.

It seemed like a bad joke.

Before I could knock, the door opened slowly and a little man invited me to enter. I could read in his lucid eyes that he already knew why I was there.

As silly as it might seem, I immediately demanded he give me back my words. I said he had no right to steal words when they needed to be spoken most. Then, I began telling him about the mountains and the sea, about the sheer joy found in delivering a baby and in the sweet scent of jasmine flowers, about the wrenching pain of finding love only to lose it. I told him about what I knew of souls, of history, of death. As I spoke, I poured out my feelings, sharing emotions that struggled to emerge through my impotence, my inability to find the right words when I needed them.

When I was done, we sat in silence for a while.

At last, he said, "I don't take the words for myself, nor do I take them forever. I also don't take the same ones from everyone, or even take them at the same time."

He gestured to another door that led to an adjoining little room. "In there, you'll find what you've been seeking, but... Would you have wanted to talk about the 'magnificence' of those mountains? Would you have preferred to qualify murders as 'atrocities' or a jail as 'dismal'? Would you have used 'lacerating' to describe the pain of losing the love of your life? To me, the descriptions you just gave me a few moments ago seemed much more vivid, much more complete. You made images appear in my mind, made me see colors and experience smells and textures in ways big words can't.

"Let me tell you what I think. Human beings look for precise words to constrain experiences, to classify them, to file them like the books in this library, thus transforming them into memories. By cataloging experiences, they stop being the present. They don't burn with the same fire. They no longer hurt. On the other hand, when we make the effort to describe those experiences over and over again, despite the anguish of not finding the right words—and perhaps because of this anguish—we keep exploring, re-discovering them.

"That's why I steal words. Life must be larger, more intense than the stories we tell ourselves." He gestured at the second door again. "Go on, enter. Help yourself. Take all the words you think you might need."

I walked hesitantly toward it, still half-expecting this all to be part of some big prank.

I opened the door and entered the new room. It was much bigger than the first one, and it was filled with shelves. I spotted all the words that I'd missed so much, every single one that I'd needed at some point: they were next to one another, in alphabetical order. Someone could touch them, take them off the shelf, one by one, and put them into a backpack.

Here was "eloquence" and "ephemeral". Over there, just in front of "fleeting" and "elusive", were "orphan" and "opacity". Suddenly, as if they were made of light, the words began to glow like artificial flames, projecting themselves into the air and illuminating the gloomy room.

I spent fifteen minutes dancing with my lost words.

In the end, I didn't take a single one with me. I left behind the myriad of abstract nouns, a good number of adjectives, and most of the adverbs.

When I emerged from the room, the Word Thief no longer sat on his stool. I asked myself where he could have gone, but I somehow knew I shouldn't wait for him. I went on my way, much lighter than I'd arrived, carrying everything that can't be described with a single word.

Silvina Palmiero was born in 1974 in the city of Buenos Aires, Argentina. She has authored five books for children and young adults, as well as various stories and poems published in Argentine and international anthologies and digital magazines. The Spanish-language version of "The Word Thief" is one of the latter, originally published in the Uruguayan magazine *Revista Mordedor.* Silvina is also a public accountant, film critic, and is currently studying for a degree in Letras at the Universidad de Buenos Aires. She is married, has four daughters, and —in addition to writing— loves reading and traveling.

Monica Louzon (she/her) is a queer writer, translator, and editor from the United States. Her translations have previously appeared in *Apex Magazine, Cosmorama, Extrasensory Overload, Futura House, MAYDAY Magazine*, and others. Her story "9 Dystopias" was a Best Microfiction 2023 winner, and her speculative poetry was nominated for the Dwarf Stars Award. She fills what free time she has with making zines, climbing on things, crocheting ridiculously large blankets, walking her dog, volunteer work, and tending to her books and houseplants. To learn more about Monica and her work, please visit https://linktr.ee/molowrites.

PART FIVE

THE RETURN

The music's deafening, with a percussive beat you can feel in your chest, and the crowd all wild as ever, dancing almost to a frenzy as ravers wave glow sticks high above their heads. Another *Climb*, another *Gather*.

The mountain stands sentinel, impervious to all of it.

You've been trying to sober Piotr up, but he's not having it, and Otto's not helping. He sets three tankards down on the table, hard, the contents sloshing over the edge.

"To Daria!" he booms. They both drink.

Your phone chirps.

Heard about you kicking ass! I always knew you could do it. So proud. xoxo

The three dots flash, then—

Coffee?? Or...?

You stare at the text for a solid minute. Then you delete it. Fuck *him*.

You look over to your friends, both barely coping. You're heartbroken, but Piotr's destroyed. The Dreamseller moves through the crowd, people laughing as they reach out to her, but when Piotr sees her across the square he turns his head away, a catch in his breath. You stare at him, questioning.

"After the drink... after I drank, I *saw* Daria dead. But it was just a dream..." He looks bewildered, hitting his fist slowly to his temple, then he sits up straight and pounds the table.

"Enough! I'm gonna do the Climb!"

"Don't do the climb."

"I'm gonna do it. For Daria!"

"That's not what she would have wanted," you tell him, but he glares at you.

"How would you know what she wanted?" The bitterness in his voice is a poison.

Because she told you, you long to remind him. *Didn't you listen?*

"You don't make your mark by dying."

"You don't make your mark by sitting around, either." He stares up at the mountain, and Otto slaps his back.

"I'm with you, my friend."

Asinine! The loss of it all sets your heart to reeling, the loss and your own powerlessness. You can't take anymore and march off across the festival floor, but as the noise, and the crush of the crowd, and the lights prisming off the mountainside disorient you, you spin and almost collide with the Dreamseller. She stares at you, her enigmatic smile settling deep under your skin. You do not feel judged, but you most definitely feel seen. Far too seen. Snow begins to fall gently, causing the crowd to laugh and cheer, their faces upturned as they reach to the sky.

And it strikes you: Piotr saw Daria dead. Otto saw *snow*.

You stare back at the Dreamseller, shellshocked.

And then you hand her a coin.

You're flying. You rise, higher and higher, catching thermals as you ascend up the side of the mountain, with veins, all luminescent, branching a course deep, deep into the mountain's heart.

You see your reflection in the glass; a crow, your feathers an iridescent blue black, and when you caw the sound you make is terrifying. And you glory in it.

Up, up and up you fly, until you finally break through the swirling snow and the cloud cover, and arrive at the summit. A roughened platform, barren but for a large, graceless throne hewn from granite; cold, its edges sharp.

And seated on the throne is the Princess.

What was once the Princess.

Tattered pieces of her robe ruffle in the harsh, biting wind, and wisps of her hair, once beautiful and wheat-golden, whirl away from a skull now bleached by the sun and the elements. There is little left of her.

How long has she been here, alone

left behind
an icon for others to fawn over
a pawn in her father's game
the design of some wizard's architect.

None of it. None of it means a fucking thing. Loved, not loved. Renowned, unknown. It's all garbage. Your heart aches for her, and for you, and for everyone left behind.

I didn't know, I'm sorry, *you caw mournfully.* Sorry sorry sorry sorry sorry... *and you fly away, back down the mountainside, even more lost than you were before.*

Morning comes too soon.

The crowd is agitated, awaiting the inevitable. Drums beat as the procession marches towards the arena, the priests first, the guards following. Amongst the candidates are Otto and Piotr. Piotr stares grimly straight ahead, but Otto gives you a small lopsided grin in acknowledgment. It's a brave but silent walk.

But then you join them, and the crowd roars with excitement. Your reputation at the lists has preceded you, and they all wonder *Will she be the one?*

"What are you doing?" Piotr whispers harshly. "Are you mad?"

"Can't I have glory, too?" you bite back.

Otto clamps his hand on your shoulder and squeezes, and you cover his hand with your own. Together you march past the in-gate, with the mountain looming overhead, the rainbow shadows the sun casts through it stretching to the village and the valley beyond. You all arrive at the centre of the ring and kneel. So many hopefuls, and so much lost hope. You look up at the mountain's summit. And then—

Without warning, as the priests are giving their blessings, you spring up and grab Otto's warhammer before he can protest.

"I'm sorry," you tell Piotr, and then, amidst the surprised cries of the crowd, you charge towards the mountain, holding the warhammer at an angle before you.

Only you don't reach high to strike. You swing low, sharply, with all your might. Right where you saw the bright veins illuminated in your vision. Over and over, as hard as you can, shouting with every blow. You put all your soul into it, through your arms, into the weapon, hoping it finds its mark. The reverberations suddenly change their echo.

And a splinter appears.

It grows wider with each sharp crack at the glass, until your arms ache, until they're numb and you can barely swing them. But you mustn't stop. Otto runs to you, and taking the hammer from your hands, he strikes hard and fast, until the fissure grows wide, the sides shattering at your feet. The mountain begins to shudder, glass shards raining down everywhere, and the crowds up in the stands all cry out again, rushing from their seats and away from the field.

Piotr looks stricken, but Otto looks feral, nodding at you in approval. You grab their hands and run back towards the village, but the shattered sides of the mountain slide towards the village's perimeter, so you keep running till you're out of breath, and till you're at the forest line. You don't care that your lungs are bursting. You don't care. It's enough. It's over.

You sit and watch the aftermath from a fair distance, your arms across your knees, you and your friends in silence. You watch the sun set over the valley, normal, no prisms.

"What am I to do now," Piotr asks, bereft, his head in his hands.

"Anything you want," you tell him.

"That's easy enough for you to say. You're *someone* now."

You pull your phone from out of your pocket, staring at the messages. "I should never have let myself believe otherwise." You scroll to *fucking store* and press *call.*

The Glass Mountain
by Altaire Gural

Altaire Gural is a screenwriter, a member of the Playwrights Guild of Canada, and a professional acting coach for stage/film and TV, where her YA fantasy novel, *Forgotten*, has recently been optioned for television. She's beyond thrilled to finally have written "The Glass Mountain" (decades in the procrastinating), a very loosely based adaptation of the Polish fairy tale of the same name.

SANCTUARY FOR STRANGE BIRDS

JE BROOKE

The road into the village was dusty from the prolonged heat of the dry season. Kula was thankful for her tinted-glass goggles as each step kicked up more of the ocher-colored powder around her. At least this leg of her journey was almost over. The confrontation was the part of her job she hated the most. The message that summoned her made this instance seem like it would be particularly odious.

The village itself was small. Anyone who hadn't been called as she had might think to describe it as picturesque. Quaint thatched roofs, whitewashed plaster walls, neat gardens, and a small brick square surrounded by a few shops and trade hubs. Nothing out of the ordinary, except for the fact that the streets were deserted in the middle of the day. Out of the eerie stillness came a twang of power... and distress. She tracked the residual frisson to a rundown farmstead on the edge of town. A couple met her outside of their house, a few young children peeking through the curtains of the window. Kula did her best to ignore the stares of the little ones as she addressed their parents.

"I believe you summoned me about—"

"The Cuckoo!" The faces of both adults broke into relief as they rapidly began explaining over each other.

"There's always been something a little off—"

"—but we never thought that it could be one of our children—"

"We thought we'd done everything to prevent—"

"—stopped talking, except to the animals or in strange tones."

"—made peculiar things happen."

"In the shadows once, I thought I saw—"

"It's eating us out of house and home!"

"What's to become of our children?"

"We tried banishing it, and it's left the house, but now it won't leave the barn."

"Show me," Kula cut in, trying to keep the weariness and exasperation out of her voice.

The barn was much older than the house. Time and the elements had eaten holes in the roof, and more than a few of the wooden planks in the walls were broken or rotted. The air inside smelled thickly of moldy straw and old cowchips. But it was quiet, dark, and secluded, which was why—Kula assumed—the child crouching in a shaded corner chose it for their hiding place. She approached slowly while the barn's owners lingered near the door, making enough noise to signal her approach to the sole occupant. The child lifted their head briefly to look in her direction, then curled back into a ball. She sat down a few hands away, not wanting to move too close too soon and add to the damage that had already been done.

"Hello," Kula said quietly. "I'm Kula. What should I call you?"

The child didn't answer, didn't move. Kula frowned and reconsidered her strategy. She reached into a pouch hanging from her belt and extracted a cube about the size of an apple. Pretending to ignore her reluctant companion, she selected a side of the cube to fiddle with. She pressed in with the pads of her thumbs, summoned a little bit of power, and channeled it through the surface of the object. Brightly colored sparks erupted from the cube with little pops. The child's head snapped back up. Their eyes fixed on the sparks and the cube with fascination, and Kula couldn't help but smile.

"Would you like to see it?"

The child nodded and reached out their hands. Their sleeves slid back as they moved, revealing a series of red, triangular welts that hadn't yet begun to heal. Kula felt hot and cold at the same time. With a smile to the preoccupied child, she rose and walked back over to the parents.

"You said you tried to banish them. How were you advised to do so?" Kula asked.

"We hired an expert from the next town over. He said the Cuckoo could be burned out."

"I see," Kula replied stonily and returned to the child, who had now moved on to another section of the cube. This side was draped in moss and studded with small rocks, an un-bloomed bud at the center. The child's amber-irised eyes widened as they channeled their power into the cube face and caused the bud to unfurl into a scarlet, trumpet-shaped flower that gave off a soothing fragrance. Kula sat back down next to them. Startled, the child looked up and let a hand slip off of the cube. The flower curled back up into the folds of the bud.

"It's alright. I won't hurt you. In fact, I'm going to take you away from here, if you'd like. Do you want to go with me?"

The child looked silently from Kula to the adults looming in the barn doorway, and then back to Kula. Kula pursed her lips together in thought, and said, "Do you have trouble speaking with your mouth sometimes?" That question received a somber nod from the child. She smiled and held out a hand. "That's alright, there are other ways I can teach you. If you want to, take my hand and send some of your power through into mine. Just like you did with the cube." The child considered Kula's upturned palm before slipping their own hand into it. Kula felt a spark a little stronger than static run up her arm as the connection was made. The child's name came first. *Vai*, a warm ringing sound.

"Vai," Kula repeated out loud and the child's mouth dropped open in surprise.

You understand?

I do. What do you think about my offer?

Kula felt a riot of emotions before a more coherent response came. *I don't want to hurt anymore. I try to be good, but it's never enough. I don't remember replacing their baby, I promise. Please, I tried to be good.*

I know you did, Kula sent back through the connection. *And you didn't replace anyone. That's just an old story. I can take you somewhere safe and help with the hurting. But it's up to you.*

Another swirl of conflicting feelings from Vai. *I don't want to hurt anymore. I'll go.*

Kula nodded and together they rose to their feet, hands still connected. As they walked out of the barn, one of the parents asked, "Will our real child come back, now that you're taking the Cuckoo?"

Kula didn't bother looking back as she hissed, "I'm afraid that isn't how this works. Good day." She pulled her goggles over her eyes as they walked, leaving the farmstead and the town behind them. Reaching into one of the pockets on her coat with her free hand, Kula extracted a second, smaller pair of goggles and offered them to Vai. The child looked at them in silence, and then put them on. Kula felt a small spark of relief and astonishment run up her arm.

"Our eyes can be sensitive to light, even when the sun is overcast like today. The darkened lenses help," Kula explained.

You're a Cuckoo like me?

"I'm not overly fond of that word, but yes, I am like you."

Are you going to bring me back to faerieland, then?

Kula thought carefully about how to explain before she answered. "Vai, we were born here in this world like other people. We're different, yes, but no one is born exactly the same as anyone else. We're just different in a way some folks find frightening, so they make up a story to give themselves answers and feel better. Even though that story is wrong."

So, my parents burned me because of the story?

"I'm afraid so, Vai. I'm sorry."

Kula could feel the child thinking, awash in a torrent of feelings, but nothing more concrete came through their forged connection. That was fine. This was a wrenching experience for anyone, let alone a scared, abused child trying to make sense of their own existence. There would be time to help them parse through what they were feeling when they arrived at the Rookery. "It's alright if you're sad, or angry," she offered. "I know that I was."

Vai didn't answer, and that was also fine.

They spent the night at the same inn where Kula had stayed the night before, on her way to Vai's old home. The lodgings had a reputation for comfortable beds, good food in plentiful portions, and being friendly to those travelers other establishments might turn away. Like Kula and her charge. They had dinner in the small tavern on the first floor, and then were shown to their room. By the time they crossed the threshold into their quarters, Vai was fidgeting fiercely. A frown of discomfort stole over their already-serious face. Kula knew the feeling.

"You can stretch them out here. It's safe," she said. Then, to demonstrate, she removed her cloak and let her wings flex free. At full length, the tips of the longest primaries almost brushed opposing walls of the room. Perlu sometimes said they reminded her of an oriole, a top-skirt of shifting orange and yellow hues along the bones gradually giving way to lustrous bands of black through the secondary feathers. Stretching them out felt marvelous after keeping them tucked in all afternoon. She'd flown in the day before, and she still felt the echo of the kind of satisfying muscle ache that only came from a long flight. With someone of Vai's age in tow, however, it was necessary to walk.

The child removed their cloak as well, revealing small wings just coming in. Their feathers were still heavily covered in down, but where more permanent feathers started to grow in Kula could see flashes of iridescent blue. She felt angry now on Vai's behalf, on the behalf of every child she'd had to remove from harm. How dare anyone seek to smother such beauty?

Kula sat in a chair by the fire to read while Vai— so exhausted from their ordeal they were falling asleep on their feet after freeing their wings--settled into one of the beds to sleep.

"Do you take everyone you're sent to find?" a voice cut suddenly through the quiet. Kula jolted in surprise, almost dropping her book. She turned around to find Vai watching her from where they lay. Their audible voice was quiet, but melodic.

"Not everyone. Sometimes, I can help people change their minds about the ones I'm summoned to see."

"But you couldn't with mine?"

"No, I couldn't. The marks on your arm told me it wouldn't be wise to leave you there. I'm sorry."

"You aren't the ones who made them," Vai said quietly and rolled over to face the wall. "Thank you."

"You're very welcome, Vai. Now get some sleep."

They set out early the next morning. Over the course of the long day, the road transitioned from packed dirt to worn flagstones, and then finally to fastidiously maintained cobbles as they approached the city Kula called home. Vai saw the aerialists first, sprinting ahead with a surprised shout and pointing at the sky above the sturdy stone walls of the city. Tiny figures that were roughly person-shaped ran atop the wall and jumped into the air, where they were carried upward by rising currents on their enormous wings. Vai looked back with Kula, grinning as they jumped up and down in elation. They pointed back and forth between themself and Kula, and then back to the flying figures.

"Yes," Kula laughed. "They're like us too. You'll learn to fly like that one day soon, once all of your feathers come in. I'll make sure of it." Vai raced on ahead, Kula increasing her pace to keep them in sight as they approached. The children's reactions to seeing the aerialists for the first time were consistent, and delightful. She never tired of them. Kula could still remember her own amazement, when she'd been brought to the city for refuge ages ago. This moment was always her favorite part of the journey. The remainder of the journey passed quickly after that. Vai continued ecstatically ahead, pointing at each new curiosity they beheld. Kula followed contentedly behind enjoying each discovery the child made. The crowds were thicker here, louder, and full of people, winged and earthbound alike. It couldn't have been more different from the village Vai, or any of the other children for that matter, had come from. Maybe someday that would change. Wind and spirits knew that this city hadn't always been so friendly. Perhaps someday other places would learn too, but for now, they were almost home.

The Rookery was a tall spire of a building rising into the sky near the city center. Perlu waited for them at the front door when they arrived. "Welcome!" the earthbound woman beamed, crouching down to get closer to Vai's level. "We're so glad to have you with us." Perlu glanced over Vai's shoulder at Kula. Kula mouthed the child's name. Perlu repeated, "Vai. Come in and make yourself at home."

Vai looked back at Kula, suddenly reluctant. Kula nodded, and some of the child's earlier enthusiasm returned. Just as Vai reached the door, they all heard an excited shout of several mingled voices. Vai darted through into the Rookery.

Kula smiled and leaned into the doorway with Perlu to see a

group of several other fledglings surrounding another flapping frantically in the air. Ah, Cetsa's new feathers had come in at last! When Kula had been sent to find her, the poor girl's wings had been plucked bare by misguided guardians trying to keep her earthbound. Her new feathers had come in over her time at the Rookery, a bold and flashing green where before they had been mousey brown, and now they carried her into the air above her enthusiastic cohort. Kula and Perlu applauded as Cetsa's feet once more touched the ground. Attention turned from the fledgling to the new child in their midst. Vai was introduced and, to Kula's relief, Cetsa took them instantly under her wing (metaphorically speaking), leading Vai over to a larger version of the cube toy. The two of them worked together in silence, using their gifts to collectively bring a whole garden into stunning bloom.

Vai wouldn't stay here forever. Almost none of the fledglings did. Most often they found places with new families after they'd healed. Some stayed longer until they were old enough to travel and see the world for themselves or pursue a vocation. A very select few, though, sometimes returned later to help shepherd and protect new children in need of shelter. This had always been the way of things at the Rookery, and Kula was its most recent custodian; a job she carried out with pride.

A hand settled gently on Kula's shoulder as she watched the children play and bond. She crossed an arm over her chest and placed one of her own hands over Perlu's. She unwound herself, turning to face her partner, still hand in hand.

"You work such wonders," Perlu murmured tenderly. Kula kissed her with a smile.

Later that evening, after supper had been eaten, the dishes cleaned, and the children settled in for the evening, Kula and Perlu sat together on the sturdy platform jutting out from the pinnacle of the

Rookery overlooking the city. The sky was awash in vivid citron hues as the sun set. It had been a long few days, and she'd rest soon, but first Kula needed to take care of the itch in her wings. With Perlu watching contentedly, Kula stood, walked to the end of the platform, and finally took wing.

JE Brooke is an anthropologist and a speculative fiction writer on the autism spectrum. When she isn't writing stories and novels, she can be found crafting, experimenting with her sourdough starter, or lost in the pages of a good book. She lives in Iowa with her husband, their dog, Arwen, and their cat, Darcy. Her work has been published in Iowa City Writers' Rooms anthologies *Writers of the Depths*, *Writers of the Ether*, *Writers of the Loam*, and *Iowa [W]rites of Winter*. She can be found on Instagram as je_brooke_thewriter.

THE OLD WOMAN AND THE SPIDER

A. KATHERINE BLACK

There once was a cottage perched on the edge of a vast forest, along a lonely road connecting two distant villages. Built years ago by an old woman, back when her muscles were thick and her joints more agreeable, the cottage was eventually home to not only her, but her grown child, her child's spouse, and her two spirited grandchildren.

The cottage provided refuge for more than just five people, of course. There were also the mice, huddled in a corner behind the stove, and the ladybugs, decorating the rafters in winter. And there was Spider, who lived not in the cottage, but in a knothole on the outside of the south wall, just above the woodpile. Most of the family, busy as they were with work and chores and play, ignored the cottage's other inhabitants. But the old woman treasured each and every scurrying creature, most especially her good friend, Spider.

"Lovely weave this morning." The old woman settled on an upturned piece of wood next to the woodpile. Spider's web spread wide and delicate just to the side of the old woman's head, while Spider herself tucked into her knothole on the wall, waiting for a morsel to happen by. The old woman, with a pile of freshly gathered green twigs on her lap, shielded her face from the angled sunlight to get a better look.

"It reminds me of a lake I once saw as a girl. The water was enormous and wild, with giant rocks pushing out of the waves." The old woman paused to gaze into the forest before clicking her tongue. "It's decided, then. Today will be a fish."

Spider rested her head on the knothole's edge and watched the old woman's gnarled fingers bend pieces of wood thicker than all of Spider's legs put together, weaving them into the shape of a fish.

The old woman spoke as she weaved, about her childhood visit to that distant lake, about their horse losing a shoe along the way, and about how she wished her grandchildren could visit the same lake one day, if only they had a carriage. If only they had spare coin. Spider didn't know the meaning of the old woman's words, of course, but as the woman leaned her sore back against the cottage wall, the comforting vibrations of her raspy voice hummed across the wood to soothe Spider's own aching joints.

Spider was old, as well. Not as long-lived as the woman, for certain, but longer lived than others of her kind. The rest of Spider's clutchmates had long since gone, males eaten by mates after only a season, females freezing to death while guarding clutches of eggs as winter settled deep in the forest floor. Spider had seen many generations pass by in this way, but with no urge to lay eggs of her own, and with fangs quick enough to make a morsel of any visiting male, she continued on.

Spider's mind did not spin with existential thoughts like those of people. There was no 'why me' or 'what's it all for' filling her mind, because that's not what spiders do. Instead, despite aching joints and slowing limbs, Spider built her web each morning, anchoring on the side of the cottage and the pile of wood, and she took the web down at the following sunrise, to bundle and consume before building a web anew. Other than that, she tucked into her knothole and waited. Waited for vibrations from a flailing morsel of food, maybe a fly or a tiny mouse, and she waited for the old woman to visit.

Spider's eyes were still keen, despite her age, and after having experienced so many seasons beyond her clutchmates, she developed the ability to recognize a fellow weaver, even one so very large and with so few appendages as the old woman.

As her child and their spouse searched for daywork at the farms and in the villages, foraged for food, and taught their children necessary skills, the old woman kept to the side of the cottage, spinning tales with words and forcing her swollen knuckles into motion, weaving soft twigs into various shapes. Some for her and some for her grandchildren, who loved to play with the twig trinkets before settling down to sleep.

As they both felt the press of advancing age across the seasons, the woman grew to appreciate Spider as a companion, of sorts. Each day she admired Spider's neat, balanced webs, and she appreciated how the quiet creature helped control the population of other critters outside the cottage. In return, the old woman entertained Spider with her weaving and soothed Spider with her raspy, reassuring voice.

When Winters grew too harsh for the old woman to endure the outdoors, she'd drag a chair inside the cottage to rest against the same wall that supported the woodpile, and from her perch she continued to weave her twigs and spin her tales. When the air became too frigid for Spider to build a web, she retreated deep into the knothole, wrapped in a thick blanket of silk, and drowsily waited for Winter to pass. Unable to see the old woman sitting inside the cottage, Spider still knew she was there, as her voice traveled through the back of her chair, and then through the cottage wall, to calm Spider's dreamy, half-frozen mind.

It seemed this odd pairing might have gone on forever, the old woman with her knotted hands and rumbly voice, the spider with her aching joints and sharp eyes, but as everyone knows, all things change, and all things end. Neither Spider nor the old woman expected to live forever.

As another Winter loomed, with biting winds promising to be harsher than the last, Spider watched the old woman perched by the woodpile as her grandchildren quietly dug two enormous holes, and then laid the old woman's child and her child's spouse gently into the earth. When it was done, her grandchildren sat before two fresh mounds, and the old woman spoke. Her voice was heavy, her hands trembling and empty in her lap.

The old woman's words trickled to nearly nothing after that, and oh how her friend Spider missed them. Still, the woman sat by the woodpile each day. Some days she wove wooden trinkets, some days she tore those trinkets apart, and other days the woman sat still as ice, eyes turned to the depths of the forest.

The cottage had grown similarly quiet, the grandchildren no longer giggling as one parent taught them to sew and another showed them the proper way to carve a fowl. Of course, Spider didn't know why the grandchildren now left the cottage each morning, didn't understand what it was like for a child to travel the long road to this village or that and beg for any work they could find, at a farm or a shop or even a larger cottage. Spider didn't understand what it was like to come home with just enough eggs or milk to last to the next morning, when the grandchildren then bundled into thinning garments and set off in search of work again.

Spider didn't understand how very tired the old woman was, so much more tired than before. She mustered all her strength to keep the table clean and the floor swept, and whether her grandchildren returned home with a generous bag of flour or only a single egg, she praised them just the same.

Winter kept its promise, setting in with deep snow, long icicles, and air eager to freeze. Spider huddled in her knothole, accepting what meager warmth seeped through the cottage wall, but her sleep was fitful, and her legs ached no matter how she re-positioned.

Spider dearly missed the comfort of the old woman's voice. She waited through the long drowsy stretch of each frigid day for the slight vibrations that arrived when the grandchildren came home at sunset. But the family ate their meals in silence. The only sounds Spider otherwise felt were the soft sobs of children late at night, drifting through the cottage wall to haunt the Winter pines. And so things were when Winter reached its depth, when forest creatures slumbered under the snow, and even the sun was too lazy to offer more than a brief bit of shine.

The depth of winter was normally a time of celebration among the villages. People reached out to pat each other's backs and look forward to the flowers to come. The old woman, though, watching her grandchildren toil as her own body knotted more tightly than ever, had nothing left for celebration or hope. And then, on the eve of the Winter Solstice, her grandchildren returned with empty hands. There was no work to be found.

Shops were closed, farms put off chores, and other households paused all else to prepare warm meals and bundle sweet treats for the following day. The grandchildren took their parents' bow into the woods, hoping to catch anything at all, but they returned with nothing. Nothing but the knowledge that there would be no work on the following day.

Tucked behind her silken blanket in the cottage wall, Spider knew nothing of celebrations that some people were unable to join. Still, she felt an emptiness too large for her knothole. She wanted something more. More than relief from her aches and more than respite from the cold. She wanted more for the old woman, to find a way back to the soothing days of weaving trinkets and spinning voices. Spider fidgeted and fidgeted in her frigid knothole until she could no longer bear it, just as she could no longer bear the pain of those in the cottage.

Breaking through her silken blanket, Spider forced her legs into motion, as she bundled and ingested the icy silk. Then she left the knothole she'd occupied for so many seasons and made for the front of the cottage, determined to provide for the old woman and her grandchildren in the only way she knew how. Spider stretched from the wall of the cottage until she reached the needles of a Winter tree. And then Spider began to spin.

She spun and spun through the long night, ignoring her aching joints and the freeze threatening to take hold. Knowing how few bugs or baby mice were about this time of year, Spider covered the tree in web upon web upon web, hoping something might be caught to nourish the old woman and her grandchildren. She spun with grief, and she spun with love, adding shapes to the center of her webs like those she'd seen the old woman create with twigs. She spun with sadness, and she spun with hope, until the tree was entirely covered, until her legs all but refused to move. Relieved that her joints no longer hurt, one small courtesy of the bitter Winter, Spider forced her legs into one last spurt of motion.

She climbed, lopsided and clumsy, up the frozen silk-covered tree, unaware that a shine had already taken to her deep-freezing body, until she reached the very top. She stood across the needles and angled all of her eyes toward the cottage door, wondering if they'd hold out long enough to see if anything came from her work.

It was the old woman who opened the door first, on her way to gather wood for the morning fire.

Spider's mind was nearly frozen by then. The feeling gone from her legs, she had no way of sensing the telltale vibration of morsels catching on her webs. But she did see a glint in the old woman's eye as she stood before the tree, and Spider even registered the tiniest vibration from the woman's raspy, soothing gasp. The old woman ran inside to wake her grandchildren, and before slipping into her long, final rest, Spider reveled in wave upon wave of comforting vibrations as the woman and her grandchildren exclaimed at the magnificent, glistening tree.

The winter pine was, indeed, a glorious thing to behold, as Spider's many frozen webs reflected beams from the rising sun. Wonderous shapes, of flowers and forest animals, sparkled from the center of the delicate, circular patterns. At the tree's very top was Spider herself, solitary and majestic, frozen to a beautiful shine.

The joy of that moment softened the children's hunger and calmed the old woman's grief. As her grandchildren danced around the tree, tears warmed the woman's cheeks. She silently thanked her quiet little friend for the exquisite parting gift.

The woman went inside the cottage and returned with an armful of woven trinkets, dusty from their pile in a near-forgotten corner. She placed all but one gingerly at the foot of the tree, and then rounded the cottage to place her wooden spider, woven years ago with gratitude and love, atop the dwindling pile of wood.

As it happened, the miller, riding by on his way to share bread with the farmer, paused in front of the old woman's cottage, taken by the joyous commotion. Leaving his carriage to admire the sparkling tree and share festive greetings, the miller noticed the many wood-woven trinkets decorating the snow below the tree. One trinket in particular caught his eye. A pig. The miller thought surely such a sweet trinket would entertain his friend, the farmer.

Apologizing for his boldness, the miller asked if the old woman would trade the woven pig for a basket of his holiday breads. Overcome with surprise, the old woman agreed with a warm smile, and soon she and her grandchildren sat at the cottage table, laughing as they feasted on breads filled with fruit and spices unlike anything they'd had for months.

Their meal was interrupted by a knock at the door. The farmer, who'd just received a lovely woven pig from her friend, asked if she could please trade a basket of eggs for the elegant, woven butterfly, which she wished to give to her sister, the village teacher.

And so Winter progressed. The tree was admired all season long, attracting people from distant villages to praise its intricate frozen webs and to place their orders for more of the old woman's playful, wooden trinkets.

Spider's pleasing webs eventually warmed, drooped in new

Spring dew, and blew away with the winds. But they would never be forgotten.

The old woman and her grandchildren sat by the woodpile each day, warmed by the sun while bending fresh twigs into shapes of various creatures, some from their forest and some from their imaginations. The children practiced their weaving and listened intently as the old woman spun her favorite stories, including the one about her very good friend, Spider.

A. Katherine Black lives in Northern Minnesota with her family, cats, and coffee machines. She loves snowstorms, multicolored pens, and dreaming up stories about creatures with bunches of legs, tentacles, and wings. Find her at flywithpigs.com or on bluesky @akatherineblack.bsky.social.

YOU ARE NOT THE CHOSEN ONE

REBEKAH POSTUPAK

"Dragons are attacking the castle!" you said and slammed the royal summons on the table.

"Save me, save me, mighty prince," I said drily, not looking up.

"Mother!" Righteous indignation, naivety; old friends, even then. You were just twenty. "The queen calls for *aid*!"

I reached for the parchment, crumpled it and, ignoring your shouted protest, tossed it in the kitchen fire. "Calm your spirit; you know perfectly well this is how they keep the economy going. In fact last month she needed... confectioners, was it? Now, *that* one I could almost support. I've been out of cinnamon brown sugar wizards for months."

"But I could—"

"You'd make a fine dragon knight, I'm sure," I said, turning back to the gingerbread dough writhing beneath my hands. "Any beast would be unlucky to face you. Still, you know what else is unlucky? My garden. I saw the beginnings of a sprite infestation out there just this morning. Take a look?"

You threw that familiar scowl at me and stormed out, and from across the table your father, halfway through his marmalade toast, heaved a sigh. "You didn't even read it this time."

"I didn't need to."

"We can't keep him here forever, you know. This isn't going to work."

"No?" I said. "Watch me."

It's true what they say about you when you're not around: the stars sang the night you were born. Sorcerers lined up to fill dragon-glass vials with the glowing overflow of your gift; centaurs lurked by the well sketching out the exact alignment of constellations above our home; even the merfolk sent couriers to collect the residue of your infant tears for their own mysterious purposes. Every day without fail, for months on end, random dryads or elves or rock-fairies gawked at us regularly through the curtains; the crowd was so thick that first year of your life, I lost track of who came and what they wanted. I'd have minded them less if they'd brought presents, like enchantments for a belly that would never go hungry or for a roof that would never leak. Or if at the very least they'd taken the leftover spell trash and mounds of half-eaten travelbread away with them, gifting us with peace and quiet.

Nobody who came to see you was interested in giving, though.

"Mama! Mama! Look!"

You were three. Our region was in the middle of a drought; I had to walk an hour to the nearest scraggly river twice a day to fetch enough water for us to survive. I'd just gotten back from that day's second trek, sweaty and exhausted, only to trip in our doorway and spill the entire bucket on my own feet. I'd hoped you were still napping—talk about a rare gift!—but you must have heard my horrified shriek, because suddenly there you were.

"Look, Mama!" you said, pointing and laughing. "A waterfall!"

Sure enough. The bucket had definitely spilled; I remembered this clearly. As further proof, the soggy grey hem of my skirt was dripping little puddles around my feet. Yet there was the bucket, now tilted and suspended mid-air, water pouring out just like you'd said.

With no small effort, your father and I eventually coaxed the bucket out to the backyard, where it bubbled into the sweet little creek that flows to this day. You were only a baby and don't remember this of course, but that undying waterfall saved our lives and the lives of everyone in the village.

Later, when you were ten or eleven, you once wondered aloud where our beloved bucket fountainhead had come from.

"Did something really cool happen here?" you asked in that eager way you have. "Is there something special about our house, that we're able to water the entire valley?"

By then I'd been lying to you for so long, I didn't even flinch in telling you it was only a visiting wizard's freak accident. Isn't it hilariously clumsy, that floating bucket! Nobody would have done that on purpose. No, dear, I love the way you think, and it would be such a clever idea; but really it was just a funny little mistake that magic-wielders are wont to make sometimes.

"Truly?" Tragedy, horror, disappointment; more old friends.

"Would your mother lie to you?" I said.

You were fourteen when barbarians invaded our kingdom. With all the bravado of youth, you assembled a junior military squad in case the enemy should assault our village. I'm sure you believed your father and I didn't know you consulted every adult in our acquaintance with military experience, begging for lessons in archery, or martial arts, or horseback riding, or metalworking.

I didn't have to be there myself to know how their eyes avoided your shining face, their fingers knotting and unknotting, wishing they hadn't answered the door when you knocked. I knew without anyone telling me, how they crushed your courage. They told me verbatim afterward anyway, though; that was part of the pact.

"I would train you in a heartbeat," one said, "except for this rotten knee. Darn the luck."

"Great idea!" said another. "How embarrassing I don't remember anything from my campaign days. So long ago."

Nobody mentioned the way their corn had been maggot-free going on fourteen years now, or how their chickens' plague-rashes healed instantly when you showed up to help, or how their grandma or child or pet phoenix defied dire medical prognoses after your visit. Not that they could have ever voiced such a thing; that, too, was part of the pact, and the pact was inviolable.

You came to me weeping after the last rejection and confessed your whole plan.

"I just wanted to help," you said. "I feel like I can. *Should.* Like I could be the world's greatest rider, if only someone would lend me a horse."

"You're already the greatest helper for miles," I said. "And walking is good for the constitution."

"I want to help *more.* Maybe someone outside our village could teach me, since no one here can. In the city—"

"Oh goodness," I said, "do you imagine any soldiers are left in the city? They're all off doing their bloody war work and surely wouldn't have time for a simple village boy, even one as wonderful as you."

"Maybe they'd let me watch them," you said. "I learn fast! Or I could carry their supplies, or wash their clothes, or dig waste pits. I would even *empty* waste pits, if it meant helping."

"Dear boy!" I said, ruffling your hair and drawing you close. "Who could love and value you more than your own family and friends? Let the soldiers do their tedious soldiering. But if it's challenge you seek, I can think of someone who needs a new shed for her goats."

In the end you disbanded your star-crossed squad and built Aunt Aggie's goat shed instead, and thanks to you though unbeknownst to you, her goats produced richer, creamier, sweeter milk than they ever had before. Aunt Aggie was all grins and praise. To the end of her too-short days she kept our larder bursting with cheese.

Wars come and wars go, after all.

Just like tears.

When you started school, the fairy godmother council sent their three best fairies to buy you.

"We will train him to be a mighty knight," the leader promised, handing me a shimmering quill. "Powerfully skilled, mind sharp as a sphinx's, brilliant dancer, bold rescuer of hapless virgins in distress, so on and so forth. A hero worthy of stories. A son to make you proud."

"You'll find all the details in the paperwork," said the second assistant.

"We won't let him die a horrible, grotesque death, screaming in torment and misery, if that's what's got you worried," said the first assistant, catching my expression. "This is all boilerplate."

"I'm worried about a lot of things," I said. "At the moment, you."

"What, pray tell, have you to be worried about?" said the leader. "I don't think you fully comprehend our overwhelming generosity here. It's not often a child other than a royal last-born achieves this level of attention."

"No?" I said. My laugh came out a little sharper than intended.

While the first two fairies, deeply annoyed, stormed off pretending to conference in another corner of the room, it was the second assistant who finally admitted the truth about the prophecy.

"Your son's fate is tied to the kingdom's," she said. "Our Council believes they're the best equipped to protect and train him, which means my boss has been given full negotiation authority. Ask for the moons if you want."

Something tickled my ear. "My son's fate?"

The fairy shrugged, sending delicate black ringlets waltzing. "The usual Chosen One stuff. Glory and wealth on offer, with doom, chaos, and despair waiting in the wings otherwise. Don't ask me to quote it. It's very poorly written."

"Right," I said. "I think we'll pass, thank you."

"Chosen Ones belong to the kingdom!" shrieked the first assistant from across the room.

"My son belongs to *me*."

"The kingdom will crumble!"

"All kingdoms crumble."

"You're a monster!" said the first assistant, wings twitching in horror. "What kind of person doesn't want to save the kingdom?"

"You might be surprised," I said.

"You've won for now," snapped the leader, wrenching her sparking quill from my hand so furiously it cut my palm open, "but we'll be back. Perhaps the queen, who is grace itself, will still offer you something, but I would not count on it. And do not imagine anyone else will give you better terms."

"That includes the unicorns," said the first assistant, angry brows a mirror of their boss's. "They double cross every deal they ever make. You should have signed with us."

"Thanks for the tea," said the second assistant a bit more cheerfully as they collected their jewel chests and turned to go. "Your rosemary scones were delicious."

The first assistant added darkly, "I'd watch out for villains if I were you."

"If you were me," I said, watching the blood pool in my hands, "the world would already be lost."

You never married. There were times I suspected you wanted to; goodness knows you had plenty of chances, and ambition flows freely in our village. As you turned forty, then fifty, then sixty, and your beard and temples greyed, even a matchmaker would have hoisted the white flag.

Still, I watched.

Everyone knows it only takes one.

"Last I checked," said the governor, her green eyes flashing, "you do not have the authority to command an outrageous pact like this."

You were eight, and off truffle-hunting with your father.

"Command?" I said. The hall was crammed so full, my words sounded faint, like little gasps. "I've never *commanded* a thing in my life, my lord. I'm only asking everyone to consider what's best for the village. For themselves."

"Your son can barely read. Perhaps we can revisit this when he's of age, and he can give his own opinion."

I choked back a laugh; our governor had stopped caring about other people's opinions by age ten. Still, I chose my next words carefully.

"With respect, lord, do you really believe a prophecy can be postponed? You're speaking as though you don't remember the last time our kingdom experienced a Chosen One. If we don't act now, my son will never become of age at all. Nor will yours. Nor *any* of your children, my friends. You heard the star-song. You've read the prophecy. You know the queen. Judge for yourselves."

The governor leaned forward in her chair. "I may be younger than you, but I do recall the last Chosen One. I also recall that we survived. We always survive."

"At what cost, lord?"

She pressed her lips together and did not answer.

"I think," I said gently, oh yes, so gently, "that our pockets are not deep enough to keep paying the price. Must I remind you, lord, how you came to govern?"

"You overstep!"

"There is grave overstepping, lord. But it is not mine."

"You ask us to trust you above the Council. Above our own queen."

"I ask you to trust your own eyes and ears."

"And you are convinced there is no other way? We must all agree to this pact?"

"Every one of us, for all the years of his life. Surely you see that."

Her voice broke at last. "You would condemn us all."

"We are already condemned. The pact may save— some."

"You condemn your own son."

I clenched my fists, palm throbbing in memory. "I have made my decision. What is yours, lord?" I turned to face the hall. "What is yours, my friends? Will you save our land? Will you sign?"

Did you hear it, beloved, out there in the forest?

Did the wind carry the thunder of ayes to you?

This morning, messengers brought the latest ruler's latest summons. There are enemies, or a plague, or an uprising, or something. My eyes aren't what they used to be, and I can't make out the words; but the kingdom is doubtless in shambles. Who are you off helping today—the carpenter? The miller? I'm a little fuzzy on this. All I know is, my treacherous legs had better get me to the fire before you come back.

Run.

But the fire is far, and my legs slow.

You stride through the door and catch me still just halfway across the room, my hand clutching the paper.

"Mama! What is that?"

"Nothing," I say. *Run.*

"Mama," you say. "May I have it, please?"

"Hurry, someone in the village needs you," I say. Or try to say. Why is my voice crumbling, today of all days?

You're already gently pulling the summons from my hand. I would sit and cradle my head in despair, if only the chair weren't so far away.

All my desperate long years' work, only to be foiled now, here, at the gate of my shadowlands.

You were forty-six when the fairies came back.

They took your father. They took Aunt Aggie.

They took the governor.

I did not let them take you.

"Mama," you're saying. "Mama, stop crying."

I don't mean to cry. You're napping in your little bed, and if I wake you, you'll never go back to sleep. It's already hard enough getting a child to sleep who with an innocent gesture can stop a chest rising. So many, too many stilled chests; if only they had kept to the pact. Let's count them together while your father digs. One, two--

"Mama," you say. "Can you hear me?"

Opening my eyes, I see your face, scarred with smile-lines — why are they called that, when it is crying that made them? — hovering close to mine. You look old. When did that happen?

"Give it to me!" My shout comes out a whisper.

"Don't be afraid, Mama," you say. "I'm here."

The floor reaches up and slams into my head. There's no pain, but I imagine blood pouring like a—like a waterfall, is that how the story goes?

"Look, Mama," you say.

You've caught me mid-fall, of course. I remember hitting the floor, yet here I am, floating like a forest wisp.

Did you know air is soft? I feel the blanket-warmth of a breeze wrapping around me.

No; not the air. It's your arms, and you're laying me tenderly on my bed, pressing your lips against my forehead.

"Rest, Mama." You stand, tall. There's a strange look in your eyes that sets my bones trembling. Do you know?? Have you guessed?

"You don't need to be afraid," you say. "I finally understand what I am."

Your eyes are aflame—your gift-glow pours from your face, your arms, your legs, your fingers, your toes—and I can't stop a laugh-cry. You're just a child; you don't understand at all, any more than your father did, may his fractured soul find peace. They will come for you at midnight, or moonrise, crawling through the cracks in the walls or down the chimney or oozing out of puddles or cupboards or mirrors.

They will recall their emissaries and come for you themselves in coaches, on broomsticks, on the backs of roaring dragons, cracking whips of raging fire.

Don't be afraid?? My fear is what's kept us alive.

With a groan I grab at the sheets, one hand trying to pull myself up, the other reaching for you. If I can just—

Wait. What—

The paper dances gracefully down, down, into the flames. It hesitates for the tiniest instant before sparks light up the gold ink and, a moment later, engulf the entire sheet in a satisfying crackle.

You... burned it?

"I told you," you say.

Your gift-glow tears are the most beautiful and terrible thing I've ever seen.

"I know what I am now," you say, "though the learning of it took my whole life. Forgive me, Mama."

Your voice sounds oddly broken. Distant, as if you're out in the garden at our— oh yes! I remember, that little bucket waterfall, where we always stand and hang our heads at somebody's— whose??— foolish, life-altering mistake.

"But you knew from the very beginning," you say. "You've been protecting the kingdom from *me*."

I'd watch out for villains if I were you

"To think," you say in wonder, "I was the villain all along."

I was the villain all along

— stillness floods the room

-no sound

-no air

-no breath

"Let the kingdom fall," you say with a burst of— light?? taking my place at the door.

SAVE THE KINGDOM! roars the hall.

Is that an earthquake?? something is slashing at my heart

at my eyes

at my hands, dripping with blood

(I can keep him here forever you know)

"You've won," says the fairy

—and the world explodes in glittering flame and a thunderclap that rattles somewhere deep in my throat

I am the Chosen One, I whisper

as somewhere above us, the stars begin to fall.

Rebekah Postupak lives on a fault line between two volcanos which, disappointingly, relates in no way to her day job of answering the phone. Her stories can be found in places such as *Penumbric, Not One of Us,* and *Daily Science Fiction*. Rebekah is an assistant producer and writer for the Nebula Awards and a chapter co-chair for Willamette Writers. She is indebted to these creative communities and so many others for demonstrating the power of words to change lives.

Other: the 2024 speculative fiction anthology
is the inaugural anthology for Bannister Press
with expectations for more to come.

A NOTE ABOUT TRADEMARKS

The story, "Maybe She's Made with It" by M.H. Bavlsik uses brand names and trademarked goods in a fictional story to express critical commentary on society, specifically about the use of make-up products and the effect it might have on people. Any brand or product mentioned could be exchanged for any other brand or product, and in no way is the story meant as an attack or defamation against any brand or trademark.

- M.A.C.™ is a trademark of Estee Lauder Cosmetics Ltd.
- Quickliner™ and Clinique's Quickliner™ are trademarks of Clinique Laboratories, LLC.
- Nars™ is a trademark of Shiseido Americas Corporation.
- Tom Ford™ is a trademark of 001 DEL LLC.
- Lancome™ is a trademark of L'OREAL.
- Monsieur Big™ is a trademark of L'OREAL.
- Armani Beauty™ is a trademark of GIORGIO ARMANI S.P.A.
- Neutrogena™ is a trademark of KENVUE INC.
- Urban Decay™ is a trademark of L'OREAL USA S/D, INC.

- Charlotte Tilbury™ is a trademark of CHARLOTTE TILBURY TM LIMITED
- Buxom™ is a trademark of BUXOM US BUYER LLC
- Power Line™ is a trademark of BUXOM US BUYER LLC
- Velour Lashes™ is a trademark of VELOUR COSMETICS INC.
- Glossier™ is a trademark of Glossier, Inc.
- Too Faced™ is a trademark of TOO FACED COSMETICS, LLC.
- Dior Addict™ is an abandoned trademark of Christian Dior Couture, S.A.
- Sunday Riley™ is a trademark of Riley, Sunday S.
- Tatcha™ is a trademark of TATCHA LLC.
- Shiseido Benefiance NutriPerfect™ is a trademark of Shiseido Company, Ltd.
- Peter Thomas Roth™ is a trademark of Peter Thomas Roth Labs, LLC.
- Smashbox Always Sharp™ is a trademark of DJF Enterprises.
- Armani™ is a trademark of GIORGIO ARMANI S.P.A.
- Color Sensational Ultimatte™ is a trademark of L'OREAL USA S/D, INC.
- Maybelline™ is a trademark of L'OREAL USA S/D, INC.
- Covergirl™ is a trademark of Noxell Corporation.
- Chanel™ is a trademark of CHANEL, INC.
- Rouge Coco™ is a trademark of Chanel, Inc.
- Glossimer™ is a trademark of Chanel, Inc.
- Big Ego™ is a trademark of Tarte, Inc.
- Essence™ is a trademark of Bora Creations S.L.
- Shape Tape™ is a trademark of Tarte, Inc.
- Tarte™ is a trademark of Tarte, Inc.
- e.l.f.™ Is a trademark of E.L.F. COSMETICS, INC.
- The POREfessional™ is a trademark of BENEFIT COSMETICS LLC.

- Benefit™ is a trademark of BENEFIT COSMETICS LLC.
- Wet 'n Wild™ is a trademark of MARKWINS BEAUTY PRODUCTS, INC.
- MegaGlo™ is a trademark of MARKWINS BEAUTY PRODUCTS, INC.
- All Nighter™ is a trademark of L'OREAL USA S/D, INC.
- Jaclyn Cosmetics™ is a trademark of Jaclyn Hill Cosmetics, LLC.
- Makeup Eraser™ is a trademark of JAPONESQUE, LLC.
- Stila™ is a trademark of Stila Styles, LLC.
- Nyx™ is a trademark of L'OREAL USA S/D, INC.
- Anastasia Beverly Hills™ is a trademark of ANASTASIA BEVERLY HILLS, LLC.
- Lilly Lashes™ is a trademark of Lilly Lashes, LLC.
- Estée Lauder™ is a trademark of Estee Lauder Inc.

ABOUT THE PUBLISHER

Bannister Press Limited was born out of a need to publish strong, unique voices and incredible new ideas. As a publisher, we aim to be our authors' greatest champion and loudest cheerleader.

We publish unputdownable books by award-winning authors. We specialize in supernatural and fantasy stories loved by adults and young adults. Our non-fiction tells the untold stories of small town Ontario.

Visit Bannisterpress.com

ALSO BY BANNISTER PRESS

Fiction:

Forgotten by Altaire Gural

No Other Love by Lori Jean Rowsell

Non-Fiction:

Historic Citizens of Kawartha Lakes by Sara Walker-Howe

Primrose Hill Manor: the history of the Janetville mansion by Paulette Sopoci and Sara Walker-Howe

Visit bannisterpress.com

Made in United States
North Haven, CT
08 August 2025

71459172R00152